Pra

"Newcomer Scott Prat... ...... a fresh voice to a crowded field in his stellar debut, *An Innocent Client*. Joe Dillard is the best defense lawyer in his small town in Tennessee. He's also desperately trying to leave the practice of law. Tired of cutting deals for the guilty, Dillard hopes to end his career on a high note—by representing one innocent client. A murder at a local strip club may give him his chance. Artfully plotted, carefully nuanced, and immensely readable, *An Innocent Client* is a terrific debut novel. Joe Dillard is an engaging, complex character who is worth rooting for. We will be hearing much more from Scott Pratt. Highly recommended."

—Sheldon Siegel, *New York Times* bestselling author
of *Judgment Day*

"A well-crafted, compelling debut, and Scott Pratt is a talent to watch." —Jeff Abbott, national bestselling author of *Collision*

"A smart, sophisticated legal thriller. Scott Pratt knows his stuff and it shows."   —Alafair Burke, author of *Angel's Tip*

"The most impressive first novel I've read in years. Think Harlan Coben meets John Grisham. Scott Pratt has written an unputdownable legal thriller, and I can't wait to see what he does next."

—Jason Starr, award-winning author of *The Follower*

"I've read *An Innocent Client* and am truly stunned. It's Scott Turow and Grisham on meth. The opening chapter is maybe the most compelling I've read in a decade."

—Ken Bruen, Shamus Award–winning author of *Cross*

"As polished and engrossing as any John Grisham or John Hart legal thriller, Scott Pratt's stunning debut novel, *An Innocent Client*, sings with intrigue, crusty Tennessee characters, and gut-wrenching personal choices. To protagonist Joe Dillard's wish for 'just one innocent client,' I'd say, 'Watch what you ask for.' To everyone else, I'd say, 'Go buy this book now.' "

—Louise Ure, Shamus Award–winning author
of *The Fault Tree*

INJUSTICE FOR ALL

Scott Pratt

AN OBSIDIAN MYSTERY

OBSIDIAN
Published by New American Library, a division of
Penguin Group (USA) Inc., 375 Hudson Street,
New York, New York 10014, USA
Penguin Group (Canada), 90 Eglinton Avenue East, Suite 700, Toronto,
Ontario M4P 2Y3, Canada (a division of Pearson Penguin Canada Inc.)
Penguin Books Ltd., 80 Strand, London WC2R 0RL, England
Penguin Ireland, 25 St. Stephen's Green, Dublin 2,
Ireland (a division of Penguin Books Ltd.)
Penguin Group (Australia), 250 Camberwell Road, Camberwell, Victoria 3124,
Australia (a division of Pearson Australia Group Pty. Ltd.)
Penguin Books India Pvt. Ltd., 11 Community Centre, Panchsheel Park,
New Delhi - 110 017, India
Penguin Group (NZ), 67 Apollo Drive, Rosedale, North Shore 0632,
New Zealand (a division of Pearson New Zealand Ltd.)
Penguin Books (South Africa) (Pty.) Ltd., 24 Sturdee Avenue,
Rosebank, Johannesburg 2196, South Africa

Penguin Books Ltd., Registered Offices:
80 Strand, London WC2R 0RL, England

First published by Obsidian, an imprint of New American Library,
a division of Penguin Group (USA) Inc.

First Printing, May 2010
10   9   8   7   6   5   4   3   2   1

Injustice for All, my third novel, is dedicated
to Lil' Smacks, the toughest girl I've ever known.

Acknowledgments

Thanks first of all to Shirley Pratt, my mom, for being my biggest fan. Thanks also to the gentlemen at the Philip Spitzer Literary Agency—Philip Spitzer, Lukas Ortiz, and Luc Hunt—for working so enthusiastically on my behalf. Thank you once again to Jon Ruetz, a man of many talents, who did a splendid job helping me get the manuscript into shape, and thank you to all the talented folks at Penguin, especially Kristen Weber and Brent Howard, who work so hard to put these projects together.

I'd also like to thank former assistant U.S. attorney Dan Smith, who took the time to explain to me how the feds allocate resources in certain situations, and Ian Harmon, who shared his computer expertise.

And finally, thank you to Kristy, Dylan, and Kody, my favorite peeps, for believing in me, for keeping me positive, and for being such a fruity bunch of human beings. I love you, I love you, I love you.

justice: the quality of being just, impartial, or fair.

—*Webster's New Collegiate Dictionary*

Prologue

May 2007

My name is Joe Dillard, and I'm leaning against a chain-link fence watching a baseball game at Daniel Boone High School in Gray, Tennessee, on a spectacular, sun-drenched evening in early May. The sky is a cloudless azure, a mild breeze is blowing out toward left field, and the pleasant smell of fresh-cut grass hangs in the air.

There are five of us watching the game from our spot near the right-field foul pole: me; my wife, Caroline; her best friend, Toni Miller; my buddy Ray Miller (Toni's husband); and Rio, our German shepherd. The Dillards and the Millers have been watching our sons play baseball together for ten years, alternately rejoicing in their successes and agonizing over their failures. Rio is a relative newcomer—he's been around for only three years—but he seems to enjoy the games as much as we do.

Ray Miller and I have much in common. We're both lawyers. After many years of practicing criminal defense, I switched to prosecuting a few years back, while Ray remains on what I now call the "dark side." I rib him on a regular basis about defending scumbags, but I know he does it for the right reasons and I respect him. He doesn't cheat, doesn't lie, doesn't try to pull tricks. He tends to see things in black and white, much as I do. We both despise the misuse of power, especially on the part of judges, although Ray is a bit more venomous than I in that regard. We're close to the same age, and we're devoted to our families.

We watch the game from our position in the outfield, away from the players and the other parents, because none of us wishes to distract our sons. We don't yell at them during games as other parents do. We don't criticize the umpires or the coaches. We just watch and worry. If something good happens, we cheer. If something bad happens, we cringe.

My son, Jack, is the star hitter on the Boone team. Ray's son, Tommy, is the star pitcher. Back in November, both of them signed national letters of intent to continue their baseball careers at the Division I collegiate level. Jack signed with Vanderbilt, and Tommy signed with Duke. It was one of the proudest moments of my life.

This evening's game has been intense. It's the finals of the district tournament, and if Boone beats Jefferson High, they move on to the regionals. If they lose, their season is over. Jack doubled off the left-center-field fence in the first inning with runners on second and third to put Boone up 2–0. Jefferson's cleanup hitter hit a solo home run off Tommy Miller in the second. Jack came up again in the fourth and hit a home run, a long moon shot over the center field fence, to put Boone up 3–1. In the top of the fifth, Tommy walked the leadoff hitter, and the next guy laid down a bunt that Boone's third baseman misplayed, leaving Jefferson with runners on second and third with nobody out and their cleanup hitter coming to the plate. Tommy threw two great pitches to get him down 0–2, but the next pitch got away from Tommy just a bit and hit the batter in the thigh. Jefferson's coaches, players, and parents all started screaming, accusing Tommy of hitting the kid on purpose. It looked as though a fight might break out, but the umpires managed to calm things down. Jefferson scored two runs when the next batter hit a bloop single to right field, but then Tommy struck out three in a row. The game is tied, with Jack leading off for Boone in the bottom of the seventh, the final inning in a high school game.

"They'll walk him," Ray says. I turn and look at him incredulously. He's wearing sunglasses that shield his dark eyes. He's an inch shorter than I at six feet two, but he's thicker through the chest and back. His long brown hair, beginning to gray, is pulled back into a ponytail, and his forearms, which are leaning against the fence, look as thick as telephone poles.

"You're nuts," I say. "They don't want to walk the leadoff man in a tie game in the last inning. They'll pitch to him."

Jack digs into the batter's box and takes his familiar wide, slightly open stance. He's a big kid, six feet two inches and a rock-hard two hundred ten pounds. He has a strong jaw and a prominent, dimpled chin—

a "good baseball face," as the old-time scouts would say. He's crowding the plate as he always does, daring the pitcher to throw him something inside.

The first pitch is a fastball, and it hits Jack between the eyes before he can get out of the way. I hear the awful thud of the baseball striking his head all the way from the outfield. Jack's helmet flies off. He takes a step backward but doesn't go down, and then starts staggering slowly toward first base. The umpire, as stunned as everyone else, jogs along beside him, trying to get him to stop. I sprint down the fence line toward the gate, watching Jack as his coaches scramble out of the dugout to his side. By the time he gets to first base, I can see blood pouring from his nose.

I make my way through the silent crowd and onto the field. Jack's coaches have taken him into the dugout and sat him on the bench. One of them is holding a white towel over Jack's face. I see immediately that the towel is already stained a deep red. The coaches step back as I approach.

"They did it on purpose," the head coach, a thirty-year-old named Bill Dickson, says. "They haven't come close to hitting anyone else."

I bend over Jack and gently remove the towel. His head is leaned back, his mouth open, and he's staring at the dugout roof. The area around both of his eyes is already swelling, and there's a deep, nasty gash just above the bridge of his nose. He's bleeding from the cut and from both nostrils.

I put the towel back over the wound.

"Jack, can you hear me?"

"Yes."

"Who am I?"

"Dad."

"Do you know where you are?"

"Boone High School. Dugout."

"What's the score in the game?"

"Three–three, bottom of the seventh."

"Has anyone called an ambulance?" I say to Coach Dickson.

"They're on the way, but it always takes them fifteen or twenty minutes to get here."

I can sense someone beside me, and I turn my head. It's Ray, Caroline, and Toni.

"He all right?" Ray asks.

"He's coherent."

"Let me see."

I pull the towel back again. Caroline gasps, and a flash of anger runs through me like an electric current. How could they do this? *Why* would they do this? It's just a baseball game, for God's sake. Jack has been hit dozens of times in the past, but never in the face. And Coach Dickson is right; their pitcher displayed excellent control until Jack came to the plate in the seventh. They hit him intentionally.

I gently replace the towel and look at Ray. I'm thinking seriously about grabbing a bat from the rack and going after Jefferson's coach.

"You don't want to wait for an ambulance," Ray says. "We need to take him now."

"Why?"

"His pupils are different sizes. There's already a

lot of swelling. I've seen this before, Joe. He might be bleeding internally." Ray was a medic in the navy for eight years, so he knows what he's talking about. At that moment, Jack leans forward and vomits on the dugout floor.

"We have to go," Ray says. "Right now."

Caroline and Toni rush off to get the cars while Ray and I each drape one of Jack's arms over our backs and lift. Coach Dickson holds the towel in place to try to slow the bleeding as we walk Jack out through the gate. Just before we reach the parking lot, he loses consciousness, and I feel a sense of dread so deep that I nearly pass out myself.

He regains consciousness after we put him in the backseat, but during the ride to the hospital, he's in and out. He keeps saying his head feels like it's going to explode. I call the emergency room on my cell phone along the way, and they're waiting when we arrive. They take Jack immediately into a trauma room, and in less than ten minutes they've taken him to surgery. A doctor comes out to talk to us briefly. He says Jack is suffering from an acute epidural hematoma. In layman's terms, he says, Jack's brain is bleeding. A neurosurgeon is going to perform an emergency craniotomy to drain the blood, relieve the pressure, and repair the damage.

We wait for three agonizing hours before the neurosurgeon comes out. The waiting room is filled with Jack's coaches and their wives, his teammates and their parents, plus dozens of his friends from school who were either at the game or heard about what happened. Everyone falls silent when the surgeon, a dark-haired, serious-looking, middle-aged man wearing scrubs, asks Caroline and me to step into a private room. My daughter, Lilly, who is a year younger than Jack and was sitting in the bleachers behind home plate when Jack was hit, grabs my hand and comes into the room with us.

"I'm told you didn't wait for the ambulance," the doctor says gravely as soon as the door closes behind us. "Whose idea was that?"

"Why?" I ask. "Was it a mistake?"

"Under some circumstances, it could have been. But this time, it was the right decision. If your son had bled for another ten or fifteen minutes, I don't think he would have made it."

"So he's all right?"

"He's in recovery. It's a serious injury, but thankfully we got to it in time. We'll keep him in intensive care for a day or two. He's going to have a heckuva headache, but we can control the pain with medication. He'll have to take it easy for a couple of months, but after that, he should be as good as new."

"When can we see him?"

"He'll wake up in about half an hour. He'll be groggy, but you can talk to him for a few minutes."

We thank the doctor, and Caroline, Lilly, and I embrace silently. Caroline and Lilly are crying, but I'm so relieved, I feel as if I could float on air. We walk back out to the crowded waiting room. Ray and Toni Miller, along with their son, Tommy, are standing just outside the door. When the group sees Caroline's tears, I can sense they think the news is bad. Ray looks at me anxiously, and I smile.

PART 1

1

The moment Katie Dean began to believe she'd been abandoned by God was on a Sunday afternoon in August 1992.

It was late in the summertime in Michigan. Katie, along with her mother and brothers and sister, had returned home earlier from the First Methodist Church in Casco Township. At seventeen, Kirk was her oldest sibling; then Kiri, sixteen; then Katie, who was just two months shy of her thirteenth birthday. Kody was the baby of the family at ten. They were gathered around the dining room table, waiting for Mother to bring the platter of fried chicken in from the kitchen.

The fresh smell of Lake Michigan floated through the open dining room windows, mingling with the sweet odors of chicken and garlic mashed potatoes. After lunch, Katie and Kiri were planning to pack a small basket with a Thermos of ice water, suntan lotion, and magazines, and hike to the sand dunes above the lake, where they would spend the afternoon lying in the sun and giggling about the Nelson boys, who lived just up the road. It would be their last visit to the dunes this summer. School was starting back the next morning.

Richard Dean, Katie's father, sat listlessly on the other side of the table, staring into a glass of whiskey. He was thin and pale, with a thatch of dark hair above his furrowed brow. He was upset, but that wasn't unusual. It seemed he was always upset.

Richard Dean was distant, as though not a part of the world everyone else lived in. He never kissed Katie, never hugged her, never told her he loved her. He was like a ticking bomb, always on the verge of another explosion. Katie's mother had told the children that Father was sick from the war in Vietnam. She said he'd been wounded and captured by Viet Cong soldiers near the Cambodian border in 1970 and had spent four years in a prison in Hanoi.

Katie's father didn't have a job, but Katie knew the family lived off money he collected from the government every month. Her mother couldn't work because she had to stay home and take care of Father all the time. He drank lots of whiskey and smoked cigarettes one after another; Katie had seen him lock himself in his room and not come out for a week at a time. Sometimes she'd hear him screaming in the middle of the night.

Father had picked them all up from the church parking lot just after noon. He didn't attend church, but he drove the family there and picked them up every Sunday at precisely twelve fifteen. When Father pulled into the church parking lot earlier, Katie's mother had been talking to a man named Jacob

Olson near the front steps. Katie didn't think there was anything unusual about it—Mr. Olson was a nice man—but as soon as Mother got into the car, Father lit into her. He called her a slut, white trash. He was yelling and spitting. The veins on his neck were sticking out so far, Katie thought they might burst through his skin. When the family arrived home, the first thing Father did was open a bottle of whiskey. He filled a tall glass and sat at the dining room table while Mother, Kiri, and Katie cooked in the kitchen and the boys went about setting the table. They all stepped lightly around Father. They never knew when he might strike, like a rattlesnake coiled in the grass.

Katie was still wearing the flowered print dress Mother had made for her out of material she bought from the thrift store in South Haven. It was Katie's favorite summer dress, light and airy and full of color. She was looking down at the hemline, which crossed her thighs, trying to imagine the pink carnations coming to life, when Mother walked in carrying the chicken.

"Here we are," Mother said. She had a forced smile on her face. She put the platter down in the middle of the table. Steam rose from the chicken, and through it Katie caught a glimpse of Father's face. He was already halfway through his third glass of whiskey. His eyes had reddened, and the lids were beginning to droop.

"Chicken," Father muttered into his whiskey glass. "Goddamned fried chicken's all we ever get around here."

Mother attempted to remain pleasant. "I thought

you liked fried chicken," she said, "and I'd appreciate it if you wouldn't use that kind of language around the children."

"The chiddren," he slurred. "Probly ain't mine anyway."

"Richard!" Mother yelled. She rarely raised her voice; Katie shuddered. "How dare you!"

Father lifted his chin and turned slowly toward Mother.

"How dare me?" he said. "How dare *me*? How dare *you*, you bitch! How long you been screwing Olson, anyway?"

"Stop it, Father," Kirk pleaded from Katie's left. Blond-haired and blue-eyed like Katie and Mother, Kirk was tall and paper thin, wiry strong but teenage awkward. Father whipped his head around to face Kirk.

"Watch your mouth, boy," he said, "and don't call me Father no more. Go look in the mirror. You don't look nothing like me."

He turned back to Mother.

"Does he, darling? None of 'em look like me. They look like . . . they look like . . . Olson!"

"Please leave the table if you're going to talk like that," Mother said.

Katie felt the familiar twinge of fear in her stomach. She watched as Father's face gradually turned darker, from pink to purple.

"Leave the table?" Father bellowed. "You think you can order me around like a goddamned slave?"

"Please, Richard." There was a look of desperation in Mother's eyes.

"*Please, Richard*," Father mocked her hatefully. "I'll give you please, by God, and thank you very much, too!"

Father stood on wobbly legs, knocking his drink over in the process. Whiskey spilled out and stained the tablecloth as he stumbled off toward his bedroom. The aroma filled Katie's nostrils, sickening her. She hated whiskey. She hated everything about it.

Katie, along with the others, sat at the table in stunned silence, waiting for Mother to say something. She'd seen Father's outbursts before—all of them had—but this one was worse, much worse and more vicious than any they'd ever experienced.

"It's all right," Mother said after what seemed to Katie like an hour. "He's just not feeling well today."

"He shouldn't talk to you that way," Kirk said.

"He doesn't mean it."

"Doesn't matter. He shouldn't do it."

Katie heard heavy footsteps coming from the direction of Father's bedroom and looked around. He was moving quickly toward them. He raised a shotgun, pointed it in Mother's direction, and pulled the trigger. Katie thought her eardrums had burst. Mother went straight over on her back. A spray of pink mist seemed to hang in the air above the table. Katie's joints froze. She urinated on herself.

She watched in terror as Father pumped the shotgun and swung it around toward Kirk—a second horrific explosion.

Then Kiri.

Then her . . .

2

As the bailiff calls criminal court into session, I look around the room at the anxious faces and feel the familiar sense of dread that hangs in the air like thick fog. Nearly everyone in the gallery has committed some transgression, some violation of the laws of man. It's an odd conglomeration of check kiters, drunk drivers, burglars, drug dealers, rapists, and killers, all irretrievably bound together by one simple fact—they've been caught and will soon be punished. Less than 5 percent of them will actually continue to protest their innocence and go to trial. The rest will beg their lawyers to make the best deal possible. They'll plead guilty and either be placed on probation or face confinement in a county jail or a state penitentiary.

The courtroom itself looks as though it was constructed by a humorless carpenter. The colors are dull and lifeless, the angles harsh and demanding. Portraits of judges, both dead and alive, adorn the walls behind the bench. There's an awkward sense of formality among the lawyers, bailiffs, clerks, and the judge. Everyone is disgustingly polite. The behavior is required by the institution, but beneath the veneer of civility runs a deep current of hostility borne of petty jealousy, resentment, and familiarity. I'm never comfortable in a courtroom. There are enemies everywhere.

Sitting next to me is Tanner Jarrett, a twenty-five-year-old rookie prosecutor fresh out of law school. He's a political hire, the son of a billionaire state senator who will no doubt soon be a United States senator. Tanner looks out of place with his fresh face and boyish demeanor. He's handsome, with well-defined jaws that angle sharply to a dimpled chin beneath inquisitive brown eyes and a thick mop of black hair. He's bright, capable, and extremely likable. It seems he's always smiling. Tanner will handle forty-seven of the forty-eight cases on today's docket. He'll resolve a few of them by plea agreement and agree to continue the rest. I'm here only to receive a date for an aggravated rape case that's going to trial.

Judge Leonard Green takes his seat at the bench. Green is mid-sixties, tall and lean, with a hawkish face and perfect silver hair. He moves with the effeminate gait of a drag queen onstage. He's as pure a son of a bitch as I've ever known, and he hovers over us from his perch on the bench, scanning the crowd like a vulture searching for carrion. Green could just as easily give my trial date to Tanner and let him pass it along to me, but since I'm handling the case for the district attorney's office, the judge insists I appear in court. He knows I have no other reason to be here, but he won't call the case early so I can go on about my business. He'll make me sit here for hours, just because he can. If I leave the courtroom, he'll call the case and then hold me in contempt of court because of my absence. Such are the games we play.

Green leans to his left and whispers in the clerk's ear. She shakes her head and whispers back. I notice a look of concern on her face, a look I've seen hundreds of times. It means that Green has spotted a potential victim and is about to indulge his ever-present, masochistic need to inflict pain or punishment on an unsuspecting victim.

"Case number 32,455, *State of Tennessee versus Alfred Milligan*," the clerk announces.

I turn to see Alfred Milligan, who appears to be in his late-fifties but is probably at least ten years younger, rise from his seat in the gallery. Milligan looks like so many others inhabiting the seemingly bottomless pit of criminal defendants. He's decimated by a lack of nutrition, probably caused by a combination of poverty and alcohol or drug abuse. He uses a cane to walk. What's left of his black hair is greasy and plastered to his forehead. He's wearing what is most likely his best clothing, a black T-shirt with "Dale Earnhardt" written in red across the front and "The Legend" written in red across the back, and a pair of baggy blue jeans. He saunters to the front of the courtroom and looks around nervously.

"Mr. Milligan, you're charged with driving under the influence, seventh offense. Where's your lawyer?" Judge Green demands.

"He told me he'd be here later in the morning," Milligan says.

"Mr. Miller represents you, correct?" The judge is talking about Ray Miller, my friend, and there's a gleam in his eye that tells me he's about to exact a little revenge. Judge Green hates Ray, primarily because Ray isn't the least bit afraid of him and lets him know it on a regular basis. They've been feuding bitterly for years, but lately it has seemed to escalate. Two weeks earlier, my wife and I were dining with Ray and his wife at a restaurant in Johnson City when Ray spotted Judge Green eating by himself at a table in the corner. Ray walked over and started an argument about the judge's practice of locking the courtroom doors at precisely nine o'clock each morning and jailing anyone who arrives late. The conversation grew heated, and with everyone in the place listening, Ray called Judge Green a "bully in a black robe." He voiced the opinion that the judge had probably been beaten up by bullies as a boy and now used his robe to seek symbolic vengeance whenever the urge struck him. I told Ray later that his indiscretion could cost him dearly. His response was, "Screw that limp-wristed faggot."

Green turns back to the clerk. "Has Mr. Miller notified the clerk's office that he would be late this morning?"

The clerk shakes her head sadly.

"Then he's in contempt of court. Let the record show that Mr. Miller has failed to appear in court at the appointed time and has failed to notify the clerk's office that he would either be absent or late. He is guilty of contempt of court in the presence of the court and will be taken to jail immediately upon his arrival."

Just as I'm about to say something in Ray's defense, Tanner Jarrett stands suddenly and clears his throat.

"Excuse me, Your Honor," Tanner says. "Mr. Miller called me early this morning. He's filed a motion on Mr. Milligan's behalf, and we're supposed to have a hearing today. But since the court doesn't typically hear motions until after eleven a.m., Mr. Miller told me he was going to take care of a matter in Chancery Court before he came down here. I'm sure that's where he is."

"He's supposed to be here, Mr. Jarrett," the judge snarls. "Right here. Right now."

"With all due respect, Your Honor, the state isn't ready for the hearing now. I told my witness to be here at eleven o'clock."

"Sit down, Mr. Jarrett," Green says coldly. He turns his attention toward Alfred Milligan, who has been standing silently at the lectern. "Mr. Milligan, your case is continued. The clerk will notify you of the new date. You're free to go."

I sit there seething impotently as Milligan walks out of the courtroom. Nothing would please me more than to jerk Green off the bench and give him the ass whipping he so desperately needs and deserves. All it would cost me would be my job, my law license, and a few months in jail. I stare up at Green, hoping to catch his eye and at least give him a silent look of contempt, but he ignores me and begins calling cases as though nothing out of the ordinary has happened. I'm afraid for Ray. I wish I could go out into the hallway and at least call him, but I know if I do, Green will call my case and do the same thing to me that he's just done to Ray.

Ray walks through the side door a little before ten.

As soon as Green sees him, he stops what he's doing and orders Ray to the front of the courtroom.

"You're in contempt of court, Mr. Miller," the judge says triumphantly. "I called your case at nine o'clock. You weren't here, and you hadn't notified the clerk's office of your absence as required under the local rules. Bailiff, take Mr. Miller into custody. His bond is set at five thousand dollars."

Ray is wearing a brown suit. His hair is pulled back tightly into his signature ponytail. He looks up at the judge with hatred and defiance in his eyes. I can see the muscles in his jaw twitching, and his complexion is darkening noticeably. I immediately begin to hope he has enough sense to keep his mouth shut. He's helpless right now. There's nothing he can do. But if he stays calm and doesn't do or say anything stupid, he can take up this fight later. If he does it right, he'll be exonerated and the judge will be the one who has to answer for his actions. But if he says something he shouldn't . . .

At that moment, Ray speaks. "I've been right about you all along, you gutless piece of shit. I hope you enjoy this, because from this day forward, I'm going to take a special interest in you. You'd better grow eyes in the back of your head."

"Cuff him!" Green yells at one of the bailiffs, who has sheepishly walked up behind Ray and is reaching for his arm.

"Keep your fucking hands off me," Ray growls, and the bailiff takes a step back.

I stand and walk to my friend. I take him gently by the arm and begin to steer him toward the hallway that leads to the holding cells. "C'mon, Ray," I say calmly. "This only gets worse if you stay." He comes out of his rage, and his eyes settle on mine. The rage has been replaced by desperation and confusion.

"I'm going to jail?" he asks in a tone that is almost dreamy.

"I'll go to the clerk's office and post your bond as soon as I can break away from the courtroom," I say. "You'll be out in an hour."

"I'm signing an order suspending you based on your threat, Mr. Miller," Judge Green says as we walk out the door. "And I'm reporting you to the Board of Professional Responsibility. You'll be lucky if you ever practice law again."

3

Six months later, I'm sitting on a metal stool in the death row visitor's section of Riverbend Correctional Facility in Nashville. Riverbend is what they call a state-of-the-art facility. It's sprawling and modern, but my experience tells me the place is misnamed. Men who spend time in a maximum security prison do not come out "corrected." They come out more cunning.

On the other side of a thick pane of Plexiglas is thirty-eight-year-old Brian Thomas Gant. I was appointed to represent Gant nearly fifteen years ago. He was my first death penalty client, accused of murdering his mother-in-law and raping his five-year-old niece. There was no forensic evidence against him—DNA testing hadn't yet become the gold standard—and seemingly no motive for the crime. But the niece, a youngster named Natalie Booze, told the police that the man who raped her "looked like Uncle Brian." The police immediately focused their investigation on Gant, and the girl's story quickly changed from "looked like Uncle Brian" to "*was* Uncle Brian." He was arrested a week after the crime was committed.

I did the best I could at trial, but I couldn't overcome the young girl's testimony. He was convicted of first-degree murder and two counts of aggravated rape a year after his arrest. He's been on death row ever since.

After her uncle was shipped off to the penitentiary, Natalie Booze had a change of heart. She told Gant's wife that she wasn't sure it was Uncle Brian. It happened so fast. She was asleep when the rapist came into her room. It was dark. The account was completely different than what she'd testified to at trial. It didn't matter, though. Gant's appellate attorneys asked Natalie to sign an affidavit swearing that she now believed she'd been mistaken when she identified Brian Gant at trial. She signed the affidavit and the attorneys filed it. Both the prosecution and the appellate courts ignored it.

Several years after Gant was convicted, after DNA testing had been developed, his wife paid a private laboratory nearly forty thousand dollars to test three pieces of evidence from the crime scene: a pair of panties his niece was wearing, a nylon stocking his mother-in-law was wearing, and a pubic hair found on the niece's sheet. The lab was able to extract DNA samples from all three pieces of evidence, and none of them matched Gant. Armed with this new evidence, his appellate attorneys were able to get a hearing in front of a judge, who summarily denied their request for a new trial. The Tennessee Court of Appeals upheld the judge's ruling, and Gant remains here in this terrible place. I'm convinced he's innocent, but once a jury finds a man guilty in a death penalty case, the odds against overturning the verdict are overwhelming.

"What are you doing down here?" Gant asks pleasantly. He's put on some weight since I last saw him, and the hair at his temples has turned gray, but he seems in good spirits.

"I'm here to witness an execution, believe it or not."

"Johnson?"

"Right. The murder he was convicted of happened in our district. My boss dumped this on me at the last minute. How's your appeal going?"

"It isn't. Unless Donna can somehow hand them the guy who did it on a silver platter, I'm the next one on the gurney."

Donna is Gant's wife. I see her at the grocery store once or twice a month, but I avoid talking to her whenever possible. Despite the fact that her mother was murdered, Donna has steadfastly maintained her husband's innocence and has become obsessed with getting him exonerated. Back when I was representing Brian, she swore to me that Brian was at home in bed with her the night the crime took place, and she testified to that at trial, but the prosecutor successfully argued to the jury that she was just protecting her husband.

"When are you scheduled?" I ask.

"Three weeks from today."

"Jesus, Brian, I had no idea. Have you run the DNA profile Donna got from the lab through the Department of Correction database? They might get a hit."

"We've tried, but they refuse to do it."

"Your lawyers can't force them?"

"How could they force them?"

"Get an order from a judge."

"What judge? Every judge I've run across has upheld my conviction. I'm just a convict now. I'm on death row. No one is interested in helping."

"Anything I can do?"

"I appreciate the offer."

"I'm sorry about everything, Brian. I'm sorry I didn't do a better job."

His eyes soften and he smiles, and I immediately feel even more guilt.

"The Lord works in mysterious ways, my friend," he says. "Don't blame yourself. You did what you could, and I have no hard feelings toward you. The Lord will take care of this, and if He sees fit not to, then I won't question His judgment. If He calls me to heaven, then He must have a purpose for me there. I'm at peace."

"You have to keep fighting."

"Like I said, I'm at peace. I've placed myself in God's hands and washed myself in the blood of the Lamb. I'll accept my fate with a song on my lips and love in my heart."

We sit there for a few minutes in awkward silence. I can't think of anything else to say. Finally, Brian stands up.

"I think I'll head on back to my cell now, Mr. Dillard, but I appreciate your coming. I really do. It makes me feel good to know you care. God bless."

*   *   *

Eight hours later, just before midnight, I'm back at the prison, only now I'm sitting on a folding chair on a polished concrete floor just outside the execution chamber. Dull gray paint covers the concrete block walls, and pale light emanates from fluorescent bulbs hidden behind sheets of opaque plastic in the drop ceiling. The room is colorless, the air so still it's stifling. I'm feeling queasy and claustrophobic, and I want nothing more than to get the hell out of here.

The condemned is a white man named Phillip Johnson. Twelve years ago, Johnson brutally raped and murdered eight-year-old Tanya Reid no more than ten miles from my house. He did unspeakable things to the child, then dumped her body in a culvert near the South Central community and covered it with brush. A couple of boys looking for frogs in the creek bed discovered Tanya two days later.

I'd been practicing law for only a few years when the crime occurred. I hung out my own shingle in northeast Tennessee as soon as I graduated from the University of Tennessee College of Law, and I wound up practicing criminal defense for many years. I was an outsider looking in during Johnson's trial, but from everything I heard and read, there was no doubt about his guilt. He was a sex offender who'd already served seven years for fondling a young girl and was on parole, living in nearby Unicoi County, the day he snatched Tanya Reid from her driveway. His semen was found on the little girl's body, and her blood and hair were all over the backseat of his car.

I've been sent here to witness the execution on behalf of the people of the First Judicial District and my boss, the man they elected as their attorney general. His name is Lee Mooney, and he was supposed to do this himself, but he called me into his office yesterday and said he'd decided to attend a conference in Charleston and would be gone until Friday evening. He then assigned this unpleasant task to me. I wasn't offered the option of refusing.

Tanya Reid's family is here—her mother, father, and three grandparents—and they smile at me tentatively. I'd introduced myself to them earlier, just as my boss had instructed. They're simply dressed, quiet, grossly out of place so near this chamber of death. I remember the parents' pleas on television the day after their child was abducted. They appear to have aged more than double the twelve years it's taken to bring their daughter's killer to what they believe is his rightful end. Their hair is gray, their shoulders slumped. They're languid nearly to the point of being lifeless.

I must admit I'm conflicted about the death penalty. Philosophically, or intellectually, I just can't cuddle up to the notion that a modern, civilized government that forbids its people from killing should be allowed to kill its people. But when I imagine putting the proverbial shoe on my own foot . . . well, let's just say I know in my heart that if someone had kidnapped, raped, tortured, and murdered either of my children, I'd want them dead. I'd want them to suffer. I also know that I'd be perfectly capable of doing the killing myself. Maybe the state legislature should consider passing a law that allows the victim's family the option of killing the condemned. They could also give them the option of killing the condemned in the same manner in which the victim was killed. Perhaps that particular form of revenge would provide the closure they seem to crave so deeply.

Sitting in the front row are two representatives from the media back home, both young female newspaper reporters, dressed in their dark business suits. So much time has passed since the crime occurred that the state and national media have moved on to more pressing matters. Tanya Reid is old news, perversely obsolete in our fast-moving society. As I look at them, I can't help but wonder what kind of effect this is going to have. These young journalists, at once inexperienced and arrogant, have a condescending air about them as they prepare their "concerned" look for the live shot outside the prison later on. I wonder how they'll feel about their love affair with professional voyeurism after they've watched a man die fifteen feet from their notepads.

At precisely the appointed time, they bring Johnson out into the death chamber in a white hospital gown, cuffs, and shackles. A steel wall separates the witnesses from the condemned. There's a window, much like the one through which newborn babies are viewed in a maternity ward. I muse over the irony for a moment, then put it out of my mind. . . .

Johnson is short and doughy, with neatly cut black hair, a double chin, and a clean-shaven face. The monster is forty-one years old, but he looks no more than thirty. He's spent nearly half of his life in prison, but if you replaced the hospital gown with a jacket, slacks, and a tie, he'd look like the neighbor who passes the collection plate in church on Sunday mornings.

The prison's representatives are here, too. Warden Tommy Joe Tester is leading Johnson into the chamber, followed by two massive prison guards in black uniforms. The chaplain, a physician, and two stone-faced medical technicians wearing white coats follow only a pace behind.

Johnson stops his shuffle and looks out over the audience mournfully. No one from his own family has come to watch him die. Until this point, he has at least attempted to remain stoic, but his lips begin to tremble and his shoulders slump. As the guards help him onto the gurney, he begins to weep. The guards remove his cuffs and shackles and replace them with leather straps attached to the gurney. Then they step back against the wall.

"That's it, cry, you son of a bitch," I hear Tanya's father mutter from his front-row seat. "Go out like the coward you are."

The warden, dressed in a navy blue suit, steps forward holding a piece of paper.

"Phillip Todd Johnson," the warden says in a nasal Southern twang, "by the power vested in me by the state of Tennessee, I hereby order that the sentence of death handed down by the Criminal Court of Washington County in the matter of *State of Tennessee versus Phillip Todd Johnson* be carried out immediately. Do you have any last words?"

There's a brief pause, and then a pitiful wail.

"I'm sorry," Johnson cries. "I'm so very sorry. I couldn't help myself. May God forgive me."

I don't know what God's attitude toward him will be, but the state of Tennessee doesn't seem to be in a forgiving mood.

"May God have mercy on your soul," the warden says as the executioners efficiently hook an IV into Johnson's left forearm.

Three different drugs will be injected into his body: five grams of sodium thiopental, which will render him unconscious, followed by one hundred milligrams of pancuronium bromide, which will block the neuromuscular system and cause his breathing to cease, and one hundred milliliters of potassium chloride, which will stop his heart. Each of the three doses would be lethal on its own, but the state wants to make damned sure he's dead and that he doesn't feel a thing. Those who are enlightened about such things consider this to be the most humane method of killing a human being.

Johnson continues to cry as the chaplain prays. Suddenly, the microphone inside the death chamber is turned off. All we can do now is watch. The prison physician steps forward while one of the EMTs walks behind a wall, presumably to release the first dose of fatal drugs. I want to close my eyes, but I can't. Even though I find the entire matter hypocritical and disgusting, I'm riveted. Thirty seconds after the EMT disappears, Johnson's chest rises, his eyes flutter, and he is still. The thought crosses my mind that the death he's just been given was so much more serene than the one he doled out to little Tanya. Even so, I wonder how what I've just witnessed could possibly be called justice.

I sit in the seat for a moment, feeling awkward, not quite knowing what to do. Then the family rises, and I do the same. The show's over—figuratively for the audience and literally for Johnson—and I hurry out into the night.

Infantry. The things I saw and did there enter into my subconsciousness randomly, like pop-up targets on a firing range, nearly always when I'm sleeping. The images don't appear as often as they once did, but when they do, they come complete with digital sound and brilliant color, and they remain as vivid as the day they happened.

If I'd had any sense, I would've chosen a career that promised to be relatively uneventful—something like accountancy or maybe pharmacy. But some irresistible force has always pushed me toward self-flagellation, and in my early twenties, I made the unfortunate decision to become a lawyer and subsequently—driven primarily by a need to support my family—entered the world of criminal justice with its sociopaths, psychotics, narcissists, and idiots. I practiced criminal defense for more than a decade, until I wound up getting shot by the deranged son of a murder victim. I took a year off after that, but eventually I was drawn back in as a prosecutor. The first case I prosecuted involved a group of Satan-worshiping Goths who murdered six people. Their leader—a psychopath named Natasha Davis—nearly killed me. Now, as I gaze into the mirror at a face that looks much older than it should, I wish I could somehow lift the top of my skull, remove my psyche with a spoon, and start all over again.

I leave the bathroom and pull on a pair of sweatpants, a hoodie, and my ragged running shoes. The hotel where I'm staying is a block from Vanderbilt University, so I spend the next hour jogging through the campus and around the park across the street that surrounds the Parthenon. By six thirty I'm showered and seated in the hotel restaurant. A couple of minutes later I see my son walk through the door.

Jack is six feet three now, the same height as me. His hair is dark like mine but cut much shorter. His eyes are a chocolate brown and reflect a natural intensity and intelligence. He's twenty years old, a junior at Vanderbilt, and a member of the baseball team, a program that prides itself on discipline and toughness. He carries himself with the confidence of an athlete, and as I stand to hug him, my heart seems to swell in my chest.

"Big Jack," I say, wrapping my arms around his neck, "you look fantastic."

"You look tired," he says as he returns the hug and sits down across from me.

"Didn't sleep very well."

"So, how are you? Want to talk about it?"

"Talk about what?"

"The execution. Are you handling it all right?"

"I'm not sure yet," I say honestly. "It's hard to believe I sat there and watched them kill a man."

"A man who murdered a defenseless little girl."

"I know. I'm just not quite sure what to think about it."

"Then don't think about it." He smiles broadly. "Let's talk baseball."

I'm relieved he isn't interested in hearing the details of the event I witnessed several hours earlier, and we begin to talk about our favorite subject while he wolfs down four eggs, two pieces of wheat toast, two apples, and a banana. We talk about coaches and teammates and opponents and Jack's prospects of being drafted by a major-league team in June. I'm in favor of his staying at Vanderbilt through his senior year, but he's a power hitter who also hits for average and rarely strikes out, and there's a good chance the pros might throw some serious money at him in the draft this year. An hour flies by, and at seven forty-five he looks at his watch and gulps down the last of a glass of orange juice.

"Gotta go, Dad," he says. "Class in fifteen minutes."

"Sure," I say dejectedly.

"Something wrong?"

"Nah. I'm just not looking forward to the rest of the week."

"What's up?"

"I have a hearing tomorrow morning that I don't think is going to go well, and your mom has invited Ray and Toni over for dinner Saturday night. She thinks they're on the verge of splitting up."

"I talked to Tommy yesterday," Jack says. Tommy Miller and Jack have remained close despite being hundreds of miles from each other. They speak on the phone often and spend time together during the holidays, which is the only time they're at home now. The last time I saw Tommy was at Christmas. He told me he loved Duke University and was doing well both in the classroom and on the baseball field.

"Yeah? What'd Tommy have to say?"

"He says things are bad. He's worried about his dad. He also says he's going to have to transfer in the fall because they can't afford the tuition at Duke anymore."

"I know. Your mom told me."

Ray Miller's situation has grown steadily worse since Judge Green threw him in jail on the contempt charge six months ago. The judge made good on the promises he made as Ray and I left the courtroom that day. Less than twenty-four hours after Ray was jailed, the judge issued an order suspending Ray from practicing law in the criminal courts of the First Judicial District. He then filed a dozen complaints against Ray with the Board of Professional Responsibility. Since the complaints were coming from a judge, the BPR—a useless bunch of paper pushers in Nashville—suspended Ray statewide without so much as a perfunctory hearing.

Green's scorched-earth campaign has resulted in Ray's being unable to earn a living, which in turn has caused him to be unable to make his mortgage payments, which will undoubtedly result in the loss of his house in the very near future. Two of his vehicles have already been repossessed by creditors, Tommy is being forced to leave Duke, and as the situation has worsened, Ray has fallen into a deep depression. He's grown a beard, is drinking heavily, and has put on at least thirty pounds. I find myself going by to see him less and less often, because watching him deteriorate is nothing short of heartbreaking.

"So why is Mom having them over?" Jack asks. "Sounds like it'll be pretty miserable."

"You know how she is," I say. "She always thinks she can help, and even if she can't, she thinks she has to try."

Jack rises from the table and hugs me again.

"Tell Mom I love her," he says, "and tell her there are some things a person just needs to stay out of."

"I'll tell her."

"And you," he says with a smile. "Can I tell you something without making you mad?"

"Depends on what it is."

"I've learned something since I've been here. It'll probably sound strange to you, but I've learned the only thing that's real is the present. If you think about it, there's really no future and no past. There's only now, and that's where we should concentrate on living."

"I didn't know you'd become a philosopher."

"It'd be good if you'd give it a try, Dad. It'd be good if you'd stop worrying about the future so much, and it'd be even better if you could forget about the past."

"Tell me about it."

"I'm serious. I know you're my father and I'm biased, but I think you're the best man I've ever known. You should go easier on yourself."

"Thank you, son. I'll try."

He turns away, and as I watch him walk out of the restaurant, I feel a tear slide down my cheek.

5

"Would you state your name for the record, please?"

The next morning I'm standing at a lectern in Criminal Court in Jonesborough, Tennessee, the seat of Washington County and the oldest town in the state. There are dozens of spectators beyond the bar, all anxiously awaiting the outcome of the hearing. The witness on the stand is an intelligent, frail-looking twenty-five-year-old with an acne-scarred face and straight, shoulder-length brown hair parted in the middle. He leans toward the microphone.

"My name is David Dillinger," he says. I notice a quake in his voice. His anxiety is understandable since he's traveled thousands of miles and is a stranger among us, but anxiety seems to be a way of life for Dillinger. When I interviewed him before the hearing, he had to leave the room half a dozen times to smoke.

"Where do you live, Mr. Dillinger?"

"I live at 401 West Fifth Avenue, Vancouver, British Columbia, Canada."

"And what do you do for a living?"

"I'm a computer programmer for Royal National Bank."

"Do you know the defendant?"

Dillinger shifts uneasily in the chair and looks over at the man sitting at the defense table.

"No. I don't know him. I've never met him."

Douglas "Buddy" Carver stares straight ahead from his spot at the defense table. There isn't a trace of emotion on his sixty-year-old face. His thinning white hair has been combed to the side and held firmly in place by a sticky product of some kind, and he's wearing a loud, red sport coat. Carver is a slumlord, one of the wealthiest landowners in northeast Tennessee. He's also an extremely popular deacon at one of the largest Methodist churches in Johnson City and hosts a local television show called *Bringing the Light* that airs at five o'clock every Sunday afternoon. Most of the people in the gallery are supportive members of his church. They stared at me coldly when I walked into the courtroom.

"Would you please explain to the court how you became involved in this case, Mr. Dillinger?" I ask.

"I received notice that Mr. Carver had downloaded some images onto his computer."

"You say you received notice. How were you notified?"

"By my computer."

"Can you explain to the court how it worked?"

"I attached what's known as a Trojan Horse virus to some pornographic material on an Internet Web site. The pornographic material depicted children. When the images were downloaded, the virus notified me. I was then able to get into the computer of whoever downloaded the images. From there, I was able to find out who was doing the downloading."

"How many pornographic images of children were downloaded?"

"Twelve the day I found out about it, but when I got into the computer, there were about fifteen hundred more."

"And what did you do, Mr. Dillinger?"

"I called Pedofind. It's a nonprofit organization that tracks pedophiles in the United States and Canada. I gave them the information I had."

"And after that?"

"All I know is that Mr. Carver wound up getting arrested, and here I am today."

Pedofind had contacted the Johnson City Police Department, and they, in turn, had followed up. They gathered enough information to get a search warrant, executed the warrant at Buddy Carver's home a week later, seized his computer, and arrested him a couple of days after that.

"Did you have any contact regarding Mr. Carver with any law enforcement agency in Tennessee before you found these images on his computer?" I ask.

"No."

"Did you have any contact with any law enforcement agency anywhere about Mr. Carver before you found these images?"

"No."

"Thank you, Mr. Dillinger."

Cut-and-dried, I think. Straightforward. Nothing to attack. But I know there's never anything cut-and-dried in the field of criminal law. I also know I'm in front of a judge who is strangely sympathetic to sex offenders in general and pedophiles in particular. I suspect he and the defendant might have something in common.

Judge Green has been taking notes and listening intently to the testimony, his glasses perched precariously on his long, thin nose. Buddy Carver's lawyer is a fifty-year-old named William Kay who brownnoses judges so blatantly that everyone calls him Fudge. He has filed a motion asking the judge to throw out all of our evidence (the pornographic images) because, he alleges, his client's rights under the Fourth Amendment to the United States Constitution have been violated. Specifically, Fudge is arguing that David Dillinger illegally searched Carver's computer, thereby requiring the court to exclude the evidence he found and subsequently turned over to Pedofind.

Were David Dillinger a police officer, Kay's argument would have legs. But Dillinger is a private citizen who took it upon himself to intervene in a situation that offended him personally. The guarantees under the Fourth Amendment don't extend to searches conducted by private individuals—only to searches conducted by agents of the government. Fudge is arguing that because Dillinger contacted authorities as soon as he found the pornographic material and sought to have Carver prosecuted, he was acting as an agent of the government and was therefore required to obtain a warrant before searching the files of Carver's computer. Fudge is wrong, but that doesn't mean a thing.

"Cross, Mr. Kay?" Judge Green asks, and Kay gets up. He's short and pudgy. His brown hair is matted and looks as though he just got out of bed.

"Mr. Dillinger," Kay says as he waddles around the

table toward the lectern, "why did you attach this virus to this particular kind of material?"

"Because it offends me."

"How did you know where to find it?"

"Excuse me?"

I'm watching Dillinger intently. He sits on his hands and his face flushes. He's already becoming flustered, so I stand.

"Objection, relevance," I say. "How Mr. Dillinger originally found the material has nothing to do with whether Mr. Carver downloaded it to his computer."

"Overruled," Judge Green snarls. "Sit down, Mr. Dillard."

"Here's the thing, Mr. Dillinger," Kay says. "I wouldn't know how to find child porn if I wanted to, and I'm guessing everyone else in this courtroom is the same way. I mean, you don't just log on to Google and type in 'child pornography,' do you? That seems like a surefire way to get a visit from the feds. So how did you know where to find it so you could attach your virus to it?"

"It isn't that difficult," Dillinger says.

"Explain it to us."

Dillinger looks at me for help, but the judge has already made his feelings known on the objection. Dillinger has inserted himself into this situation, and Judge Green and William Kay are making sure he has to live with the consequences.

"People find it through chat rooms, mostly," Dillinger says reluctantly.

"And you have personal experience with this?"

"Yes."

"Why? Are you some kind of pervert?"

I could stand and voice the objection of badgering or argumentative, but I don't want Dillinger to come across as being spineless. I decide to let him handle it himself. His eyes tighten, and he leans forward.

"I believe your client is the pervert in this room," he says angrily. *Attaboy. Don't let him intimidate you.*

Kay looks immediately to the judge. "Will the court instruct the witness to answer the question, please?"

"Answer the question," Green says curtly.

"I don't remember the question," Dillinger snaps.

"The question is why," Kay says, starting to reframe the query. "Why do you know how to locate child pornography on the Internet?"

Dillinger pauses, and I feel for him. I've asked him the same question, of course, during our preparation for the hearing. It initially seemed as odd to me as it does to Kay, but once I heard the answer, I understood. Kay should have learned the answer himself before he asked such a dangerous question. The word *why* can be a powder keg in the courtroom.

"I know how to locate it because I was raped as a child by a man who showed me the same kind of smut that your client downloaded onto his computer."

Dillinger's tone is one of indignation and disgust. He lifts his chin and folds his arms, glaring at Kay, who is surprised but manages to recover quickly.

"So what you're telling me is that your motivation in finding child pornography on the Internet and attaching this virus to it is anger, correct?" Kay says.

"I don't know."

"Anger, and maybe revenge? You regard yourself as a cyber vigilante of some sort?"

"I don't regard myself as anything. I just find the perverts and report them."

"So you've done this before? How many times?"

"I don't know exactly. A few."

"Would a few be more than ten?"

"Not that many."

"More than five?"

"Maybe five. Maybe six. I don't keep a log."

"And these reports, do they usually wind up in the hands of the police?"

"Sometimes. I guess so."

"So what you're doing is helping the police find people who might be pedophiles; isn't that right?"

"What I'm doing is alerting Pedofind when illegal images of child pornography are downloaded from the Internet."

I let out a slow, deep breath. Dillinger is doing fine. He isn't letting Kay back him into a corner on the issue of whether he's working specifically for the police.

"But Pedofind reports what you tell them to the police, don't they? Isn't that the point?"

"They do what they do."

"Of course that's the point," Kay says. "You wouldn't report it to them if you thought they were going to ignore you, would you, Mr. Dillinger?"

"I don't know."

"Let me ask you this. What's to keep you from attaching your Trojan Horse virus to some other kind of file, something harmless, and then going into Mr. Carver's computer and downloading these images yourself?"

I pop to my feet again. "Objection. Foundation. There's absolutely no evidence in the record to suggest that Mr. Dillinger did any such thing."

"Overruled."

"Judge, he's trying to suggest that Mr. Dillinger picked Mr. Carver randomly out of all the people in the world who have access to the Internet and intentionally set him up. There's no evidence to support it. It's ridiculous."

"Did I stutter, Mr. Dillard? I said your objection is overruled."

"It didn't happen like that," Dillinger says. He seems to be nearing his breaking point.

"But it could, right?" Kay says, holding on to the line of questioning like a bulldog to a forearm.

"I said it didn't happen like that."

"That's all I have," Kay says, and he sits down.

"Anything else, Mr. Dillard?" Judge Green asks.

"We rest, Judge."

"You can step down, Mr. Dillinger. Do you want to say anything before I rule, Mr. Dillard?"

I've already laid out the argument and all the case law for the judge in a brief that I filed two weeks earlier. I've called two witnesses prior to Dillinger. The first was the president of Pedofind, who outlined what the organization does, how they do it, and specifically what happened in this case; the second was the Johnson City detective who investigated the report, obtained the search warrant, and arrested Buddy Carver. Both of them testified that Dillinger was not working on their behalf when he hacked into Carver's computer. The detective testified that she'd never heard of Pedofind or Dillinger prior to the investigation. The Pedofind executive admitted that they'd obtained information from Dillinger before, but that Dillinger received no compensation, no direction, and no encouragement from their organization. He just popped up on their radar every so often and gave them information about suspected pedophiles actively downloading child pornography from the Internet. The Pedofind executive also testified that his company receives no funds from the government— no grants, no loans, no stipends, nothing. The organization is funded entirely by private donations.

As an aside, I've reminded the judge that Dillinger isn't a citizen of the United States and wasn't in the country—let alone in the city or the state—when he alerted Pedofind. Therefore, I've argued, he could not possibly be acting on behalf of any U.S. governmental agency. The protections of the Constitution simply do not apply.

I stand up and lay it all out for the judge one last time. He won't look at me, which is always a bad sign.

Kay gets up and argues his side of the case again. Pedofind is obviously an agent of the government, he says. They report illegal activities to law enforcement whenever the opportunity arises. Their activities have resulted in the prosecution of more than a dozen pedophiles. Dillinger, he says, is an agent of Pedofind. He's given them information in the past, they've turned it over to government authorities, and the information has resulted in criminal prosecutions. Because both are acting on behalf of the government, the search of Carver's computer is covered by the Fourth Amendment. A warrant is required. Since there was no warrant, the search is illegal. The evidence must be suppressed.

When Kay is finished, I experience the same feeling of gloom that I experienced so many times as a defense lawyer. I'm going to lose. The judge's attitude, his mannerisms during the hearing—his interest when Kay is talking and his distance when I'm talking—have tipped his hand. I know he's going to rule against me as sure as I know it's going to rain when a thunderhead rolls in over the mountains to the west.

"Do you require findings of fact and conclusions of law, Mr. Dillard?"

I remain seated, unwilling to stand and show him the respect required by tradition because I regard him as a small man in terms of intellect and morality. Despite the fact that he's sitting above me on his throne and could possibly do the same thing to me that he's done to Ray Miller, I can't force myself to genuflect.

"Is there any point?" I mutter from my seat at the table.

"Speak up!"

I lift my head and glare at him. "I think you made up your mind before we walked in the door."

Judge Green stiffens briefly but manages to control his anger. He knows the press is in the audience. He knows this is a big story. He knows he has a rare chance to deal a blow to the prosecutor's office and me personally, and he's relishing it.

"I am an elected official," the judge says deliberately, "whose primary responsibility, in my view, is to interpret and uphold the law. The people of this district elected me because they trust me. They've trusted me for many years, and I've served them faithfully."

I drop my head into my hands, certain that this is a preamble to a decision that only he can rationalize. I've already considered what I'll do if he rules against me, and I resign myself to the fact that this battle will be fought elsewhere.

"However," Green continues, "a judge must occasionally make a ruling that is not popular. He must do what's right under the law. He must protect the very foundation of our laws and our government, the Constitution of the United States of America."

He's making dramatic pauses while he speaks. I want to throw up.

"I hope those who read about this in the newspaper tomorrow morning or watch it on the evening news will understand that this ruling is for all of you. It will protect you from future illegal intrusions into your privacy. There is no doubt in this court's mind that the state's primary witness in this case, Mr. David Dillinger, was acting as an agent of the government when he hacked into the defendant's computer. Mr. Dillinger has testified that he was abused as a child by someone he believes was a pedophile, and that he has undertaken a mission to see that other pedophiles are exposed and brought to justice. In order to accomplish his mission, Mr. Dillinger intrudes on the privacy of other citizens by clandestinely hacking into their computers with the intent to have them prosecuted under the criminal laws of this country. The court finds that the fact that the governmental agencies involved in this particular case were unaware of Mr. Dillinger's activities is irrelevant. At the very core of it, Mr. Dillinger is a wannabe police officer, a 'cyber vigilante,' as Mr. Kay so adroitly pointed out. Mr. Dillinger obviously regards himself as a sort of charitable mercenary, working on behalf of the government without the expectation of compensation or recognition, but in reality, he's no different than a common burglar. Instead of stealing jewelry, he steals information, and he does so by secretly invading the privacy of his victims' computers. He then expects his targets to be prosecuted, which in this court's view, makes him an agent of the government. His warrantless search of Mr. Carver's computer was illegal, and any evidence obtained as a result of that search is hereby suppressed."

Kay stands. I'm sure he wants to get out of the courtroom as quickly as possible. I also stand and turn to look at Dillinger. I want to apologize to him on behalf of the state of Tennessee, on behalf of the entire U.S. criminal justice system. But he's already out of his seat, heading for the door. He slams it as he leaves, and the bang rips through the courtroom like a gunshot.

"Bailiff!" Judge Green shouts. "Stop that man and bring him back here."

I fix a stare on the judge as the bailiff hurries out the door. I hear shouting in the hallway. Thirty seconds later, the bailiff walks back through the door, holding Dillinger by the elbow. The look in Dillinger's eyes is one of fear and humiliation.

"Bring him to the lectern," the judge says.

Dillinger stands before Judge Green, looking down at the lectern.

"You're in contempt, Mr. Dillinger. Your punishment is a hundred-dollar fine, payable in the clerk's office before you leave the building. If you don't pay it, I'll have you arrested and jailed. Go back to Canada where you belong, sir. The Canadian government may allow you to invade the privacy of others to your heart's content, but this is the United States of America. We don't tolerate such behavior."

Dillinger's shoulders drop, and he walks out of the courtroom like a condemned man. As soon as he leaves, I speak up.

"In light of your ruling, Judge, the state moves to dismiss the indictment against Mr. Carver."

"Really, Mr. Dillard? You mean you don't plan to appeal?"

He's smug. He knows an appeal will take two years. Even if his ruling were reversed—and I feel certain it would be—so many things can happen in two years. Evidence is lost. Witnesses die or move away. They become uncooperative. After what Dillinger's been through today, I'm certain he won't return in two years.

"No, Judge. I'm not going to appeal."

"Very well. Case dismissed. Costs taxed to the state. Mr. Carver, you're free to go."

6

Katie Dean spent two months in the hospital after she was nearly murdered by her father. The blast entered the right side of her chest, smashed her sternum and several ribs, and blew out a large part of her right lung. She didn't remember what had happened for at least two weeks after the shooting. There was only blackness—a vast hole in her life. She didn't even remember dreaming.

When she had finally healed enough to leave the hospital, Katie's aunt Mary took her to the cemetery. It was mid-October 1992. The weather had turned cold, the wind was howling in off Lake Michigan, and leaves were falling from the trees and swirling in the air like giant, colored snowflakes. Katie's mother, along with Katie's brothers and sister, were buried side by side. She knelt and laid fresh cut flowers in front of the headstone that marked her mother's grave, and she wept so hard her stomach cramped. She couldn't believe she'd never see them again. She couldn't believe what Father had done. She wished he'd killed her, too.

Father's grave wasn't there. Aunt Mary said he'd

been placed in another cemetery. Katie didn't ask where it was. Mother always said he was sick, but Katie couldn't find it in her heart to forgive him for what he did.

Aunt Mary was Mother's older sister, and she bore a striking resemblance. She was slender, not very tall, with blond hair, blue eyes, and a kind face. She looked tired most of the time, as though she never got enough sleep. Mother had taken Katie and her brothers and sister to Tennessee to visit Aunt Mary once, not long after Aunt Mary's husband was killed in a logging accident. She lived in a farmhouse at the base of a mountain near a place called Gatlinburg. Katie was just a little girl, but she remembered they went there late in May, right after Kirk and Kiri got out of school for the summer. Aunt Mary was pregnant.

It was the first time Katie had ever seen the Great Smoky Mountains and the purple haze that hung over them in the evening. They were so beautiful. She would go out onto the front porch in the evening and sit for hours, just looking up at the massive humps and gentle slopes shrouded in mist. Sometimes after dark the mountains would sparkle with tiny lights, as though thousands of fairies were flying among the leaves on the trees. The image made her think of magic kingdoms, filled with wonder and mystery.

Aunt Mary took Katie back to her farmhouse in Tennessee the day after she visited her family's grave sites. Katie supposed Aunt Mary was the only person in the family who wanted her. Father's parents had both died of cancer before Katie was born. Mother's mother died of an aneurysm in her lung when Katie was nine. Her grandpa Patrick was still alive, but he'd married another woman and was living in Oregon.

Katie was sitting in the front seat beside Aunt Mary in the car on the way to her house. They crossed into Tennessee near a town called Jellico. Rain was beating against the windshield, and the tires on the tractor trailers were throwing up huge plumes of water like geysers. Darkness was falling.

"Katie," Aunt Mary said, "we don't have much, but what we have is yours. You're my daughter now."

Katie scooted over and buried her face in Aunt Mary's shoulder. She started to cry.

"There, there now," Aunt Mary said. "Everything's going to be all right. I can't imagine how hard this is for you, child, but you have to keep on going. God chose you to go on living. He *chose* you, Katie, and for a reason. We don't know what His reason is yet, but you have to be strong. It's what God wants, and it's what your momma would have wanted."

Katie had thought a lot about God when she was lying in the hospital, after Aunt Mary told her that everyone in her family was dead. She was angry with Him. Katie and her mother and brothers and sister had gone to church every Sunday morning, and every night since she could remember, Katie knelt down next to her bed and prayed before she went to sleep.

> Now I lay me down to sleep,
> I pray the Lord my soul to keep.
> If I should die before I wake,
> I pray the Lord my soul to take.

At the end of the prayer, she always asked God to bless Mother and Father, her sister, and her brothers. If there was anyone she knew who was sick or having problems, she'd ask God to bless them, too. She never asked Him to bless her; she thought it would be selfish. She never asked Him for a thing. Maybe she should have asked Him to keep her family safe.

When they finally arrived in Tennessee in the middle of the night, Aunt Mary and Katie carried their things inside. The house was dark except for a lamp near the front door. The hardwood floors creaked under Katie's feet with every step, and the wind was rattling the shutters outside the windows. The house smelled odd, like a doctor's office.

A light came on down a short hallway to Katie's right, and a door opened. A black woman stepped into the hall and walked toward them. The woman stopped and looked down at Katie. She smiled. She had the darkest eyes and the whitest teeth Katie had ever seen, and her face was as shiny and round as a ceramic dinner plate. She was much bigger than Aunt Mary. Her hair was wrapped in a blue bandanna, and she was wearing a faded blue flannel robe.

Katie heard a muffled sound coming from the other side of the door. It sounded almost like a sheep bawling.

"Welcome home, Mary," the black woman said to Aunt Mary. They embraced.

"It's good to be here," Aunt Mary said.

Aunt Mary put her hand on Katie's shoulder. "This is Katie," she said. "Katie, this is Lottie, my good friend."

"Nice to meet you, Miss Katie," Lottie said in a soft, smooth, Southern way. She knelt down and hugged her. "You're gonna be real happy here. Real happy."

Katie heard the sound coming from behind the door again—"*nnggghhaaaaah*"—and looked nervously up at Aunt Mary.

"He knows you're here," Lottie said to Aunt Mary. "He's missed you something terrible."

"Why don't you take Katie upstairs and get her settled?" Aunt Mary said. "I'll look in on him."

Lottie picked up Katie's suitcase with one hand, wrapped the other around Katie's hand, and led her toward the stairs. Katie looked back over her shoulder and saw Aunt Mary disappear into the same room from which Lottie had emerged. She heard the bawling sound again, this time much louder.

"That's Luke," Lottie said as they made their way slowly up the stairs. "He's a special boy. I expect you'll meet him tomorrow."

7

"I gave these damned things up a long time ago," Ray Miller says as he blows a smoke ring toward the night sky and leans against the rail on the deck. "Now look at me."

Dinner was awkward. Caroline fixed lasagna and salad, and she and Toni chatted while we all downed a couple of glasses of wine. After dessert, Ray stepped outside to smoke, and I tagged along to keep him company. I don't know how much he had to drink before he came over, but he seems lethargic and distracted. He hasn't uttered a complete sentence since he walked in the door.

I, too, lean against the rail, not knowing what to say. I know all about the turmoil surrounding his life, but I don't know whether he wants to talk about it. I finally decide to breach the line.

"So, how are you holding up?" I try to be nonchalant as I search out the Big Dipper to the north. I hear him take a short breath, as though I've startled him.

"You don't want to know," Ray says. He's a substantial man, and his voice is a deep baritone.

"Sure I do, Ray. I'm your friend, remember?"

Ray takes a long drag off the cigarette. The smoke rises slowly around his tired face, framing it eerily for a brief moment before disappearing into the darkness.

"We got a foreclosure notice in the mail this afternoon," he says. "We're three months behind on the mortgage."

"Why didn't you say something? I'll loan you some money."

"I appreciate it, but I don't borrow money from my friends."

"You'll pay it back."

"You don't understand, Joe. I'm three months behind now. It's going to be at least another six months before I can get a hearing in front of the board. If I get my license back, which isn't guaranteed by any means, it'll take me another six months to get back on my feet. The mortgage is twenty-five hundred a month. You want to loan me thirty grand that I won't be able to pay back for a year or two?"

"Sure. Caroline has taken good care of our money. I can handle thirty grand."

"Thanks, buddy," he says, "but I can't accept. I just can't. I wish I'd had your foresight. Saved a bunch of money, you know? God knows I've made a lot of it in the past fifteen years. But I grew up with nothing, and I've always wanted Toni and Tommy to have the best of everything. Nice home, nice cars, nice clothes, good food. And Christmas? I'm a damned fool at Christmastime. Toni calls me Santa."

"I know," I say, smiling at the thought. Ray spends thousands on food and gifts for underprivileged families every year. He donates to churches and welfare organizations. "I've seen what you do at Christmas."

"I'm not that far in debt except for the mortgage, but Tommy's college expenses ate up almost all of our savings."

Duke University's baseball program gave Tommy a scholarship that paid for half of his tuition and his books. But Ray pays the rest: the other half of the tuition, Tommy's food and clothing, his car and insurance and gasoline, the rent for his apartment, his walking-around money. Ray has told me that it costs him nearly forty thousand dollars a year to keep Tommy in school at Duke.

"If it weren't for Toni's job, we'd starve," Ray says.

I shake my head and sigh. "Amazing, isn't it? The power that one man can have over another just because he wears an ugly black dress."

"I can't tell you how many times I've dreamed about killing him. I'd like to kill him slowly."

His tone is ominous. I decide to change the subject.

"Isn't there anything else you can do for a while? For money?"

"Like what? I've been on the front page of the newspaper four times already. Green's got everybody thinking I'm some kind of criminal, a whack job lurking in the shadows, just waiting for my opportunity to take down the entire system. Nobody around here is going to hire me. Besides, the only thing I know how to do is practice law."

"I heard about Tommy having to leave Duke." I look over at Ray. "I'm sorry, Ray, truly sorry."

Ray's shoulders slump forward and his head drops. I can hear him breathing slowly in the stillness.

"That's the worst part of all this," he says. "The effect it's having on my wife and son. Tommy acts like it's no problem. He hasn't complained, hasn't said a word about it other than to tell me he knows I didn't do anything wrong."

"And Toni? Everything good with her?"

"I think it's beginning to wear on her. I'm not exactly a joy to live with these days, and she loves the house. Losing the house will tear her up. And the thought of her being torn up tears me up."

I look at him and see a tear glistening on his cheek. He wipes it away with the back of his hand.

"Jesus," he says. "I'm acting like a child."

"Don't apologize. I probably would have fallen on my sword by now."

Ray turns toward me. His eyes lock on to mine briefly, then drop toward the ground.

"Do you remember a couple of years back?" he says, his head still down. "I think you'd just started at the DA's office. Judge Glass had charged Sheriff Bates with contempt over something stupid, and your office refused to prosecute. Didn't you handle that in court?"

I remember it vividly. Judge Ivan Glass, the cranky, seventysomething judge, was presiding over an afternoon hearing two years ago when a question arose about a policy at the sheriff's department. Judge Glass told a bailiff to telephone Sheriff Leon Bates and order him to come to court to testify and clear up the matter. Sheriff Bates politely told the bailiff he was busy. Judge Glass told the bailiff to call back and tell the sheriff if he didn't come to court immediately he'd be charged with contempt. The sheriff told the bailiff to tell the judge to kiss his biscuits, and the judge filed the contempt charge. When the day came for the hearing, I went into court, and on behalf of the district attorney's office, told Judge Glass he had no authority to order the sheriff into court, that the charge had no basis in law or fact, and that the district attorney's office refused to prosecute the case. The courtroom was packed with Bates's political supporters, and Judge Glass was forced to back down and drop the charge against the sheriff.

"Yeah, I handled it," I say.

"I hate to ask you, but what are the chances of your doing the same thing for me? I have to go in front of the son of a bitch on Monday."

"Who? Judge Green?"

"Plea deadline on the contempt charge. All you'd have to do is go in there and say the DA's office refuses to prosecute. It's a bullshit charge and everybody knows it."

"I've already talked to Mooney about it. I begged him. He doesn't want to get involved."

"Why?" Ray says. "What's the difference between me and Bates? What's the difference between Glass and Green?"

"Think about it."

Ray flips the ashes off his cigarette and puts the butt in his pocket. He pauses for a long moment.

"Oh, I've thought about it. Believe me."

"Bates is probably the most popular sheriff we've

ever had in this county," I say. "Mooney helped Bates out, hoping it would benefit him politically somewhere down the road. That's all it was."

"And Green has already announced he's not going to run for another term, assuming someone doesn't kill him before this term expires. So there's no upside for Mooney if he gets involved."

"Exactly. I'm sorry, Ray."

"Forget it."

"Take it to trial. Surely a jury will see what's happening and do the right thing."

"I appreciate the advice," he says, "but if you can't help, I've got something a little more dramatic in mind."

"Like what?"

"You'll see on Monday," he says, and he turns and walks back into the house.

8

"Aren't you coming to see the show?"

I look up from an attempted murder file into the face of Tanner Jarrett. He's wearing his perpetual smile.

"What show is that?"

"Ray Miller's in court. Judge Green sent word that he's going to call Miller up first thing."

"Yeah, I was planning on coming down." I've been thinking about what Ray said, about his doing something dramatic, all weekend.

"I hate this," Tanner says. "It's a lousy case, and Miller seems like a good guy. Being the new kid on the block sucks sometimes."

"Why don't you just walk in there and tell Green there's no case and refuse to prosecute? Show everybody you've got some balls, son."

"Mooney and my dad would both cut them off as soon as I walked out of the courtroom," Tanner says. "I'll leave that kind of stuff to you old guys."

I stand and smile at Tanner. "Is Mooney coming?"

"He took a week of vacation."

"You're kidding. He went to a conference last

week. He didn't say anything to me about going on vacation this week."

"He's the boss. I guess he can do whatever he wants."

Tanner and I make our way downstairs to the courtroom, and I take a seat in the jury box. The place is full of defense lawyers and prosecutors, most of whom have no business with the court; they're there just to see if a battle erupts. There are about thirty people in the gallery, two television news camera crews, and a smattering of reporters. The atmosphere is tense and subdued. I look around and see Ray sitting in the back row. Toni isn't with him. Ray won't let her come. He's told me he's too ashamed.

Judge Green enters the courtroom and his clerk calls the case of *State of Tennessee versus Raymond Miller.* Ray walks slowly, almost unsteadily, toward the front, wearing a black suit, a black shirt, and a black tie. His hair, which has grayed significantly over the past six months, is pulled back tightly into a ponytail. His forehead is deeply lined, his eyes dark and intense. His back looks to be as wide as a sheet of plywood. He attempts to stand straight at the defense table, but I notice he's swaying slightly. He stares at Judge Green. Tanner silently rises from his seat at the prosecution table.

"Mr. Miller," Judge Green says, "you've been charged with contempt of court in the presence of the court based upon your failure to show up at the appointed time and your failure to notify any court personnel. You're here today for a plea deadline. I see you haven't hired counsel."

"I don't need counsel," Ray says curtly.

"You know what they say about the man who represents himself in court," the judge says. "He has a fool for a client."

There is a lingering silence in the courtroom, and as I sit there watching, I imagine that the entire building is shuddering, as though it's trying to shake off the tension inside. Ray's jaw tightens, and his chin juts forward. He begins to speak, very slowly.

"Because of you, I've lost nearly everything I've spent my life working for." His speech is almost imperceptibly slurred. Only someone who has spent as much time with Ray as I have would notice. He continues, "I've also lost my livelihood, my reputation, my—"

"Anything that's happened to you, you've brought on yourself," Judge Green interrupts.

"*I'm not finished!*" Ray roars, and Judge Green, suddenly intimidated, seems to sink in his high-backed leather chair.

"What you've done to me is inexcusable. I've done everything in my power to try to put a stop to it, but you just won't quit. You're a pathetic excuse for a man, an embarrassment to the judiciary, and I'll be *damned* if I'm going to stand here and let you call me a fool!"

"You're in contempt again," Judge Green says, trying unsuccessfully to look brave. "Bailiff, take Mr. Miller over to the jail."

"You're right about that." Ray lets out a sardonic chuckle. "I have more contempt for you than you could ever imagine."

Ray's right hand slides quickly inside his jacket. When it reappears, it's holding a revolver. Without saying a word, he points the pistol at Judge Green.

Boom!

The shot is deafening in the confined area of the courtroom. I see smoke pour out of the gun barrel and I freeze, unable to believe what I'm witnessing. Ray pulls the trigger a second time, and another ear-splitting roar reverberates off the walls. I glance at Judge Green. He's scrambling to get beneath the bench. I'm conscious of women screaming, men yelling, bailiffs dashing forward. I start climbing over the two rows of seats in front of me, yelling Ray's name.

A bailiff moves to within five feet of Ray, his gun pointed at Ray's head.

"Put the gun down! Now!" the bailiff screams. Another is approaching from the rear.

Ray looks at the bailiff. Then he looks back at the bench, where Judge Green—dead, wounded, or cowering—has disappeared.

Then Ray looks at me.

"Good-bye, my friend," he says calmly. "I didn't deserve this."

He opens his mouth wide, inserts the pistol barrel, and, before I can get to him, pulls the trigger.

9

Katie Dean awoke to a house filled with the smells of clean cotton sheets and pillowcases, coffee brewing, and sausage frying. Sunlight was spilling through her window upstairs, and when she lifted her head to look outside, the view nearly took her breath away. The mountains to the east were dazzling with color—deep reds, brilliant oranges, and golds. It looked as though they'd been covered with a gigantic, multicolored quilt. She pulled the covers back and looked around at her new bedroom. The walls were plaster and had been painted gold. The hardwood floor next to the bed was covered by a dark orange woven rug. There was a small closet just off the foot of the bed and a chest of drawers against the wall near the door. Framed photographs of Katie's mother and brothers and sister covered the chest and a small nightstand next to the bed. Some of her drawings had been hung on the wall by the window. She walked to the closet in her stocking feet and saw that her clothes had already been unpacked and were hanging neatly in a row.

Katie slowly descended the stairs. When she was halfway down, she saw him for the first time. His bed had been rolled into the living room. His head was turned away from her, toward a television set. He was covered from the neck down with a sheet and blanket. All Katie could see was his hair, which was the same color as that of the bright red squirrels that lived in the trees in her yard back in Michigan. Katie stopped, sat down on the stairs, and watched him through the railing.

Lottie walked into the den from the kitchen a few seconds later. She noticed Katie immediately.

"I knew the smell of sausage would bring you outta that bed. Come on down here and meet Mister Luke."

Lottie reached her hand upward from the bottom of the steps, but Katie hesitated.

"Don't be scared now, child. Like I told you last night, Luke's a special boy."

Lottie's voice and manner were soothing, so Katie stood and took her hand. Lottie led her to the side of the bed. Katie noticed it was just like the bed in which she'd lain for two months at the hospital.

"Mister Luke," Lottie said, "this is Miss Katie. Ain't she just a beautiful angel?"

Katie looked curiously into Luke's brown eyes. He was small and incredibly thin, his skin as pale as the white sand beaches on the shores of Lake Michigan. The boy's eyes widened, his body began to jerk, and he let out a strange, guttural wail.

"See? He's happy to meet you," Lottie said.

"Hi," Katie said softly as Luke continued to squirm. She was a bit uneasy, because she'd never seen anyone quite like Luke. He obviously couldn't talk or move around on his own. The noises he made were unsettling, and the jerky motions were almost frightening, but Katie continued to smile.

"You go back to watching your TV now," Lottie said to Luke. "I'm gonna get this young lady some breakfast. I'll bring yours in directly. The two of you can get acquainted later on."

Once again, Lottie took Katie by the hand and led her into a small kitchen surrounded by windows that overlooked the back of the property and the mountains beyond.

"Do you know where you are, honey?" Lottie said.

"Tennessee," Katie said quietly.

"Gatlinburg, Tennessee. One of the most beautiful places on God's green earth." Lottie pointed out a side window. "That's Roaring Fork Road, and just a few miles over that ridge is the town of Gatlinburg."

Lottie waved a hand toward the mountains.

"And all of that, as far as the eye can see, is the Great Smoky Mountains National Park. We live right on the border. Now you just sit yourself right down here and let me get some food into you. We believe in a good breakfast around here."

Katie watched in fascination as Lottie piled two eggs, two sausage patties, fried potatoes, and a slice of tomato on her plate. On another plate was a biscuit. Next to it was a small bowl of gravy, a saucer with a stick of butter on it, and a jar of blackberry preserves. On yet another plate was a mixture of apple and banana slices and grapes, flanked by a tall glass of orange juice.

"Dig in, child. Don't be shy."

Katie began to eat, slowly at first, but then with more purpose. She didn't remember the last time she'd had a decent meal, let alone enjoyed it.

"Good?" Lottie said as she dropped a fried egg and a couple of sausage patties into a blender.

"Yes, ma'am," Katie said, nodding her head. "This is the best sausage I've ever had."

"Most everything is fresh," Lottie said. "We buy fresh sausage from Mr. Torbett. He's our closest neighbor; lives up the road a ways. The eggs come straight from the henhouse out back. Potatoes and tomatoes come from the garden. And your aunt Mary makes the best biscuits this side of the Mississippi."

"Where's Aunt Mary?" Katie said.

"She's at work. She's a nurse down at the hospital, you know. They let her work a special shift so she can spend more time with Luke. She leaves here at three in the morning and gets back home a little after noon."

Luke let out a loud wail from the den.

"I'm coming, baby," Lottie called as she pushed the button on the blender. "Just one second."

"How old is he?" Katie said.

"Luke? He's seven."

"What's wrong with him?"

"He has cerebral palsy," Lottie said. "It's a sickness that keeps him from being able to do things other folks do. But we don't look at it as something that's wrong with him. He's just another one of God's beautiful creatures. And don't you go letting him fool you. He may not be able to walk and talk like other folks, but he's a smart young gentleman. And sweet? That boy's sweeter than those grapes you're eating."

"Will he get better?" Katie asked.

"No, honey. Your aunt and her husband, God rest his soul, took Luke to doctors all over the country. They took him over to Duke University and up to the Mayo Clinic and a couple of places in between. There's nothing anyone can do."

As Lottie talked, she poured the sausage and egg paste from the blender onto a plate. She looked up to see Katie staring at her.

"He likes the taste of meat," Lottie said, "but he can't chew it himself and he doesn't swallow real good. I'm just getting it to where he can handle it. We do the same thing with vegetables and fruit, pretty much anything he eats."

"So he's like a baby?" Katie said.

"I suppose he is. He's as helpless as a baby. He wears diapers, and we give him a sponge bath every day. He don't ever get outta that bed. But we don't talk to him like a baby. We talk to him like any other seven-year-old boy. And those sounds he makes, he's trying to talk, but the muscles in his mouth and lips don't work good enough to form the words. But me and your aunt Mary can understand him. You will, too, soon enough."

Katie took one last bite of the fruit and set her fork on the plate.

"Finished?" Lottie said.

"Yes, ma'am. Thank you."

"C'mon in here with me. I'll show you how to feed Luke."

*   *   *

Katie spent the rest of her first morning on the farm exploring her new surroundings. To her delight, she found that the barn out back was home to a black-and-white border collie named Maggie, three calico cats named Winkin, Blinkin, and Nod, and a billy goat named Henry. There were five Black Angus cattle in a fenced-in pasture with a stream running through it and six chickens in the henhouse—five hens and a rooster named Ernie. Every animal on the property was named except for the cattle.

Aunt Mary arrived home shortly after noon and, after feeding Luke, gave Katie a tour of the outer edges of the property. Every time Katie looked at her, she saw Mother. She was there in Aunt Mary's mannerisms, in her way of speaking, in the way she moved. The thought crossed Katie's mind that had Aunt Mary not been such a kind and gentle person, her similarities to Mother would have been painful.

The property was beautiful—twenty-five acres of rolling pasture and five more of wooded land that bordered the national forest. The stream dissected the property from the northeast to the southwest, and the mountains rose like great sentinels all around.

"They're spectacular, aren't they?" Aunt Mary said when she noticed Katie staring up at the peak of Mount LeConte. They were rattling along through the pasture in an old green pickup truck that Aunt Mary had backed out of the barn.

"Yes, ma'am," Katie said.

"But they can be dangerous, too. You have to respect the mountains, Katie."

"Yes, ma'am."

As they topped a small ridge heading back toward the house, Katie noticed movement to her left. She looked toward a logging road that led back into the heavy woods and the mountains and saw a line of trucks heading down toward Roaring Fork Road. She counted ten of them, large trucks like those that carried soldiers in the movies, with huge tires and covered in canvas. At the front of the line was a Jeep with a star on the door and a bar of lights across the top.

"What's that?" Katie asked, pointing in the direction of the convoy.

Aunt Mary's face turned cold.

"It's nothing," she said. "If you ever see them again, you just act like they're not even there."

10

The immediate aftermath of Ray Miller's public suicide was confusion, followed by the horror of realization. Numbed and silent, I moved slowly across the courtroom floor to where his body lay, and I knelt beside him. Ray had dropped straight to the ground between the prosecution and defense tables, partially on his side, his open eyes staring blankly ahead, his face frozen in a look of eternal defiance. The gun lay at his side, and a dark pool of blood spread slowly on the gray carpet beneath his head.

Judge Green emerged from his hiding place a few moments later. The first bullet had struck his high-backed chair an inch from his right ear; the second had actually caught the sleeve of his robe. But the judge was unscathed, and he soon began muttering to himself as he leaned against the wall and walked stiffly toward his chambers. I noticed that nobody went to Green's aid, at least not until the emergency medical people showed up. One of the paramedics found him later, sitting on the toilet in his private bathroom, fully clothed, babbling about miracles and the mysteries of life.

The sheriff's department quickly learned that Ray

had managed to get the gun into the courtroom by avoiding the security station. He simply walked in a back door of the courthouse—a door frequently used by attorneys and county government employees—and came up the stairwell past the property assessor's office. That door is now locked, so that anyone entering the courthouse has to pass through the metal detectors. Too little. Too late.

The medical examiner found a note in Ray's pocket. It was a long and rambling good-bye to Toni and Tommy, but it established a reason, at least in Ray's mind, for his suicide. He believed the two million dollars in insurance money his wife would collect would take care of his family far better than he could. Toni told Caroline that Ray had owned the policy for ten years, so the two-year suicide clause standard in life insurance contracts had long expired. Toni has become an instant millionaire, but I know she would gladly trade every dime for an opportunity to turn back the clock and save her husband.

I'm standing now at the back of a hearse in the immaculate burial ground at the Veterans Administration at Mountain Home. It's two o'clock on Sunday afternoon, and dozens of people are milling around beneath an overcast sky. A brown canopy has been erected over Ray's grave. I'm one of eight pallbearers. Jack has driven up from Nashville and is standing next to me, and across from him stands Tommy Miller. Tommy, tall and lean and dark haired, has adopted the affect of a zombie. I haven't heard him utter a single word since we arrived. His cheeks are without color, his dark eyes empty and trained on the ground.

The group of pallbearers stands silently as the funeral home director slides Ray's casket out of the hearse. We carry the flag-draped casket solemnly through the crowd toward the tent. As we place the casket on the stand above Ray's grave, I hear Toni sobbing behind the black veil she's wearing. Jack and I step out of the tent and stand next to Caroline and Lilly. Caroline is sniffling into a pink handkerchief.

"This is terrible," she whispers. "So senseless."

A debate has been raging in the legal community over the past few days. Who's to blame for Ray Miller's killing himself has been the central question. Many blame Ray, reasoning that his aggressive style in the courtroom and his bravado with judges made him an inevitable target for someone like Judge Green. Had he kept his head down, played nice, and got along like nearly everyone else, he wouldn't have found himself in such a desperate situation. It's as though they believe he got what he deserved.

Others, of course, blame the judge. There's little doubt that his vicious campaign against Ray was personally motivated and largely unfounded. Nearly everyone believes that had any other lawyer made the same mistake Ray made, nobody outside of the judge's office would have heard about it. But Ray had been suspended, jailed, and bankrupted. The local media sharks had gone on a feeding frenzy, and Ray was the bait fish of the month. His reputation had been shattered.

Then there are those who call Ray a coward. He didn't have to kill himself, they say. He could have taken his medicine, apologized to the judge, gone through a bar hearing, and he would have been back practicing law within a year. I find myself empathizing with Ray on that point. I'm a proud man, just as he was. If a judge had taken away my ability to earn a living and care for my family and the media had ruined my reputation without giving me a chance to defend myself, I might have considered doing the same thing Ray did. The only difference, I think, is that I wouldn't have missed when I fired the shots at the judge.

A minister is talking, saying something nonsensical about a basket representing Ray's life and that he had filled his basket to overflowing with love for his family and friends, service for his clients, and genuine feeling for his fellow man. He's speaking in banal generalities. It's obvious the minister didn't know Ray.

"Follow his example," the preacher says. "Fill your basket."

He drones on about how we shouldn't judge Ray for taking his own life, that God never gives us more than we can handle, and that the bullet that ended Ray's life was somehow an instrument of God's love. It's sophistry of the worst kind, worthy of an appellate court, and I find myself wanting to tell the preacher to shut up and let us bury Ray with some dignity.

But I stand there quietly, grieving for my friend but grateful I'm still alive, still with the people I love, and once again I think about how fleeting life is, how fragile, how dangerously unstable. One minute Ray Miller was a fine specimen of a man, a strong and brave spirit standing defiantly in front of those who sought to persecute him, and the next he was a mass of dead matter, lying in a heap on the ground, his spirit gone to some mysterious place.

I lean over and kiss Caroline gently on the cheek. She's been battling breast cancer, along with the sickness and mutilation that comes with the treatment, for a year and a half. I love her so much it almost hurts, and I can't imagine how I'd go on if she were the one being lowered into the ground.

"Oh death, where is thy sting?" the preacher says. "Oh grave, where is thy victory? The sting of death is sin, and the strength of sin is the law. Therefore, my beloved brethren, be ye steadfast, unmovable, always abounding in the work of the Lord, forasmuch as ye know that your labor is not in vain in the Lord."

I look around at the men and women who work in my profession, men and women who make judgments each day about the lives of others, who decide what is right and what is wrong and what punishment is to be doled out for violations of our laws, and I'm reminded of how futile the endeavor is. A man like Ray commits a minor transgression, at worst, and ultimately pays with his life, while so many others who do so much more harm walk away unscathed. How do I reconcile that? Why do I want to continue on this path?

At last, the preacher delivers his final prayer and dismisses the crowd. I hook my arm in Caroline's as Jack drapes his arm around Lilly, and we walk up the hill away from the grave, leaving Toni and Tommy to grieve in private.

11

That evening, I walk up the stairs toward the kitchen after spending a couple of hours in my study. Rio, my German shepherd, tries to slip past me and nearly sends me sprawling. It's close to ten o'clock, and the emotion of the last few days has drained me. I hear voices talking as I approach, but as I round the corner and enter the room, they fall silent. Jack, Lilly, and Caroline are sitting at the table.

"Okay, I'm paranoid," I say. "What were you talking about?"

"We were talking about Ray," Caroline says.

She'd lost her beautiful auburn hair during chemotherapy but it has grown back now and is shimmering beneath the light above the table. The glow is back, too, that aura that surrounds her like a halo. She still has a long way to go with her treatment, but she no longer looks like a dead woman walking.

"Mom said you were in the courtroom when he killed himself," Jack says.

I nod my head, not wanting to relive those awful moments.

"So you saw it? You were looking at him when he pulled the trigger?"

"Yes."

"What did he say?"

I sit down at the table and look at the three of them. "He was talking to Judge Green about Green's ruining his life, and then Green said he was in contempt, and the next thing I knew, he pulled the pistol out and took a couple of shots at the judge."

"Too bad he missed," Lilly says.

"Lilly!" It's Caroline, but the tone is more of surprise and amusement than anger.

"I mean it," Lilly says. "What Judge Green did was cruel. He had no right."

I'm grateful for the interruption. I didn't want to tell them I was the last person on this earth Ray spoke to. I didn't want to tell them about his good-bye.

"Ray would be in jail if he hadn't shot himself," I say. "As much as I hate to say it, he's probably better off." I look at Jack. "Have you talked to Tommy?"

"I've called him five or six times, sent a few text messages, but I haven't heard anything back. I thought about going over there, but if he doesn't want to talk to me on the phone, he probably doesn't want to talk to me in person."

"When are you going back to school?"

"Day after tomorrow. I have to leave early."

"Try to get him on the phone tomorrow and if he doesn't answer, go over there. I'm sure he could use a friend right now."

We talk for a while and I lose myself in the conversation, happy to be able to speak to my children face-to-face. They were such an intimate part of my life for so long, and now I'm lucky to see them thirty days a year. I marvel at their intelligence, their outlook, their honesty and maturity, and I'm humbled to think I played a part in creating them.

Around eleven, Lilly stretches her slender arms toward the ceiling and lets out a yawn.

"I'm tired," she says. "I hear my bed calling." She gets up, kisses me on the cheek, and wanders out of the room. Jack follows her lead, and a couple of minutes later Caroline and I find ourselves alone.

"Something's bothering you," Caroline says.

"Why do you say that?"

"Because I know you."

So much for the mystery in our relationship. When I was younger, there were things I didn't tell her. I'd rationalize by telling myself she didn't need to know, probably didn't want to know; that she was somehow better off staying clear of the deepest recesses of my mind. But she'd broken through a few years earlier, and now, at only forty-three years old, I feel almost naked in her presence, as though she can see everything. I believe she only makes inquiries to test my honesty.

"It keeps running through my mind," I say.

"What? Ray?"

"It was surreal. It happened so fast. I keep thinking I should have gotten to him quicker, but after he fired the first shot, I froze for a split second."

"There you go again," Caroline says, "blaming yourself for something you couldn't have changed."

"I keep seeing the back of his head explode."

The image of Ray's suicide has now been added to the long list of digital clips in my subconscious mind. I've rerun the scene a hundred times in the past few days.

Caroline stands and walks around the table. She puts her arms around me and pulls me close.

"I thought about you today at the funeral," I whisper. "About the cancer, about what it would have been like if you hadn't—"

"Shhh," Caroline says, putting a finger to my lips. "I told you when I was diagnosed that I wasn't going to leave you. I meant it."

The touch of her finger is soothing, and I close my eyes and kiss her hand.

"We need to clean it," she says.

"Okay."

A few minutes later, I'm sitting on the edge of our bed. Caroline is on her back. She's removed her shirt to reveal the mangled mess that was once a breast. The surgeon who attempted to reconstruct the breast originally transplanted a flap of skin and fat from Caroline's abdomen. She was in surgery for twelve hours. It seemed to work, but as soon as she began her radiation treatments, the flap began to develop large, open wounds. They leaked constantly and gradually enlarged. Then the flap began to shrink.

The surgeon explained that the radiation was destroying the tissue in the flap. Fat necrosis, he called it. Three months later, he took her back into surgery, this time removing a large portion of muscle from her back and moving it to the breast site. The result of that surgery was a staph infection that nearly killed her. When she finally recovered from the staph, a large blister began to rise on the edge of the new flap. It, too, developed into a large, open wound.

The responsibility for cleaning the wound has fallen to me. Caroline lies back and closes her eyes while I pull on a pair of latex gloves. I remove the bandage and reach into the wound carefully—it's about the circumference of a quarter on the surface—and begin to pull out a long, thin strip of medicated gauze tape that I'd packed into the wound earlier in the day. The tape is slimy, covered with a mixture of blood and dead fat that smells like rotten eggs. I place it in a small trash bag that I'll carry outside when we're finished.

Each time we do this I ask her whether she's okay, and each time her answer is running down her cheeks. I reach over and pull a tissue out of a box on the mini-trauma center I've set up next to the bed and wipe the tears away.

"Just a few more minutes, baby."

I irrigate the wound with sterile sodium chloride and then unwrap a long, cotton-tipped applicator and dip it into a mixture of hydrogen peroxide and water. I insert the applicator into the wound and begin to swab. The applicator reaches a full four inches beneath the skin.

"It's getting smaller, Caroline. It really is."

At its worst, the hole beneath the skin was as large as my fist. It's healing now, but the progress is painfully slow. I finish swabbing, pack it with fresh gauze tape, and fashion a new bandage out of gauze pads. I tape the bandage in place and rub Caroline's forehead.

"Are you ready?"

She nods, and I begin the difficult task of massaging the reconstructed breast, or at least what's left of it, with my fingertips. The tissue around the scars left by the incisions is as hard as packed clay. The massage is necessary, the doctor says, to try to soften the tissue and improve the range of motion of Caroline's left arm, which she can no longer lift above her head. She winces several times but doesn't complain. This is the worst part of it for me, knowing that I'm inflicting pain on her, but the doctor says it has to be done and she refuses to do it herself.

After several minutes of massage, I stop and put away the supplies.

"All done. Can I get you anything?"

Caroline gets up and heads toward the bathroom. I remove my clothes, hang them in the closet, put on a pair of pajama bottoms, and crawl into bed. Caroline comes in a few minutes later and turns out the light. I retreat into the comfort of my wife's arms and stay there deep into the night.

12

I'm out of bed early the next morning. It's Monday, and I want to get to the gym by six and get in a decent workout before I go back to the grind. It always makes me feel sharper and fresher, helps me to better cope with the insanity I deal with on a daily basis.

As I back out of the garage, I see an unfamiliar car parked in the yard off the driveway. It's a white Honda Civic, an old one that's beginning to be consumed by rust. I get out of my pickup and look inside the car, but there's nothing that tells me who the owner might be.

I walk around the house and see nothing out of place. I walk back into the house and go upstairs. Lilly's sound asleep, and I don't see any of her friends crashed on the floor or anywhere else. I head downstairs to Jack's room and as soon as I get to the bottom step, I know who owns the car. Tommy Miller is on the couch, fast asleep. The car outside is symbolic of the family's financial collapse. The last time I saw Tommy, he was driving a new Jeep. I creep back up the stairs and head off to the gym.

A couple of hours later, I'm standing in the doorway of my boss's office. Lee Mooney has just returned from yet another of his frequent weeklong vacations, one he decided to take immediately after the conference he attended in Charleston. Between the vacations and the time he spends at conferences and seminars, he's out of the office at least two and a half months a year.

I find it difficult to look Mooney in the eye these days because I've come to know he isn't what he seems to be. Not long ago, I sent his nephew—a fellow prosecutor named Alexander Dunn—to prison for extorting money from gamblers. Alexander said Mooney was involved. I believed him, but I couldn't prove it.

Then there's the progressive alcoholism. I've seen Mooney drink himself into stupors at two office functions in the past six months, and I smell the lingering odor of vodka on him often. There are persistent rumors that his marriage is failing. I'm certain he stands to lose a great deal if his wealthy wife divorces him, but his lechery has become legendary. He believes himself to be a gift that must be generously bestowed upon women of all shapes, sizes, colors, and ages. He pursues women at office parties and bar association meetings with both a dogged determination and a complete lack of discretion. His behavior has become increasingly erratic, and his life seems to be spinning out of control; yet he seems totally oblivious.

Mooney is sitting behind his desk, bracketed by the American and Tennessee flags. There's a large, framed photograph of former president George W. Bush behind him. He has handsome features, with a strong jaw that outlines a lean face, but large, dark bags have formed beneath his eyes, and there's a hint of purple in his cheeks. He has salt-and-pepper hair and a handlebar mustache that he fiddles with constantly. He's wearing a brown tweed jacket over a white shirt and beige tie. His gray eyes are angry.

"What the hell's going on with you?" he barks disdainfully. "I go away for a little while, and you dismiss a case outright after you've gotten your ass kicked in a hearing. Have you no sense of the public's perception of this office?"

He's talking about my case against Buddy Carver, the pedophile Judge Green allowed to walk away. He's Monday-morning quarterbacking, and I don't appreciate it.

"I'm taking Carver to the feds," I say. "The federal laws are tougher, the jail terms are longer, and they don't have a judge down there who sympathizes with pedophiles."

"We need to make sure the public knows it when the federal grand jury issues an indictment," Mooney says. "I'll put out a press release."

"Do you remember Brian Gant?" I say, changing the subject. "He was convicted of killing his mother-in-law and his niece a long time ago. I guess it was before you moved here."

"What about him?"

"He's about to be executed, and I think he's innocent. I was wondering whether you might be interested in taking a look at the case. Maybe we should get involved."

Mooney starts to answer, but is interrupted by the

buzz of his intercom. He speaks in muffled tones, then looks back up at me.

"Let's go," Mooney says.

"Where?"

"I said let's go!"

I shrug my shoulders and walk out the door behind him. When we get to the parking lot, he tells me to follow him in my truck. He's tense and upset, more so than usual. He leads me to a wooded lot in an exclusive subdivision called Lake Harbor near Boones Creek. The driveway is asphalt and winds nearly a quarter of a mile through a stand of sugar maple trees toward a massive colonial-style brick house. We round a curve and top a small hill, and as we descend into a shallow valley about halfway to the house, I see it—the unmistakable activity of a crime scene. Vehicles, flashing lights, yellow tape, uniformed men moving slowly about. Mooney pulls over into the grass about a hundred yards short of the tape, and I do the same. As soon as I get out of the truck the smell hits me—the unique, acrid smell of burned flesh, and I jog to catch up to Mooney as he hurries toward the group of officers and paramedics.

"Jesus, Mary, and Joseph," Mooney mutters, and I follow his gaze toward one of the trees.

A blackened body is hanging by its neck from a rope, which has been wrapped around a branch about eight feet from the ground and tied off around the maple's trunk. The body appears to be a male, but beyond that, it's virtually unrecognizable. Chunks of charred flesh cling to the limbs and torso. The lips and most of the face have been burned away, leaving only a garish snarl.

Ten feet to my right, a smaller tree—a Bradford pear—is lying across the driveway. A black Mercedes is parked perhaps five feet from the tree. A TBI agent is photographing the car. I recognize him and walk over.

"Agent Norcross," I say. "Long time, no see." I'd gotten to know Norcross when he worked a murder case with me a little more than a year ago—the Natasha Davis case.

"Well, I'll be damned," Norcross says. He straightens to his full height, around six feet seven, and reaches out to shake my hand. "Joe Dillard."

"Good to see you again. What can you tell me?"

There's a large lump in Norcross's left cheek—chewing tobacco—and he steps off to the side and spits a stream of brown juice onto the ground.

"This your case?" Norcross asks.

"Will be as soon as you catch the killer."

"Looks like somebody hid out in the tree line over there for a while." Norcross motions to a spot where two other agents are walking a grid. "Not really sure how long he was here, but from the look of it, he moved around quite a bit before he decided where he was going to set his little trap."

"Trap?"

"The tree. The perp cut it down—looks like he used a saw of some kind—and it falls across the driveway. He waits back in the trees. When the victim leaves, he has to stop right here. He lives alone, and he's far enough away from everyone else that nobody sees or hears a thing—at least we haven't found anybody yet. The victim walks around to the trunk of the tree, starts tugging on it, and he gets whacked. There's some blood on the tree trunk and scuff marks where the body was dragged across the lawn to the other tree over there. Then the perp douses him with kerosene or gasoline, strings him up, and sets him on fire."

"Who's the victim?" I ask.

Norcross grins. "You don't know?"

"No. Why should I?"

"You're serious? Nobody's told you yet? He's almost as famous as you."

I shrug my shoulders.

"His name's Green," Norcross says, and a chill immediately goes down my spine. "As in Leonard Green. *Judge* Leonard Green."

PART 2

13

I hate to admit it even to myself, but as I stand watching the paramedics untie the rope and slowly lower what's left of Judge Leonard Green to the ground, I feel no sympathy for him. I've practiced law as both a defense lawyer and a prosecutor in front of Green for fifteen years. I've seen him at the gym almost every weekday morning—where he has invariably ignored me—for at least eight years. I should feel something, especially considering the horrible death he's experienced, but I don't. His destruction of Ray Miller's life and career was simply the latest in a long line of cruel acts I've seen him commit from his perch of power, and I'm almost relieved to know he won't be doing it again.

Lee Mooney has been scurrying around the crime scene like an ant. I can sense that he's angry as he approaches me. His cheeks are flushed with pink, and there are small beads of sweat on his forehead. He stands next to me as the coroner begins to look at the body.

"I've been screwed," Mooney says.

"How so?"

"They assigned it to *her*." Mooney jerks his head to his right and shoots a glance toward a black woman wearing a black baseball cap and a navy blue jacket, both with "TBI" emblazoned across the front. Her name is Anita White.

"So? She's smart. She's tough. She's experienced. Seems like a pretty good choice to me."

"I don't like it."

"Why?"

"Look around, Dillard. What do you see? Swinging dicks, that's what. *White* swinging dicks. I've got a dead judge in my district, and the TBI assigns a black woman to lead the investigation."

"It's a new age, boss."

"New age, my ass. I don't give a damn if a black man got himself elected president, a murder investigation requires cooperation between agencies, especially when the TBI is involved. How many cops around here do you think are going to cooperate with a black woman?"

"I think you'd be surprised."

Mooney looks at me in disgust and stomps away. I've seen glimpses of racism in his behavior before, but this is the first time he's been blatant about it. As I watch him walk away, I wonder whether the reason he's been able to hide it so well is because he rarely, if ever, interacts with people of different races. The county where I live has a very small number of African Americans, less than 3 percent of the population. There are no black lawyers, no black office holders, only a couple of black police officers in Johnson City, and no black person works for the sheriff's department. The world in which we both work is staffed by whites.

Anita White is in her late thirties. She was transferred to the Johnson City field office about a year ago. She's medium height and slim, her smooth skin is the color of cocoa powder, her ebony hair is touched with red highlights, and her eyes are a clear green. She has an easy, dimpled smile with a barely noticeable gap between her front teeth and a small mole on her left cheek. She's truly stunning, almost to the point of being intimidating.

I've worked only one case with her so far, a prison murder in Mountain City shortly after she arrived. It was a particularly gory stabbing and all of the witnesses were cons, but working with Anita was a pleasure. I found her to be extremely intelligent. I learned that she loves to read and once dreamed of being a concert pianist. She has a bachelor's degree in criminal justice and a law degree from what used to be Memphis State University, now the University of Memphis.

As the coroner continues to gingerly look over Judge Green's body, Anita walks up. I, too, step toward the gurney.

"Morning, Counselor," Anita says.

"Agent White."

"Unpleasant way to go out, huh?"

"I can give you a time of death."

"Really?"

"He got to the gym every morning at five. He

worked out until six, took a shower, and was out the door by six fifteen. I saw him in the locker room almost every day."

"Were you there this morning?" Anita says.

"Sure was."

"I take it you didn't see him."

"Nope."

"Which gym?"

"The one on State of Franklin Road."

"Which is about ten minutes from here, give or take a few?"

I nod.

"So he leaves here around ten minutes to five, and that should be pretty close to the time of death?"

"Should be."

"I'd like to hear your thoughts on who might have done this," Anita says. "You've known the judge a lot longer than I have."

Something pops to the front of my mind, but I push it back quickly. Could it be possible? No. No way.

"Who found him?" I ask.

"A man he hired to trim some shrubbery. He showed up about eight this morning."

I take a moment and think back on the judge's career on the bench. When it came to making enemies, he was truly an artist.

"Your list of suspects is probably pretty long," I say. "Green sent thousands of people to prison over the past thirty years. His decisions were emotional more often than they were rational, and he couldn't restrain himself from sticking a knife into anyone who gave him an opening. Add the fact that I think he was a sexual deviant, and the list gets even longer."

"What makes you think he was a sexual deviant?"

"Things he's said over the years, things he's done, the way he acted. He was always talking about staying up until three or four in the morning reading legal opinions on the Internet. Used it as an excuse for being grouchy. But since he didn't know very much about the law, he was either lying or just plain stupid. Plus, he's always been soft on sentencing sexual offenders. He let a pedophile walk last week on a legal technicality."

"I heard about that," Anita says. "Didn't some witness come all the way from Canada?"

"Yeah, Vancouver, and Green made him look like a fool. I guess he just couldn't help it. But as far as suspects go, maybe Green molested someone and the victim decided to get even. Maybe someone was trying to blackmail him and he resisted. This is personal. Beaten, hanged, burned. Whoever did this was extremely pissed off."

"Anyone in particular come to mind?"

I shrug my shoulders. "Like I said, long list. I guess you could start by finding out if anyone he sent to the penitentiary has been paroled lately."

"We're already working on that. What about this Ray Miller? How well did you know him?"

"He's dead. I don't think he killed the judge from beyond the grave."

"Quite a coincidence, though, don't you think? Green suspends Miller. Then Miller commits suicide in his courtroom after taking a couple of shots at Green. Miller is buried yesterday, and the judge is found this morning."

"Ray Miller's gone, Anita. That story is over."

"So how well did you say you knew him?"

I look directly at her and her eyes narrow slightly. She's testing me.

"Forgive me, but I'm really not in the mood to be jerked around right now."

· "Really? It was an innocuous question. I just thought you might be able to help."

I smile inwardly for a brief second. She may be the first cop I've ever heard use the word *innocuous*.

"Sorry," I say. "Mooney's had his foot up my butt for the past hour and a half. I guess I'm a little touchy. I knew Ray well. His son and mine played baseball together for years. We were friends."

Anita looks toward the sky. "Storm's coming," she says. "We'd better button this up."

I follow her gaze toward a thunderhead over Buffalo Mountain. It's moving steadily toward us. The newly sprouting leaves on the trees that cover the mountain are a dull gold against the blackening sky. The breeze stiffens, and I shove my hands into my pockets.

"How old is Miller's son?" Anita asks.

"Another innocuous question?"

"Feel free to regard it any way you'd like."

I look down and start digging at the grass with my shoe. I realize Tommy has to be a suspect, but I just can't wrap my mind around the idea that he'd be capable of killing anyone, even the judge. I could tell

Anita about finding him sound asleep on the couch earlier, but I know the drill. If I tell her, I drag myself and my son smack into the middle of a murder investigation. They'll probably even want to talk to Caroline and Lilly. The TBI agents will separate us and interrogate us. Anyone who refuses to talk to them will be deemed to be hiding something. If there's any small discrepancy in any of our stories, they'll all think we're lying.

Then again, if I don't tell her, am I committing a crime? Am I somehow obstructing justice? Tampering? Failing to disclose a material fact in a criminal investigation? I run the possibilities through my mind quickly and decide that though I might have some ethical obligation to tell Anita that Tommy was at my house this morning, I'm not breaking any laws by keeping it to myself. The kid's been through enough, and even though I know she'll do everything in her power to question him, I also know that he has a right to remain silent. He doesn't have to tell her a damned thing.

"He's twenty, and I think you're wrong if you suspect Tommy Miller of doing this," I say. "I've known him since he was a little kid. He's spent the night at my house at least a hundred times over the past ten or twelve years. He's eaten with us, gone to movies and ball games with us, spent holidays with us. We've even taken him with us on vacation a couple of times. He's my son's best friend, and my wife and I would adopt him in a heartbeat. He's a fantastic kid. There's no way he could have done this."

I hear the distinctive sound of a zipper as the paramedics close the body bag. Anita and I watch as they begin to roll the charred remains of Judge Green toward the ambulance.

"That's quite an endorsement coming from an assistant district attorney," Anita says.

"I know him, and I know he didn't do this."

"So if I arrest him for murder, I guess somebody else will be prosecuting."

I hear a clap of thunder in the distance as she turns her back to me and walks away. I hurry off toward my pickup. I need to talk to Tommy.

14

Instead of going to the office, I head straight back to the house. By the time I get there, the thunderstorm is beginning to unleash its fury. As I pull into the driveway, I can see whitecaps on the channel below, and the young birch trees at the edge of the woods are bending with the howling wind. Small raindrops are whizzing by the windshield horizontally, and the thick cloud cover has transformed morning into dusk.

The Honda Civic that I assume belongs to Tommy Miller is gone. I open the door from the garage into the kitchen and Rio almost knocks me down. He's excited to see me, unaccustomed to my coming home so early in the day.

Caroline is standing at the stove, while Jack sits at the kitchen table. There's a stack of pancakes in front of him, and the smell of bacon fills my nostrils. Both of them look at me in surprise.

"What are you doing here?" Caroline says.

I ignore her and walk straight to the table.

"Where's Tommy?" I say to Jack.

"What?"

"You heard me. Where's Tommy? I saw him sleeping downstairs before I left."

"I guess he went home."

"Did you talk to him? What did he say?"

The questions I'm firing at Jack are quick, and the tone of my voice is intense. It's not the kind of treatment he's used to getting from me. Caroline walks over from the stove and sets a plate of scrambled eggs down on the table.

"What time did Tommy show up?"

"I don't know," Jack says. "Why are you so pissed off?"

"I asked you a question, and I want a straight answer. *Now, what time did Tommy show up?*"

"Don't yell at him," Caroline says evenly.

"Stay out of this."

Jack is looking at me with wide eyes. We haven't exchanged a cross word since his first year in college when he got a little too deep into the Nashville party scene. Caroline doesn't reply. She knows how I feel about Jack, and she knows I wouldn't be acting this way without a good reason.

"I don't know what time he got here," Jack says, looking back down at his plate. "I woke up this morning and he was here. He was already awake."

"Did you talk to him before he left?"

"Yeah, a little bit. He said he got hammered last night."

"What time did he leave?"

"About ten minutes ago."

"What else did he say?"

"Not much. He was pretty quiet. I don't think he felt good."

"How did he look?"

"What do you mean, 'How did he look?' He looked like someone who buried his father yesterday and tried to drown the memory in a liquor bottle."

"Did he look like he'd been in a fight?"

"I didn't notice anything."

"No cuts? No blood? No bruises?"

"Not that I saw. What's going on, Dad?"

"What about his clothes? Did you see anything on his clothes?"

"Not really. I mean, he was wearing some of my clothes."

"What the hell happened to his clothes?"

"I don't know."

I take a deep breath and sit down across from him. Caroline returns the pan to the stove and walks back to the table.

"You'd better sit down," I say to her.

For the next few minutes, I describe to them the crime scene, how someone apparently planned the murder, lay in wait, then brutally assaulted, hanged, and burned a man. When I'm finished, I stare straight at Jack.

"They haven't positively identified the body yet. But there's no doubt in anyone's mind who it is."

"Who?" Caroline asks.

"It's Judge Green." I'm still staring at Jack. "And Tommy Miller is at the top of their list of suspects. The TBI is going to be crawling all over this."

Jack's face slowly turns pale, as though a valve has been opened and has drained every bit of blood from above his shoulders. Suddenly he stands.

"I'm going to be sick," he says, and he sprints for the bathroom.

15

Caroline and I sit in silence for a few minutes, listening to the retching from the bathroom echo off the walls down the hall.

"You don't really think Tommy did it," Caroline says.

"It's possible."

"But you knew Ray. You know Tommy. You're his friend, Joe."

"Not if he committed a murder and brought it to my doorstep. That's not my idea of friendship."

"Tommy didn't kill anyone, and you know it. They're just going after Tommy because of what happened with Ray."

"Oh, they're going after him, all right. You can count on that. My guess is Special Agent Anita White will be knocking on his door within the hour."

Caroline stands and starts walking toward the counter. She picks up the telephone.

"Then I'm calling Toni," Caroline says. "I have to warn her."

I get up and walk toward her, holding out my hand.

"No way, Caroline. One of the first things they'll do is get a subpoena for their phone records. If you call, you'll probably get a visit. Now give me the phone."

"She just buried her husband. I can call to check on her if I want."

"But you can't call to warn her that the cops are coming to question her son about a murder."

"Why not?" She turns her back on me and begins to dial.

"Because you could wind up getting charged with obstruction of justice, that's why. Caroline, don't be reckless. Stay out of this."

"That's twice you've said that to me in the past twenty minutes. In case you've forgotten, I'm not one of your underlings at the office. I don't take orders from you."

"Please."

"If it were me, I'd expect her to do the same."

I put my hand on her shoulder and turn her toward me.

"What do I have to do to make you understand this isn't a game? You're about to commit a crime, and you're forcing me to be a witness."

"Calling my friend is *not* a crime. And you don't have to listen."

The look in her eyes tells me she's made up her mind. She walks toward the bedroom, the phone to her ear. I turn, frustrated, and catch a glimpse of Jack coming down the hall, wiping his mouth with a washcloth. The aura of self-assuredness that usually surrounds him has vanished. He trudges through the kitchen on heavy legs and plops back into his seat at the table.

I begin to rub my fingers through my hair and notice that they're trembling. I feel anger—anger that Judge Green set all of this into motion, anger that I'm helpless to do anything about it, anger that my wife is acting like a stubborn fool—but I also feel fear. I know what the system is capable of. I know what it can do to the guilty, and I know what it can do to the innocent. My mind conjures up an image of Tommy strapped to a gurney, an IV hooked to his arm. I fear for Tommy, but I also fear for my son.

"I can't believe this," Jack says quietly. He stares down at the table, as though in a trance.

"Think," I say. "Think about everything he said and did."

"Why? Even if I remember something that might help the police, do you think I'm going to tell them? We're talking about my best friend here. We're talking about someone whose life was ripped apart for no good reason, someone who didn't deserve it. Even if he did kill the judge—and I don't believe for a second that he did—I'll be damned if I'm going to help them pin it on him."

His words shock me to the point of incredulity. I bore in on him, my voice much louder than I intend it to be.

"What the hell is going on here? Has everyone in this house suddenly gone insane?"

He doesn't respond, and I look away in silence, not wanting to comprehend what I'm hearing. Jack has worked hard all his life. He's been an excellent student, a great athlete, a great kid. He has a promising future. He's going to earn a degree from one of the finest universities in the country. He has a chance to achieve his lifelong dream of playing professional baseball. And now he sits in front of me telling me he's willing to take a chance on throwing it all away over a sense of misguided loyalty. I turn back to him.

"Jack, listen to me. You don't know what you're up against. A man has been killed, and not just any man. A judge. I don't care what you thought of him or what I thought of him or what anyone else thought of him. The position he held is as symbolic as it is powerful. He wore a robe, Jack. Think about that. A black robe. Do you think the people around here are just going to sit by and let someone kill one of their most powerful symbols and get away with it? Somebody's going to burn for this. If Tommy did it, they're going to catch him, and they'll probably kill him. If you get in the way, you'll go down with him."

"What are you talking about?" he yells. "I didn't *do* anything. I went to bed last night, and I woke up this morning. That's it."

"He was here when you woke up. That's all it takes."

Jack tenses. The muscles in his neck, shoulders, and chest ripple beneath his skin like waves on a pond.

"All it takes? For what? For the government to invade my life, my privacy? For them to drag me down to the police station and force me to betray my best friend, even though I have no idea what he did last night and I don't believe he committed a crime?"

"If they ask you if you saw him, you have to tell them the truth. And believe me, they'll ask you."

"I don't have to talk to them! Listen to yourself! You sound like a freaking Nazi! Don't forget, Dad—I grew up in this house with you. I've heard you say it a thousand times. 'People don't have to talk to the police.' How many times have I heard you say, 'If he'd just kept his mouth shut, he would've never been caught'?"

"This is different."

"How?" His tone is now defiant. "How is it different? If the police come knocking on my door, I can tell them to piss up a rope, right? I can tell them to go to hell. As a matter of fact, I don't have to tell them anything."

He's right, to a degree. A private citizen doesn't have to speak to the police if he doesn't want to. But unless he's the target of a criminal investigation, he can be subpoenaed to testify in front of a grand jury. If he refuses to answer questions, the presiding judge can throw him in jail until he changes his mind or until the grand jury's term ends. It's a practice used regularly by the federal government. They convene investigative grand juries all the time. I've seen the feds use them to the point of extortion.

On the other hand, the locals have never used the grand jury as an investigative tool; not once, to my knowledge. Local grand juries are nothing more than rubber stamps for cops and prosecutors, largely because the only people who ever appear before them are cops and prosecutors. The prosecutors ask all the questions and the cops provide all the answers, meaning they can choreograph the proceedings to suit their needs. Sadly, the old saying that a local prosecutor can indict a ham sandwich is true.

"They can force you to answer questions if they want to," I say. "If you refuse, they can throw you in jail."

"What about my right to remain silent?"

"The fact that you grew up in a house with a lawyer doesn't make you a lawyer. There are a lot of things about the law you don't know."

"Enlighten me."

I throw up my hands in frustration.

"What do you want me to do, Jack? I'm an assistant district attorney. Before I leave for work this morning, I find Tommy Miller asleep in my house. After I leave for work, I find out that Judge Green has been murdered and Tommy is a suspect. I come home to try to figure out what's going on, and my wife decides to jump into the middle of it and my son tells me he's going to hide behind his constitutional rights. Put yourself in my place."

"Hide?" Jack says, his voice rising again. "You think choosing to exercise my right to stay out of this is hiding? You've really changed, haven't you? Whatever happened to the dad who always told me, 'Don't ever let the government in your life, son. You can't trust them'? Whatever happened to the dad who always told me that real friends should be treasured and that loyalty is important? What happened to that guy?"

"You need to calm down."

He rises from the chair, his fingertips pushing

against the table. His face, so pale earlier, is now flushed with anger. I've never seen him like this.

"Do you know what I *need*, Dad?" he says through tight lips. "Right now, this very minute, do you know what I really *need*?"

"Tell me."

"What I *need* is a lawyer! A good one! One who's on my side! Now, are you going to help me or not?"

16

"What do you think? Have I broken through the glass ceiling? Tell me the truth."

At thirty-eight years old and after twelve years of busting her backside as a special agent with the Tennessee Bureau of Investigation, Anita White was finally the lead investigator on a high-profile murder case. She looked over at Mike Norcross, the superhero look-alike who sat in the passenger seat as they drove through the rain.

"I don't know," Norcross said. "Depends on why the suits gave it to you. I mean, the boss was one of the first people on the crime scene. He knows how tough it's going to be. I'm glad he didn't drop it on me."

Anita pondered for a minute. She and Norcross had become friends over the past year, and she knew he'd give her an honest opinion, one unaffected by racism, chauvinism, or jealousy. She liked Norcross. His massive physical presence belied the personality beneath. Anita's experiences with Norcross both in the office and in the field told her he was a smart man, honest and hardworking, gentle at his core, who somehow managed to balance the strenuous demands of the job with the needs of a family.

"So you think I'm a sacrificial lamb?" Anita said.

"I think you're in for a rough road. It's a tough crime scene. We won't get squat as far as physical evidence goes. So unless somebody talks or we get lucky, we might be screwed."

Norcross was right. The crime scene was difficult. To start with, it was outdoors, and now it had been drenched by a thunderstorm. The judge had apparently been killed outside his vehicle, which meant the inside of his Mercedes would probably yield nothing of value. The killer had stayed primarily in the grass, except when he dragged the judge across the asphalt driveway, which meant there were no usable footprints. The Mercedes had been loaded onto a covered truck before it rained and hauled away for forensic examination, but Anita doubted they'd find any fingerprints that would help identify a suspect.

The judge had apparently been ambushed when he attempted to move the tree from the driveway. There was blood on the tree trunk, and a few samples had been taken from the grass near the driveway and along the path where the judge had been dragged, but Anita expected the blood to turn out to be Judge Green's. They'd collected some cuttings of grass and some soil that smelled like kerosene. They'd collected the rope the killer used to hang the judge. They'd collected portions of the trunk of the Bradford pear tree that had been lying across the driveway in hopes they might be able to determine exactly what kind of saw had been used to cut it down. Finally, they'd collected two cigarette butts, Marlboro Lights, from the grass beside the driveway. That was it. Anita also believed the judge had been beaten with a blunt object of some sort, but no weapon was found.

So, based on the evidence at the crime scene, they were looking for a man strong enough to drag the judge and string him up in the tree and who might smoke Marlboro Lights, a saw of some sort, and a container that held the kerosene. Not much to go on. Not much at all.

Anita had also learned that two witnesses reported seeing a white compact car in the vicinity of the crime scene around the time the murder was committed. Four blocks away, a neighbor of the judge's, a retired air force colonel named Robbins, had been unable to sleep and had gone for a walk sometime between 5:15 and 5:20 a.m. He'd seen the car driving out of the neighborhood. It wasn't speeding, but Robbins said it might have been swerving. He didn't pay attention to the tag number, and he didn't get a look at the driver. All he knew was the car was small and white. He thought the car also had a taillight out, but he didn't remember which one.

Another witness, named Deakins, had called 911 at 5:26 a.m. to report that a white compact car had swerved across the center line on Highway 36 near Boones Creek and nearly hit her head-on. The witness said the car was traveling south, toward Boones Creek. It disappeared before a sheriff's deputy could respond to the call.

It had taken Anita less than fifteen minutes to determine that one of her primary suspects in the case,

Thomas Raymond Miller, age twenty, son of dead lawyer Ray Miller, owned a white 1995 Honda Civic.

Anita pulled the Crown Victoria into the driveway at 1411 Park Drive, the address she'd been provided for Tommy Miller. The large house, stained a deep red, had a cedar shake roof. She felt awkward about showing up less than twenty-four hours after Ray Miller was buried, but this was a murder investigation, and time was important. The fact that Norcross was with her was comforting. The big man was more than a good agent; he was intimidating without having to try. Witnesses tended to talk when Norcross was around. Sometimes he didn't have to say a word.

Anita stopped the car and looked at her watch. Ten thirty; probably about five and a half hours since the murder. If Tommy Miller killed the judge, he'd certainly be surprised to see them so soon.

As the agents walked toward the front door, Anita saw there was no Honda in the driveway. She peered into the garage through the windows as she passed. A midsized black Toyota sedan was parked inside. Anita followed a concrete sidewalk to the front door, rang the bell, and waited.

After a minute, a red-haired woman opened the door, wearing a pair of pink sweatpants and a white T-shirt. The woman was pretty, but she looked disheveled. Her hair was unbrushed, she wasn't wearing makeup, and the skin around her blue eyes was puffy. She looked as though she'd been crying.

"Mrs. Miller?" Anita said. She and Norcross displayed their identification. "I'm Special Agent White, and this is Special Agent Norcross. We're with the

Tennessee Bureau of Investigation. May we come in, ma'am?"

"What do you want?" Her demeanor was not one of compliance and cooperation.

"We'd just like to ask you a few questions," Anita said.

"About what?"

"Please, Mrs. Miller, it shouldn't take long."

"Don't you know I just buried my husband? Can't this wait?"

"I'm sorry to have come at such a difficult time, but it's extremely important."

"Tell me what you want." It was obvious she wasn't going to let them in, so Anita decided to forge ahead.

"Actually, we were hoping to speak to your son, ma'am."

"Why?"

"We'd prefer to discuss that with him. Is he here?"

"I don't think that's any of your business."

"It's a yes or no question, Mrs. Miller. Is your son here or not?"

"I prefer not to answer the question."

Anita noticed a tremble in Toni Miller's voice. Her face was stern and emotionless, but she was obviously frightened. She'd moved behind the open door so that only her head was visible. Perhaps she'd heard about the judge's death and drawn her own conclusions.

"Is there any particular reason why you're being so difficult?" Anita said. Norcross stepped back off the porch and began to wander away toward the back of the house.

"*Me? I'm* being difficult? You come to my home

unannounced less than a day after my husband's funeral, you try to barge in, you're asking me questions about my son, and you won't even tell me why you're here." She pointed toward Norcross. "And now *he* is trespassing on my property!"

"We can come back with a warrant," Anita said.

"For what? Are you going to arrest me for something? Have you forgotten what my husband did for a living, Agent . . . what was your name?"

"White."

"He was a lawyer. I know my rights."

"All right, Mrs. Miller. I'll tell you why we're here. We're investigating a crime, and we think your son may have some information that could help us."

"My son doesn't know anything about any crime."

"We'd like to hear that from him."

"Well, good luck with that," Toni Miller said, and she slammed the door in Anita's face.

17

Anita White knew she was being stonewalled, but she wasn't the kind to sit on her hands and wait for something to happen. With the sound of the slamming door reverberating in her ears, she walked to the neighbors on the east side of the Millers' home and sent Norcross to the neighbors on the west side. Both agents worked their way down and across the street. An hour later they were back in the car.

"There's always somebody in a neighborhood like this who can't keep their nose in their own business," Anita said as she pulled back out onto the rain-soaked street and headed for the TBI offices on Boone Street. "It never fails. This one is priceless. She lives right across the street, but she still uses binoculars. Her name's Goodin. Trudy Goodin."

"And what did Trudy Goodin have to say?" Norcross asked.

"Tommy didn't come home last night. Showed up here about a half hour before we did and left about fifteen minutes later. We didn't miss him by much."

"Would this nosy neighbor have any idea where he might be?"

"She said he was in a hurry. Made a couple of trips in and out of the house, threw a bunch of stuff into his car, and took off. She thinks he probably went back to school."

"And where's school?"

"Durham, North Carolina. He goes to Duke."

"So let's lay this out," Norcross said. "Our suspect's father commits suicide in Judge Green's courtroom less than a week ago after publicly blaming the judge for his legal and financial problems. They bury the father yesterday. Our suspect doesn't stay at home and mourn like a normal person. He doesn't stay home to comfort his mother or look out for her in her time of grief. He spends the night out. The judge is killed sometime during the night or early this morning. We go to our suspect's home, and his mother is totally uncooperative, almost confrontational. She even shuts the door on us. So we canvass, and we find out from a neighbor that our suspect has arrived home this morning not long before we arrived, hurriedly thrown his belongings into his car, and left. What do you think? Enough for a warrant?"

"Not an arrest warrant, but maybe a search warrant. Especially when you add the fact that we have two sightings of a white car in or near the vicinity of the murder, around the same time as the murder, our suspect owns a white car, and our victim is a judge."

"So we search the mother's house? The kid's car?"

"The house for sure. But the car could be a problem. We'll go ahead and list the car on our warrant here, but if he's gone back to school, he's out of state.

We'll have to hook up with the cops over there and get a judge in North Carolina to issue a warrant."

Anita turned to Norcross.

"How well do you know Joe Dillard?"

"Not that well on a personal level, but I've worked with him. The Natasha Davis case, the one where Fraley got killed. Fraley loved him. Why do you ask?"

"Just wondering what you think of him."

"I think a lot of him. He's always been straight with me. Good lawyer. Tough guy, honest. I hear he was a Ranger in the army."

"Know anything about his son?"

"All-American boy. Almost too good to be true. I saw him play baseball a couple of times when he was a senior in high school. He can flat-out crush it. Why are you asking about Dillard?"

"I got a weird vibe from him this morning," Anita said. "And the nosy neighbor said Tommy Miller was wearing a bright red T-shirt with 'Tiger Baseball' on the front and a name and the number thirty-five on the back. Guess what the name was."

"No clue."

"Dillard."

"I think you should dismiss the charges against Rafael Ramirez," he says.

"Beg your pardon?" I can't believe he's even thinking about Ramirez. "I seem to remember your busting my balls just a little while ago about the public's perception of the office."

"The case is weak. Stinnett is representing him. You're going to wind up embarrassing us again, just like you did with Carver. We'll put out a press release that says the evidence is insufficient to proceed to trial, but that we'll continue the investigation. Maybe we'll come up with something more."

I shake my head in disbelief. Rafael Ramirez is a career criminal, and a dangerous one at that. He's been on the regional drug task force's radar for several years, but because he's stayed on the move and has killed anyone he thought might be a snitch, the task force hasn't been able to make a case on him. They've told me he's a Mexican national who, in the country illegally, began his drug career working for a farmer outside of Pigeon Forge sometime in the early 1980s. According to the drug task force, the farmer, a man named Duncan who was found shot to death in his barn twenty years ago, taught Ramirez the intricacies of raising marijuana in the Great Smoky Mountains National Park near Gatlinburg. Once Ramirez learned to grow, conceal, harvest, and cure the crop, he realized he could wholesale the drug to his Mexican connections. They, in turn, distribute it all over the country. Ramirez is a multimillionaire who lives like a pauper, often sleeping for months in the woods near his vast patches. He's apparently content to smuggle his cash back to his family in Mexico. The drug task force says the Ramirez family lives like royalty on a five-thousand-acre ranch outside Guadalajara, while Rafael lives primarily in the woods and does all the work.

Ramirez controls a group of around twenty fanatical followers who help him with the crops each year and help him maintain his wholesale network. He's also dabbling in contract killing, according to the drug task force's informants, none of whom are willing to say anything on the record or testify. I can't blame them. Ramirez's record regarding betrayal is straightforward and consistent. If anyone within the organization gets out of line, they wind up dead. If anyone outside the organization tries to screw Ramirez, they wind up tortured and dead.

About four months earlier, Ramirez made the first big mistake of his illustrious career. Based on information the task force had gathered from informants, we knew that Ramirez's young nephew, Ramon, had come up last year from Guadalajara to learn the marijuana production and wholesale business at the elbow of Uncle Rafael. Maybe Rafael was growing tired and thinking of retirement, or maybe his business enterprise had grown so much that he needed a family member he could trust to help him run it. Either way, Ramon was chosen.

During the winter months, when business was slow, nephew Ramon had taken up residence at an apartment complex in Johnson City and had decided to take advantage of the local party scene. At a college bar called Plato's, Ramon ran into a cocaine dealer named Roberto Sanchez. Sanchez was flashy—he drove a Porsche, tossed cash around like candy, and had a small stable of women who followed him everywhere he went. The more Ramon drank, the more jealous of Sanchez he became. When Sanchez went to the bathroom late that night, Ramon followed him and ambushed him with a pool cue.

As soon as Sanchez was released from the hospital, he set up a little ambush of his own. He waited outside Ramon's apartment building until three in the morning, and when Ramon showed up after another night at the bar, Sanchez shot him twice. The first bullet went through Ramon's jaw. The second one hit him as he tried to run away. It went in under his scapula and out beneath his right arm. Ramon didn't go the hospital. Instead, he called his uncle Rafael.

It took Rafael two months to set Sanchez up. He summoned another family member from Mexico, who started hitting the bars and convinced Sanchez he was a high-level cocaine dealer. He offered Sanchez two kilos for the bargain-basement price of seventeen thousand dollars. When Sanchez went to a rural road in Washington County to buy his coke, the fake dealer was waiting for him, along with Rafael and Ramon Ramirez. Their plan was simple. They intended to kill Sanchez and take his seventeen thousand dollars. They didn't need the money. It was the principle of the thing. Sanchez had shown great disrespect to Ramon when he shot him in the back.

But Sanchez didn't go down without a fight. He managed to squeeze off close to thirty rounds from a Mac-9 machine pistol before he was hit twice in the head. Three of those rounds hit Rafael Ramirez: one in the neck, another in the left thigh, and a third lodged against a kidney. The fake drug dealer, who remains unidentified, was shot through the heart and died at the scene. Young Ramon was also hit, although we don't know how many times. He left a blood trail from the passenger side of the car, where he was firing from near the front fender, to the driver's side, where he got into the vehicle and fled. He must have been in a panic, because he left his uncle behind, along with the seventeen thousand dollars.

Uncle Rafael survived his wounds. A benevolent God and a skilled surgeon made it possible for him to continue to share his talents and his bountiful spirit with the rest of us. After convalescing in the hospital at state expense for two weeks, he was transported to the Washington County Detention Center. I'd convinced a grand jury to indict him for felony murder based on the evidence the police found at the scene.

"We've got enough to convict him," I finally say to Mooney. "We've got a ballistics match from the slugs in Sanchez's head to the gun that was lying next to Ramirez when the police found him. We've got Ramirez's fingerprints all over the gun, and he had gunshot residue all over him. We've got the money from the trunk of Sanchez's car. Some of it's circumstantial, but it's enough."

"I disagree," Mooney says, but he's interrupted once again by his intercom. He talks for a minute and then looks up at me.

"It isn't like her."

"What?"

"Hannah," he says. "It isn't like her."

"Hannah Mills?"

"She didn't show up for work this morning, and she hasn't called. How about going out to her house and checking on her?"

As if I don't have anything else to do. Mooney is strangely dependent on me sometimes, but this seems a little over-the-top, even for him.

"Why me?" I say. "Am I a trial lawyer or an errand boy? If you think something might be wrong, why don't you call the sheriff's department and ask them to send a deputy?"

"Just go by and take a look around, will you? Maybe she just overslept."

"Until one in the afternoon?"

"Just go. I've got enough on my mind right now."

I sigh and start to walk out the door.

"What's the address?"

"How the hell am I supposed to know?" Mooney snaps. "I've never been to her house. Get it from Rita. And dismiss on Ramirez!"

19

Hannah Mills is the victim/witness coordinator for the district attorney's office. As the title suggests, she deals with victims of crime and their families, offering comfort and reassurance, helping them through the difficult experience of dealing with the criminal justice system. She keeps them up-to-date on the prosecution, lets them know when they need to show up for court, helps them file paperwork for the victim's relief fund if they're eligible, and sits with them in the courtroom.

Hannah has been with us only a few months. Mooney hired her away from a similar job in the Knoxville district attorney's office after he met her at a conference in Nashville. She's thirty-one years old, holds a master's degree in sociology, and is compassionate and dedicated. She's also drop-dead gorgeous, with stunning blue eyes, a trim, athletic body, and a head of long, wavy sandy blond hair that seems to have a mind of its own.

When I first met Hannah, I sensed we had something in common. She was friendly and outgoing, but there was pain behind her blue eyes, the same kind of pain I've seen in the mirror. She must have sensed the same thing, because we hit it off immediately. A week after I met her, I invited her out to the house to meet Caroline. The two of them have become shopping buddies. One thing Caroline and I have both noticed about Hannah is that she never speaks of her childhood. Life for her seems to have begun after college.

The address the receptionist gives me is off Bugaboo Springs Road, a couple of miles outside of Jonesborough. It's a small brick house surrounded by poplar trees, set about a hundred feet back from the road. The yard is neatly trimmed, and the gravel driveway is lined with red and yellow tulips. It's an idyllic setting, especially since the storm has cleared out and the sun is shining brightly. I park my truck behind the blue Toyota Camry that belongs to Hannah and walk to the front door.

I knock a few times and immediately hear a puppy whining. I cup my hands around my face and peer through the windows in the door and, sure enough, a small puppy—it looks like a floppy-eared cocker spaniel—is scratching at the bottom of the door from the inside. Hannah's mentioned that she picked up a puppy at the animal shelter, but I can't remember whether she told me what she named it. I knock several more times and then try the door. It's locked.

I walk around the house, calling Hannah's name, looking in and knocking on the windows. There's no movement inside, save for the puppy, which follows the sound of my voice and continues to whimper. The back door is unlocked, and I debate for a second whether I should go inside. I decide she could be sick or injured, and I open the door. An odor of urine and feces greets me along with the puppy. I pick up the puppy, and it wriggles excitedly. I look down and see two small bowls, both empty. The dog apparently hasn't been fed or watered. I scratch its ears as I walk slowly through the kitchen and continue to call Hannah's name.

It takes only a few minutes to go through the house. Besides the kitchen, there's a small dining area and a den, a bedroom that has been converted into an office, another bedroom, and a bathroom. Given the way the day has gone so far, I expect to find something horrible around each corner. I step into the bedroom and see that the bed is made. A small leather purse is sitting on the pink comforter along with a red Windbreaker. There's an empty glass in the sink in the kitchen, but aside from that and the feces and urine the puppy has deposited on a mat near the back door, the house is spotless.

I open a door off the kitchen that leads to a basement and peer down into the darkness.

"Hannah? Hannah? Are you there?"

No one answers, so I flip on the light and walk down the steps. The floor is concrete, and the walls are unpainted concrete block. There's a washing machine and a dryer in one corner and some gardening tools in another, but otherwise the basement is empty. I go back to the kitchen and open the refrigerator. A disgusting odor makes me gag. I look around in the refrigerator and quickly find the source—an unopened package of chicken breasts that has spoiled.

I walk back through the house again, this time looking for some telltale sign of disturbance, some small clue as to what has become of the occupant. I pick up the telephone and go back through the caller ID. She's missed five calls over the weekend. I don't recognize any of the numbers. I see there are messages but can't bring myself to listen to them. I already feel like I'm invading her privacy.

Nothing seems to be out of place, but something is wrong. The abandoned puppy, the foul smell in the air, the purse on the bed, the rotten chicken, the car in the driveway. I put the puppy down, hoping it might lead me to something or someone, wishing it could talk, but all it does is put its front paws up on my knees and whimper.

I pick the dog back up, walk outside, and call the sheriff's cell phone.

20

Sheriff Leon Bates shows up in less than twenty minutes. Bates is immensely popular with the voters in Washington County. He's in the final year of his first four-year term, but there is no political opposition on the horizon that will keep him from being elected again. He's so popular that when visiting politicians come around, they make a beeline for him. They all want to kiss up to him, to have their photograph taken with him. They want to gain his favor in the hope that he'll endorse them come election time. He has a vast network of political connections, and even includes the governor of Tennessee among his closest friends. His political aspirations go far beyond the office of county sheriff, but for now, he's content to stay put and wait for the right opportunity to come along.

Bates is the hardest-working law enforcement officer I've ever known. He sleeps at the office, a habit that cost him a wife, but even she still likes him. He knows every newspaper and television reporter around, gains their confidence by being honest and straightforward, and then is smart enough to gently persuade them to do stories that cast both him and his department in a positive light. He teaches a criminal justice class at East Tennessee State University for free, and speaks at churches, civic clubs, schools, pancake breakfasts, fish fries, and spaghetti suppers. I've never seen it, but I feel certain he helps little old ladies cross the street. Bates is a savvy Andy Taylor, a throwback to the days when sheriffs were admired in their small communities. But he's also a man confronted on a regular basis by real crime in a county that continues to grow and develop. I was suspect of him when we first met—a natural inclination of mine—but in the past few years I've come to respect him as a man and admire him as a law enforcement officer.

"Now what has my old buddy Dillard gone and got himself into today?" Bates says as he unfolds from a year-old black BMW and sets his cowboy hat atop his head at a slight angle.

"Nice ride," I say as he walks around to the trunk and retrieves a pair of latex gloves. "When did you start driving that?"

"Last week. Took it off a meth dealer out toward Sulphur Springs." Bates smiles, admiring the vehicle. "You'd think them drug dealers would have enough sense to lease. But this old boy paid cash, and what was once his now belongs to the Washington County Sheriff's Department." He chuckles under his breath. "I love taking their stuff."

"Where's the guy you took it from?"

"I turned him over to the federal government, which means he'll most likely be resting and relaxing at the medium security penitentiary in Beckley, West

Virginia, for the next thirty years or so. I understand the inmates up there got a nice view of the mountains. That your pup?"

"It must belong to Hannah."

I follow Bates back toward the house. He's mid-forties, perhaps an inch taller than I, and has the sturdy build of a farmer. His hair is medium length and light brown beneath the tan cowboy hat. He's wearing his ever-present khaki uniform with the brown epaulets and cowboy boots. I've already filled Bates in on the details over the phone. He said he's talked to Hannah Mills a few times and found her to be a "sweet little ol' gal."

Bates stops just short of the back door. "Say you've already been through the house?"

"Yeah."

"Touch anything?"

I think for a second. *Did I?*

"Just the handle on the refrigerator door. Oh, and the knob on the back door . . . and the knob on the door leading to the basement and a light switch. And the phone."

Bates shakes his head.

"Don't touch anything else," he says, and walks in. "Lord, what's that smell?"

"Spoiled chicken."

"Make you think twice about eating such a *foul* animal," he says, smiling at his lame pun.

I follow silently as he retraces my earlier route through the house, including the basement. He grunts occasionally, but other than that, he offers no comment. When he's finished with the house, we walk the edge of the property, finding nothing. Finally, Bates attempts to open the driver's-side door on the Camry. It's locked, so he walks back inside the house, reappearing a moment later with a set of keys.

"Got these out of her purse," he says, dangling them gingerly from his latex-covered fingers.

Bates opens the door and looks through the interior of the car, then opens the trunk.

"This ain't good," he says.

"What?" I haven't noticed anything out of the ordinary.

"Take a look at this."

I walk around to where he's standing and follow his pointing finger to a dark spot on the carpet in the trunk. The circumference of the spot is about the same as a coffee cup.

"Blood," he says. "Bet my badge on it."

"That could be anything," I say.

"It ain't anything. It's blood."

"What makes you so sure?"

"C'mon back here and take a peek at this."

We walk around the car, and he points to the driver's seat. I look at him stupidly. I have no idea what he's trying to tell me.

"Good thing you're a lawyer instead of a cop," he says. "The unsolved-crime rate would skyrocket."

"So you think there's been a crime?"

"I think we're gonna have some problems finding this gal," Bates says. "And when we do find her, I'll bet you a poke full of cash to a pig's ear she's gonna be dead."

21

I leave Leon Bates to what he believes is his crime scene shortly thereafter. There isn't anything I can do. He's already put in a call to forensics, a department he's also funded with money seized from drug dealers. He's hired and trained specialists so he doesn't have to go begging to the Tennessee Bureau of Investigation every time he finds himself with a serious crime on his hands. His department even has a mobile minilab. It won't surprise me if Bates winds up funding his own full-fledged lab sometime in the not-too-distant future. He's become so proficient at arresting drug dealers that I find it hard to believe there are any left in the county. But I guess they're like rats, multiplying in the darkness while the world around them pretends they're under control. I take the puppy to a woman in Jonesborough who boards dogs, then drive back to the office.

I find Mooney in his office, sipping coffee, fiddling with his mustache, and reading the Johnson City newspaper. He must read every word, including the obituaries and the classified ads, because he pores over it for hours every day.

"No luck," I say as I peck on the door frame.

"No luck? What do you mean?"

"Her car's there, her purse is on the bed along with a jacket, but she's nowhere to be found."

"You looked all over?"

"Twice."

Mooney leans back in his chair and rubs his chin. "Christ, I guess we ought to start checking around to see whether anybody's heard from her."

"Don't bother," I say. "Bates is on it."

"*Bates?* What do you mean, Bates?"

"I called him."

"Why the hell did you do that?"

"Because there's a puppy in the house that's obviously been alone for a while. Because there's meat spoiled in the refrigerator. Because her house is outside the city limits, so it's his turf. Something's wrong, Lee. Bates thinks there's blood in the trunk of her car."

"Bates is a redneck."

"Bates is a good cop."

Mooney leans forward and puts his face in his hands.

"My God," he says, "she's such a sweet kid. I'll never forgive myself if something's happened to her. And with what's happened to Judge Green . . . what will people think?"

What will people think? We have a murdered judge and a young woman missing, and he's calculating political fallout. My distaste for him is growing faster than a garden weed.

"There has to be some reasonable explanation," I say.

"I'm the one who talked her into coming here, you know." Mooney's voice takes on a dreamy sort of monotone. "She gave a seminar in Nashville about the importance of compassion for victims in the district attorney's office. She was so convincing, so persuasive. Bright, funny, attractive. When she finished, I felt like I'd been saved at a revival. I saw her in the hotel lobby a little while later and introduced myself and asked her if she'd like to have a cup of coffee. We ended up talking for a couple of hours, and I convinced her she'd love northeast Tennessee and she'd enjoy working here."

"No offense, but what you're saying sounds like a little more than professional interest."

"No!" Mooney says, slamming his palm onto the desktop. His eyes open wide, and he glares at me. "Why is everybody's mind always in the gutter? It wasn't anything like that. I just thought she might bring some fresh air into this place. Besides, I'm not a cradle robber. I'm old enough to be her father. That's the way I felt about her. Fatherly. Protective, you know?"

"Sorry, I didn't mean to upset you. I just wanted you to know where it stands."

I leave him with his head in hands, surprised at the depth of his emotion and relieved that he didn't mention Ramirez again. But there's something that's bothering me, something he said: "That's the way I felt about her. Fatherly. Protective, you know?"

Felt about her. He's referring to her in the past tense.

Maybe it was just a slip of the tongue.

Or maybe he knows something I don't.

22

Anita White sat across the desk from Judge Ivan Glass while he read over her application for search warrants for Toni Miller's home and Tommy Miller's car. She'd drafted the affidavit carefully, laying out everything she knew about Ray Miller's relationship with Judge Leonard Green, the suicide in the courtroom, the subsequent funeral, the judge's murder, and her reasons for believing she had probable cause to search for evidence.

Anita had gone back to the Lake Harbor neighborhood and obtained a signed affidavit from Colonel Robbins, the neighbor who saw the white car. She'd gotten the nosy neighbor, Trudy Goodin, to sign an affidavit saying she'd seen Tommy Miller arrive early that morning in his white Honda. She'd also picked up a tape recording of the 911 call from the motorist who was nearly run off the road by the white car near the time of the murder and had it transcribed. She'd obtained copies of the vehicle registration from the Department of Motor Vehicles that said Tommy Miller was the owner of a white Honda Civic. She'd attached everything to her written application for the warrants.

She'd done everything she could think of. Now it was up to the elderly judge to sign the warrants so she could proceed with this part of her investigation.

Anita had also followed Dillard's suggestion and collected the judge's computer. She'd sent it to Knoxville, but it would be at least a couple of weeks before the techs could sift through all of the information on the computer and report back to her. The investigation into people whom Green had sent to the penitentiary revealed that only two had been released in the last six months—a burglar named Wayne Timmons who'd moved to Jackson, and a nonviolent, drug-addicted check kiter named Melanie Buford. Anita didn't think either of them a likely suspect.

She'd already contacted a detective in Durham, North Carolina, a veteran named Hakeem Ramakrishna—they called him "Rama"—and faxed him a copy of her application. Rama was doing the same thing in Durham that Anita was doing in Jonesborough. He was asking a North Carolina judge to issue a search warrant for Tommy Miller's car and an order allowing the police to collect a DNA sample from him. Anita thought the logical place for Tommy to go would be back to Duke University.

Judge Glass finished reading, removed his tinted glasses, and began rubbing the bridge of his nose. This was the first time Anita had been in Glass's office; the first time, in fact, she'd ever spoken to him. His reputation was that the pain medication he took for his plethora of health problems made him cranky and erratic, and that he suffered mightily from black-robe fever. But he was also known as an ally to law enforcement, a judge who would stretch the limits of probable cause.

Glass quit rubbing his nose and gave her a fierce look.

"This is pretty goddamned thin," he said. "The core of this application is a white car. It doesn't say what *kind* of car it is, what make or model; just that it's *white*, that it *might* have been seen in the vicinity of the murder *around* the time it was committed, and that your suspect owns a white car. Very little specificity here."

"Yes, Your Honor," Anita said.

She knew Glass had been around forever and had probably seen and heard every trick cops use when trying to get warrants. There was no point in trying to bullshit him.

"But when you add everything up," Anita said, "and look at the totality of the circumstances, I think there's enough probable cause to at least search."

"Totality of the circumstances?" Glass said. "They teach you that at the academy?"

"I have a law degree, sir," Anita said.

"I didn't like the son of a bitch, you know," Glass said.

"Beg your pardon?"

Glass leaned back in his chair and looked up at the ceiling. The folds in his neck looked like string cheese.

"Green. Didn't like him worth a damn. You know he campaigned openly against me during my last two elections? He was jealous because I was the senior judge in the circuit. He wanted to be the big shot. But he was dumber than a coal bucket and had the personality of a goddamned salamander. And those teeth, Jesus. He could eat an ear of corn through a picket fence. I don't know how he kept getting elected."

Anita attempted to maintain her professionalism. She'd never heard a judge speak in such a manner. His reputation was well deserved, at least the part about being erratic and cranky.

"Whatever his shortcomings, Your Honor, I'm sure you agree he didn't deserve the death he received."

"I heard he was hanged and burned," Glass said. "That right?"

"Yes, sir, that's correct."

"Been a few times when I would like to have hanged the bastard myself."

Glass chuckled, obviously amused with himself.

"Yes, well, as far as the standard for probable cause for a warrant goes, I think the affidavit is sufficient," Anita said. She wasn't about to indulge Judge Glass in bashing a murder victim.

"He was a fag, too, you know," Glass said. "Never saw him with a woman, not once. You'd think a man in his position would at least *try* to fake it. Not Green, though; he was so goddamned arrogant. But you know what? He probably couldn't have faked it even if he wanted to. It was just too obvious."

Anita wished she'd brought a tape recorder. Norcross and the rest of the agents in the office would have loved this.

"Is there anything else I can tell you?" Anita asked. "Any more information you'd like to have before you decide?"

"You married, young lady?"

"No, sir. Never been married."

"Lesbo?"

Anita stood. Enough was enough. She reached out and picked the warrant application up from Glass's desk.

"Thank you for your time, Judge," she said.

"Wait just a goddamned minute," Glass said. He reached out and snatched the papers from Anita's hand. "I'll sign your warrant. What're you getting so goddamned touchy about?"

23

Late in the afternoon, I receive a telephone call from Roscoe Stinnett. He's the lawyer defending Rafael Ramirez, the drug dealer and murderer Mooney wants me to set free. Stinnett is from Knoxville, and he and Mooney are close friends. Both of them are Texans. They did their undergraduate work at Texas A&M together, and both of them were heavily involved in the ROTC program. Mooney wound up going to law school in Texas and then enlisted in the Marine Corps, where he served as a JAG officer, while Stinnett migrated to the University of Tennessee and stayed in Knoxville. He carves out most of his living defending crack cocaine dealers in federal court, but Ramirez has hired him on the murder case. During each of the few discussions we've had, he's made sure to tell me how close he is to my boss.

"What can I do for you, Mr. Stinnett?"

"My client has some important information for you. He wants a face-to-face meeting with you at the jail. I think he wants to make some kind of deal."

"You *think* he wants to make a deal? You mean you don't know?"

"He won't tell me anything. I don't think he trusts me."

"Imagine that. A client not trusting his lawyer. What kind of information does he have?"

"He won't tell me."

"So when do you want to set up this meeting?"

"Now."

"Now? Where are you?"

"At the jail. Waiting for you."

There doesn't seem to be anything that demands my immediate attention going on with the investigation into Judge Green's murder, so I make the short journey to the Washington County Detention Center. On the way over, I ponder how strange it is that Stinnett would call and want to make a deal after Mooney has told me to dismiss the charge against his client. I have no intention of dismissing the charge, however. I've decided that if Mooney wants it done, he can go into court and do it himself.

After I walk through the maze of gray hallways and sliding steel doors, I find myself sitting across a table from Stinnett and his client, fifty-three-year-old Rafael Ramirez, known on the streets as "Loco." Ramirez's skin is olive colored and leathery. His hair is graying and no more than an eighth of an inch long, his eyes as black as a moonless night, and he has a jagged scar running from his hairline to the tip of his left eyebrow.

Ramirez looks defiant, his eyes hardened with anger and resentment. He smells of perspiration and cigarette smoke. Stinnett is leaning over, whispering forcefully in Ramirez's ear. The longer I'm away from criminal defense law, the more horrified I become that I once did the same thing Stinnett is doing now. Ramirez is handcuffed, waist chained, and shackled. He shrugs his shoulders violently and pulls away from Stinnett. The scar in his forehead becomes ridged as his forehead crinkles in anger.

"No, motherfucker!" Ramirez snaps. "I walk out of here. Now. I don't want to spend another minute in this jail. That's the deal."

"If he thinks he's walking out of here, you're wasting my time, Roscoe," I say to Stinnett.

"He says he has some information he thinks is worth it."

"He could tell me who killed JonBenét Ramsey and he wouldn't walk."

"This is better," Ramirez says with a smirk. "I got something you might care about personally."

"Really? And what might that be?"

"I want to hear you say it."

"Say what?"

"That you'll dismiss your bullshit murder charge against me if I tell you what I know."

"Not a chance."

Ramirez smirks at me. "She might still be alive," he says.

I'm temporarily stunned. Could he be talking about Hannah Mills?

"You've figured out by now she's gone, right?" Ramirez says. "Been gone, what, forty-eight hours or so? Ticktock."

I fight to keep my composure. I want to rip his throat out.

"Exactly what are you talking about, Mr. Ramirez?"

"I'm talking about a little *punta* who may work in your office, you know? Something bad may have happened to her, and I might know something about it."

"Is she alive?"

"Could be. Can't really say."

"Do you know where she is?"

"Maybe."

My mind starts racing through the possibilities. He obviously knows something about Hannah, but how? He's been in jail. Has she been kidnapped? Maybe to get back at us for charging Ramirez with murder? Maybe some of his people are holding her for ransom. We let him go; he lets her go. That's it. It has to be.

"I'm not going to let your client extort me," I say to Stinnett. "If he knows something, he needs to tell me now. If the information pans out, I'll ask the judge to take his assistance into consideration when he's sentenced for the murder."

"The deal is I tell you what I know about the girl and you dismiss the murder charge," Ramirez says. "No negotiation."

I stand up.

"Not interested. Can I talk to you outside for a minute, Roscoe?"

I push the button on the wall to let the guards know I want to leave. As I'm waiting for them to release the air lock on the door, Ramirez gives me his parting shot.

"Somebody wants her dead real bad," he says, "and I might know who that somebody is."

The lock releases, and Stinnett follows me back through the maze, through the lobby, and out into the parking lot. I don't say a word until we're clear of everyone else, and then I turn on him.

"What the hell was that?"

Stinnett looks as if he's seen Satan himself. Sweat is running down the side of his face, and he's gone pale.

"I swear I didn't know what he was going to say," Stinnett says. "He called my cell yesterday and said he wanted me to come up today. Said it was urgent. Given the fee he paid, I drove up. When he said he wanted to meet with you, I advised against it, but he insisted. I didn't know what kind of information he had. I still don't."

"Do you remember Hannah Mills? She worked in the Knoxville DA's office for a while. Victim-witness coordinator."

"Yeah, yeah, I remember her." Roscoe is distracted, almost panicked.

"She's missing. We just found out about it a few hours ago, and your boy is already offering information. I'm sure that's what he's talking about. Nobody's seen her since Friday."

"Sorry. Like I said, I had no idea."

"I want you to go back in there and give him a message. You tell him if we find her dead, and if he's withholding information that could have saved her, he won't have to worry about a murder trial. I'll put the word out that he's snitching on everyone he's ever known. He won't live a week."

*   *   *

Roscoe Stinnett hurried back into the jail and through the steel doors and bland hallways. Rafael Ramirez was still sitting at the table. Stinnett walked in and banged his fist down on the table dramatically.

"What's wrong with you? Are you crazy or something? I told you I had this taken care of."

Ramirez stared at him coldly. Despite Ramirez's being cuffed and shackled, Stinnett feared him. He was more intimidating than any defendant Stinnett had ever represented, and Stinnett had represented more than his share of sociopaths and psychopaths.

"All you have to do is be patient," Stinnett said. "It will happen."

"Sit your ass down, Counselor," Ramirez said, "and don't ever raise your voice to me again."

Stinnett lowered himself weakly into the chair, making sure he was out of Ramirez's reach.

"That wasn't smart, Rafael. You could have jeopardized the whole thing."

"You came to me with a job," Ramirez said. "You said you needed it done quick and clean. I put you in touch with the right man. The job is done, yes?"

"Yes."

"I didn't ask you to be patient, did I? I didn't try to put you off. I didn't refuse your request. I just did what you wanted me to do, and now it's your turn to do what you promised. I want out of this place, and I want out now."

"It's a delicate matter. It has to be done a certain way. It has to at least appear to be legitimate. It will just take a little time."

24

Katie Dean laid her walking stick aside, took off her pack, and sat down on a fallen log to eat. It was mid-afternoon on a Saturday in June 1998. The sun was shining, the temperature in the mid-sixties, the mountain air clear and crisp as the breeze rustled through the canopy above. Taking out a Baggie filled with a trail mix of peanuts, raisins, dried bananas, and chocolate, she began to munch.

"You want some?" she said to Maggie, the border collie who had become her constant outdoor companion over the past five years.

The time had passed like a single night for Katie. Her life on the small farm outside of Gatlinburg was simple. The days were long and the work was hard, but Katie had grown to love the animals, the land, and, most of all, the people who surrounded her. She kept her mother and brothers and sister close to her heart always, but she'd come to accept that Aunt Mary, Luke, and Lottie were her family now.

The awful memory of that faraway Sunday crept up on her occasionally. A couple of weeks after she moved in, Lottie had fixed fried chicken for dinner on a Friday evening. The smell sent Katie running out of the house and through the pasture, screaming. Aunt Mary had caught up with her in the old pickup truck, and after she calmed down, Katie had tearfully told Aunt Mary what she remembered about the day her family was slaughtered. She never smelled fried chicken in the house again.

There were other things that triggered nightmares sometimes; little things, such as the sound of church bells, a glimpse of someone who reminded her of one of her siblings, or the sound of shotguns firing in the fall when the hunters took to the nearby cornfields in pursuit of doves. But the reminder Katie saw most often was in the mirror, because in the place where her right breast should have been was an ugly, pink, concave scar. She'd learned to cover herself with a towel or a robe before she looked in the mirror after showering, but it was impossible not to be self-conscious. Katie had dealt with the deformity through high school by wearing a prosthetic—a "falsie," she called it. She'd stayed away from boys and had avoided discussing it with girls until her closest friend, a townie named Amy, told her one day that nearly everyone in school had heard about what happened to her. It was a small town, Amy said. It was hard to keep secrets.

Despite the missing breast and the memories, Katie had willed herself to overcome. She forced herself to concentrate on what was good in her life, and there was plenty. Luke was her closest friend. She spent hours reading to him, watching television with him, and caring for him. Katie had learned to feed him, bathe him, and change his diapers. He quivered with excitement every time she walked in the door from school or from doing her chores around the farm. She read him stories and watched cartoons with him on Saturday mornings. Lottie had been right. He was a smart young gentleman. He communicated by different sounds from his throat and by the expressions in his eyes. He had a wonderful sense of humor, and Katie thought he was the sweetest, gentlest creature on earth.

Because Aunt Mary had collected a substantial amount of money when her husband was killed in the logging accident, Katie was on her way to college. Aunt Mary had never said how much, only that it was more than enough to take care of her and Luke and Lottie and Katie for the rest of their lives. Katie was already enrolled at the University of Tennessee. She would start classes late in August. She was a year older than most of her classmates because she took a year off after her family was killed, but no one seemed to notice. Inspired by the beauty that surrounded her in the mountains, she was planning to major in horticulture and perhaps work for the forest service one day.

Aunt Mary had also given Katie another gift, the best she'd ever received. For Katie's seventeenth birthday, Aunt Mary had accompanied her to Knoxville to a cosmetic surgeon. The surgeon had first placed a tissue expander beneath the skin where her breast should have been. Over the next few months, he pumped increasing amounts of water into the expander, stretching the skin and making room for a breast implant. When he did the surgery to install the implant, he'd also fashioned a nipple out of a small amount of skin he took from Katie's rump, and he'd tattooed the nipple and surrounding skin pink to match the other breast. Then he'd injected a pigment to lighten the skin that covered the implant. It still wasn't perfect—it was a bit darker than her other breast, and the skin was still numb—but for the first time in years Katie had begun to feel normal.

She swallowed another bite of trail mix and resumed her hike. Each year, Katie had ventured farther away from Roaring Fork and deeper into the park. She'd scaled Mount LeConte, visited the cabins and farms of the early settlers, and marveled at the beauty of Grotto Falls, Rainbow Falls, and the hundreds of species of plants and wildlife.

Katie had become an expert at orienteering and camping. It had taken her nearly a year to convince Aunt Mary that she was capable of staying out overnight in the park. Now she'd made at least a dozen overnight trips. She'd encountered bears and snakes and even the occasional wild boar, but she felt safe in the woods, especially with Maggie along.

Her plan for the weekend was to head east along the Grapeyard Ridge trail to Greenbriar Cove and then travel south, cross-country and off-trail, toward Laurel Top on the Appalachian Trail. She'd made good time to Greenbriar and was relieved to be off the beaten path used by an increasing number of tourists each year. Katie topped a ridge and checked her map. She'd make the trail by nightfall, no problem, and then hike back home tomorrow.

As she descended the other side of the ridge into a cove, Katie stopped suddenly. Something wasn't quite right ahead. She peered through the branches of a rhododendron and could see that the forest had been cleared in the cove below and replaced by a vast field of . . . what was it? Whatever it was, it was a fluorescent green, almost glowing. She crept toward the break in the trees and reached into her pack for her binoculars.

The marijuana patch was vast, close to five acres, Katie guessed. The plants were at least four feet high and waved gently back and forth in the breeze. As Katie scanned with her binoculars, she saw two all-terrain vehicles at one end of the patch. At the other end, about a hundred yards to her right, she saw three men sitting on lawn chairs. They were eating. All three of them appeared to be Latino, probably Mexican.

Maggie must have caught their scent, because she started to growl.

"Hush, Maggie," Katie whispered. She knelt down next to the dog and reached out for her collar with her left hand. Maggie's ears were standing up straight, as was the hair on the back of her neck. She let out a weak bark.

"No, Maggie, no." Katie took another look through the binoculars. One of the men was standing now, pointing in her direction. He'd seen her.

"Let's go, Maggie." Katie turned and started running as fast as she could back up the ridge. Maggie followed her but continued to bark.

When Katie reached the top of the ridge, she heard the sound of engines. They were coming after her. She veered left through a large area of Fraser fir deadfall, scrambling over tree trunks and branches, crawling beneath rhododendron. Even if they saw her in the deadfall, they wouldn't be able to follow on the four-wheelers, and Katie felt confident she could outrun or outhike anyone in these mountains.

When she heard the engines top the ridge behind her, maybe three or four hundred yards back, she crouched behind a huge tree trunk, wrapped her hand around Maggie's snout, and waited. About twenty seconds passed before she saw two men on four-wheelers tearing through the trees, heading in the direction she'd been going before she broke for the deadfall. They stopped at the edge of the deadfall, turned off the engines, and listened.

"Shhh," Katie whispered as she clutched Maggie close to her. "Shhh."

After an agonizing minute, the engines started, and the four-wheelers tore off up the ridge. As soon as they were out of sight, Katie started running due west. The sound of the engines faded with every step she took.

Katie kept telling herself she was safe now.

She was safe.

25

Katie arrived home after dark on Sunday. The route she took back after her run-in with the men at the marijuana patch had taken longer than she expected. The terrain was as difficult as any she'd encountered in the park. As soon as she walked through the back porch and into the kitchen, Aunt Mary appeared.

"Oh, Katie, are you all right?" Aunt Mary asked. She immediately embraced Katie.

"I'm fine."

Aunt Mary stepped back and took stock of her.

"Look at you. You're scratched all to pieces."

Katie had debated much of the way home about whether she should tell Aunt Mary what she'd seen. Aunt Mary despised the "druggers," as she called them. Every year in the fall, they hauled their harvest out of the mountains past the farm, led by a sheriff's department vehicle. A couple of years after Katie moved in, Aunt Mary finally told her what the annual parade of trucks contained.

"They hide deep in the mountains where no one can see them, they do their business, and they pay off the sheriff," Aunt Mary had explained. "Everyone's afraid of them. It's best to just let them be, but I swear it goes against my grain. They're making millions of dollars illegally, and nobody'll do anything about it."

"Why are you so late?" Aunt Mary said. "We've been worried sick about you."

Katie couldn't bring herself to lie.

"I had to take a detour. A big one. It took a lot longer than I thought it would."

"What kind of detour? Why?"

"I ran across something I wasn't supposed to see. I was hiking cross-country toward Laurel Top. I came to a clearing in a cove and it was full of marijuana plants. There were some men there, and they chased me."

"Oh my Lord!" It was Lottie, who had just walked into the kitchen. "Chased you? You mean they saw you, child?"

"I think they may have seen me from a distance," Katie said. "They chased me on four-wheelers, but I ran and hid in some deadfall, and they didn't see me again."

"Thank God you're all right," Aunt Mary said. "I've told you to be careful in those woods."

"I'm sorry," Katie said. "I wasn't looking for them or anything. I just sort of stumbled across them."

"How big was the field?" Aunt Mary said.

"Big. Really big."

The three of them were silent for several seconds. Katie wondered what her aunt and Lottie were thinking.

"How's Luke?" Katie said, hoping to get the focus off her ordeal.

"He's sleeping like a little angel," Lottie said. "He missed watching cartoons with you yesterday."

"I missed him, too," Katie said. She began to pull her pack off.

"Katie," Aunt Mary said, "do you know where this marijuana field is? I mean, could you tell someone how to find it?"

"Sure, I know exactly where it is."

"Miss Mary, I want you to slow down just a bit now," Lottie said. "We don't need to be getting involved in something like this. You know they got the sheriff in their pocket."

"I wasn't thinking about the sheriff," Aunt Mary said. "I was thinking about maybe the DEA. They're always on the news making big drug busts. I'll bet they have an office in Knoxville. Maybe they'd be interested. It's time somebody put a stop to this nonsense."

"I don't know," Lottie said. "I don't believe in meddling in other folks' business. Nothing good ever comes of it."

On Monday afternoon, as soon as Aunt Mary got home from work, she and Katie drove to Knoxville. The DEA offices were housed in the rear of a nondescript shopping center off Kingston Pike. Aunt Mary told Katie that she'd called that morning and spoken to an agent. He asked her if she could come in immediately and bring Katie with her.

There was a security keypad on the door and a dead bolt lock. Aunt Mary knocked on the door, and a few seconds later it opened. A young man with short dark hair was standing on the other side. He was medium height, muscular, and wearing a shoulder holster that carried a pistol. Katie immediately noticed a deep cleft in his chin. "Butt chin" was what the kids at school called it.

"I'm Mary Clinton," Aunt Mary said, "and this is my niece, Katie. She's the one I told you about on the phone."

The man introduced himself as Agent Rider and led them through a large, open room filled with desks. There was no carpet on the floor, and the steel beams that framed the building were exposed. The space was very much like a warehouse, with several people milling about, talking on telephones, talking to one another. Most of them were men, and nearly all of them were armed. They passed a cabinet filled with rifles and came to a small office with paneled walls and a fake fern in the corner. On the wall behind the desk was a map of East Tennessee. Agent Rider motioned for them to sit down.

"So, Katie, right?" Agent Rider said. "How old are you?"

"Eighteen."

Agent Rider folded his hands in front of him on the desk. His fingers were thick and leathery, and the veins running down his arms looked like rivers and streams on a map.

"Your aunt tells me you may have some information."

"Before we get into that," Aunt Mary said, "I want assurances that there is no way this will ever come back on us. I don't know whether you know it or not, but the sheriff protects these people. He knows what's going on. If you tell him where your information came from, he'll tell them. I don't know what they might do, but I don't care to find out."

"The sheriff doesn't have anything to do with this operation," the agent said. "We're a federal agency. We have people from state and local agencies on our task force, but we share information on a need-to-know basis only. The sheriff certainly doesn't need to know. We've been aware of his activities for quite some time now. We just haven't been able to make a case against him yet. But I assure you, if we make any kind of move based on information you or your niece provides, we won't be talking to the sheriff about it."

"You're positive," Aunt Mary said.

"It takes a lot of courage for people to do what you're doing right now, Ms. Clinton," Agent Rider said. "We need people like you, and we take great care to protect our witnesses."

"Witnesses? You're not saying that Katie will have to testify in court, are you?"

"No, ma'am. You indicated over the phone that your niece has information regarding a large field of marijuana. The chance of our actually catching some-one during the raid is minimal. What will most likely happen is that we'll cut down the marijuana that's there and burn it on-site. If it's as big as you indicated, it'll cost the grower hundreds of thousands, if not millions, of dollars. We'll be hitting them where it really hurts. Right in the pocket."

"Do you know who this grower is?" Aunt Mary asked.

"I have a pretty good idea, but the less you know, the better."

"All right, Katie," Aunt Mary said, "tell him what you saw."

Katie spent the next half hour telling Agent Rider about her experience hiking in the Great Smoky Mountains National Park and how she happened to come upon the marijuana field. Then, using a map of the park she'd brought along with her, she showed him the exact location of the field.

"Five acres? Are you sure?" Agent Rider said when she'd finished.

"Pretty sure. Maybe a little smaller, maybe a little bigger," Katie said.

"This is impressive. Looks like we'll have to go in by helicopter because of the terrain, which means they'll hear us coming, but this will be one of the largest marijuana seizures we've ever made around here."

A few minutes later, Agent Rider led Katie and Aunt Mary back through the room full of desks and people and to the door. Katie could feel eyes on her, and as the agent thanked them one last time at the door and said good-bye, she couldn't help but wonder who was looking at her, what they might find out about her, and what they might do.

26

I wanted to check on what was happening with my son and Tommy Miller, but after my meeting with Ramirez, my first phone call is to Sheriff Bates.

"We need to meet," I say. "Someplace private."

"Where are you?"

"Just leaving the jail."

"You know Highland Church?"

"Yeah."

"Parking lot. Ten minutes."

He's waiting when I pull in. I get out of my truck and climb into the BMW. I tell him about the meeting with Ramirez.

"He said it was a girl who works in our office," I say. "He knew how long she'd been missing. Before I left, he said somebody wants her dead. He said he *might* know who it is."

Bates considers the information silently for a minute.

"I reckon the first question we gotta ask ourselves is how," he says. "How does Ramirez know? It ain't like it's been in the papers. Hell, we just found out about it a few hours ago. So since he knows she's gone, and he says he knows where she is, he has to be involved somehow, right?"

"I'm thinking maybe he had some of his guys kidnap her and he's holding her for ransom. We let him out; he lets her go. That's the deal he wants."

"Is that what he said? Did he say he'd let her go?"

"No. He said he'd tell me what he knows. But he did say, 'Ticktock,' which makes me think she's still alive."

"Wishful thinking, Brother Dillard."

"Do you really think she's dead? I can't imagine anyone wanting to hurt her."

"It ain't good."

"How do you think Ramirez is getting his information? He'd have to get it either over the phone or through a visitor. I don't think Ramirez would take a chance on them listening to his phone conversations at the jail, and it'd be risky to talk to a visitor about something like this."

"For a smart hombre, you sure can be naïve sometimes," Bates says. "Open your eyes."

"What are you talking about?"

"Who's the only person he can he talk to without having to worry about anybody listening?"

It hits me. Stinnett. His lawyer. Stinnett is his information courier. That's why he was acting so strangely.

"Son of a bitch," I say.

"Don't act so surprised. You used to do the same thing."

"If I did, I didn't do it intentionally."

We sit for a moment while I ponder this latest

possibility. Stinnett probably took a phone call from someone and relayed a message to Ramirez. Maybe Stinnett didn't even know what the message meant; at least that's what I'd like to think. Then again . . .

I ask Bates what he's learned thus far.

"A little," he says. "Whoever drove her car last was a man or a damned tall woman. When I asked you to look at the driver's seat, I was trying to get you to notice that it was pushed all the way back. Hannah's a short gal. And I noticed something else. She got her oil changed Friday afternoon. It was on the little sticker in the windshield, along with the mileage. When I looked at the odometer, more than a hundred miles had been put on that car since the oil change, so either she took a quick trip before she disappeared or somebody hauled her away in her own car, dumped the body, and then brought the car back."

"You were right," I say. "It's a good thing I'm not a cop."

"The key to her car had been wiped clean—not a print on it, not even hers. The inside of the car had been wiped down, too, but we lifted a partial from the exterior of the door. There was quite a bit of clay on the floor around the gas pedal, along with something else. My guys say they're not sure yet, but they think it might be lime. Same stuff in the carpet on the passenger side. We lifted some hair and fiber from the car, and we're still going through the house. There might be something in there, too."

"Damn, Leon, you don't mess around, do you?"

"Trail gets cold in a hurry. I'm gonna stay on this one until I find out what happened to her or we fall flat. The sheriff's department doesn't get that many murders, you know. It's kinda fun."

Fun. Alternate flashes of Hannah run through my mind. Flashes of her beautiful smile. The pain behind her eyes. The way her hair flipped when she turned her head. Her battered body dumped somewhere, slowly decomposing, covered by insects. I let out a long sigh.

"Sorry, brother," Bates says. "You knew her better than I did. I guess this ain't exactly your idea of fun, is it?"

"Not exactly. So what do you think about Ramirez? Should I make some kind of deal with him?"

"That'd be between you and your boss, wouldn't it?"

"My boss tried to get me to dismiss the murder case against him this morning."

Bates is silent for several seconds. He begins scratching his head, which I know is his way of manifesting confusion.

"Why would he want you to do that?"

"He said it's a weak case, and he doesn't want the office to be embarrassed if I lose at trial."

"How strong is your case?"

"It's not the strongest I've ever had, but I think it's enough."

Bates shoots me a sideways glance and raises his eyebrows. "Anything else you need to tell me?"

"Nah, it's probably just a coincidence. There's just something about Mooney that bothers me. Something isn't right with him."

"You just now figuring that out? He sure does like the ladies. You think he was chasing Hannah?"

"Nah. Hannah doesn't seem to be too interested in men. So what about Ramirez?"

"Give me a little more time. Let me find Hannah's family and friends, talk to them, see if I can find out who might have wanted to hurt her. If we don't come up with something in forty-eight hours or so, maybe you should pay Ramirez another visit."

Bates's cell phone begins to chirp the melody of "When the Saints Go Marching In." He looks down at the phone, then back at me.

"One of my forensics boys," he says. "Better take it."

Bates speaks quietly on the phone for a few minutes. Finally, he says, "Well, I'll be," and closes the phone.

"You say you know this gal pretty well?" he says.

"Yeah. We're friends."

"My boys went through her garbage and found something interesting. Did she mention anything to you about being pregnant?"

27

I call Caroline and ask her to meet me at the Peerless in Johnson City for dinner. The restaurant is known primarily for great steaks and Greek salads, but I'm more interested in taking advantage of one of the private rooms they offer. Caroline doesn't mention anything about Hannah's disappearance over the phone, so I assume she doesn't know. The news will upset her terribly, so I decide to tell her later at home. I have something else I want to talk about at the restaurant.

I'm greeted at the door by the owner, an elderly Greek gentleman named Stenopoulos who's owned the restaurant for forty years and still goes to work every day. He leads me down a hallway to a small, private dining room. I order two beers. Caroline shows up less than five minutes later. She's wearing a red jacket over a black turtleneck and a short black skirt that shows off her incredible legs. She sits down across the table from me without saying hello and takes a long pull off the beer. No glass for Caroline when she's drinking a beer; I've always liked that.

A waitress walks in and we order dinner. I'm not hungry—my stomach has been in knots all day—but

I order a steak anyway. If I don't eat it, I'll take it to Rio.

"You're angry," I say as soon as the waitress leaves the room. No point in fencing. We might as well get down to it.

"I'm not angry. I'm scared for Tommy," she replies.

"What did you say to Toni?"

"I thought you didn't want to know."

"I changed my mind. What did you say to her?"

Caroline takes another drink from the beer bottle and reaches for a basket of crackers. She's avoiding eye contact, a sure sign she's upset.

"I told her that TBI agents were probably coming," Caroline says. "I told her to get Tommy out of there."

"Did she?"

"Yes. He's gone back to school."

"Did they show up?"

"Two of them. A black woman and a huge white guy."

White and Norcross.

"What did she tell them?"

"Nothing. She told them to go away. She was married to a lawyer, too, you know. I didn't have to tell her what to do."

"Did they ask about Tommy?"

"Of course they asked about Tommy."

Her tone is edgy, impatient. I find myself wishing we were simply having a pleasant dinner, a civil conversation. But the events of the past twenty-four hours have swept us up. All I can do now is hope no one else gets hurt.

"Caroline, I need to ask you a few questions, and I'd appreciate it if you'd be honest with me."

"I'm always honest with you."

She's right. It was a stupid thing to say.

"Did you see Tommy this morning?"

She nods her head.

"Talk to him?"

"He said he needed to go home. I made him an egg sandwich."

"How did he look?"

"You already went through this with Jack this morning, and I don't appreciate your asking me to come out to dinner and trying to interrogate me. You said you didn't want to know anything about my involvement. Why don't we just keep it that way?"

"Fine, then let's try the old lawyer's cat and mouse game. Let's talk hypotheticals."

"Hypotheticals? What do you mean?"

"I'll make a supposition and then ask you a question. It's sort of like make-believe."

"I know what a hypothetical is, Joe. I just don't understand what you want from me."

"Let's suppose Tommy went to somebody else's house last night, okay? Another friend's house. And let's say that friend's mother just happened to see Tommy this morning. And maybe she heard him say something about where he went last night, what he did, that kind of thing. Hypothetically speaking, what do you think he might have said to her?"

I see the slightest upturn at the edge of her lips. She's willing to play.

"Hypothetically?" she says.

I nod.

"He might have said something to her about not remembering what he did last night. He may have been drinking heavily."

"So you don't think Tommy would have made any admissions to her about being involved in a crime."

"No. I don't think he would have."

"And do you think this woman, this friend's mother, would have noticed any injuries of any kind on him?"

"I don't think she would have noticed anything like that, no."

"What about his clothing? Do you think she would have noticed anything unusual about his clothing?"

The waitress walks into the room carrying a tray with two Greek salads and two more beers. Caroline remains silent until she leaves.

"I think his clothing may have smelled bad. His shirt, his pants, his shoes."

I sit back and let this sink in. We're back in dangerous territory. I should change the subject, keep silent, break into song, anything but continue this line of questioning. But I have to keep going. If she's done something she shouldn't have done, I have to protect her, and I can't protect her unless I know the truth. I'm reminded of the days I was practicing criminal defense. I push my salad away and lean forward on the table.

"And what might his clothes have smelled like?" I ask.

"I'm not sure. Maybe gasoline?"

Shit. My stomach churns. I can feel my mouth going dry. I gulp down a few swallows of the beer.

"Okay, now let's be sure to stay in the hypothetical. Far, far in the hypothetical, all right? So if Tommy goes to this other friend's house and this other friend's mother notices that his clothing smells like some kind of fuel, do you think she might have asked him why?"

"She might have asked him what happened. He might have said he thought he must have stopped for gas somewhere when he was drunk and spilled some on his clothes, but he doesn't remember."

"So what else do you think might have been said?"

Caroline's eyes lock on to mine. She seems to relax completely, as though she's experienced some kind of spiritual awakening. Her voice is steady.

"First of all, I think this woman might believe him. Then she might ask him to take the clothing off and borrow some from her son. She might just intend to clean the shirt and shoes for him, since he and his mother have so much grief in their lives right now. She might have just been trying to be nice. She might have just been trying to help."

"And what would she have done with his clothes?"

Caroline lifts the beer bottle to her lips, then sets it back down without drinking.

"She might have put everything in a garbage bag and taken it to the laundry room in the basement."

I relax a little. This isn't as bad as I thought. Even if Tommy's clothes are in our house, she would have taken them before she knew anything about Judge Green's murder. That doesn't make her guilty of any crime. The question is whether she now has a legal obligation to make the police aware that she has the clothing and turn it over to them. And now that she's told me, even hypothetically, I'm wondering whether I, too, have a legal obligation to tell the police.

"So this hypothetical clothing in this hypothetical laundry room," I say. "Do you think it might still be there?"

"I don't think so."

"Why not?"

"Well, the woman might have put the clothing in the washing machine right after the boy left. Then maybe she started fixing breakfast for her son. Her husband shows up unexpectedly and starts making wild accusations about Tommy. So after her husband leaves, maybe she does something she knows she probably shouldn't do, but maybe she loves this boy like a son and believes with all of her heart that he didn't commit a crime. Maybe she wants to make sure that clothing can never be used against him in any way."

I hold up my hand to stop her. I can see it in her eyes. I know what she's done.

"Don't say anything else," I say.

"After her husband leaves, maybe she makes a decision that she knows she might regret someday, but she relies on her heart. She doesn't want to do anything to hurt her husband, but she *knows*, she absolutely *knows*, that this boy she loves so much simply

28

Three days after Katie Dean visited the DEA agent, Aunt Mary called her into the den from the kitchen.

"They just did a teaser for the news about a big drug bust," Aunt Mary said. "I think this might be it."

Katie sat on the edge of Luke's bed. A male reporter appeared on the TV screen. He was wearing a camouflage uniform and holding a microphone. He was outdoors. Behind him was a wall of gray smoke.

"Local law enforcement authorities are saying this marijuana field is the biggest ever discovered in the Great Smoky Mountains National Park," the reporter said. "Agents from the U.S. Drug Enforcement Agency, the Tennessee Bureau of Investigation, and the Sevier County Sheriff's Department descended from helicopters into this five-acre field early this morning after receiving a tip from an anonymous informant. More than twenty-five hundred plants have been cut and burned. Police estimate the marijuana's wholesale value at more than three and a half million dollars. The street value is estimated at close to ten million dollars. Sevier County Sheriff Hobart Brackens says the marijuana was most likely meant for out-of-state buyers."

A heavy man with jowls like a bulldog came onto the screen. He was wearing a cowboy hat with a silver star on it. Beneath his face were the words "Sheriff Hobart Brackens."

"An operation like this has to be a wholesaler," the sheriff said. "We've had information in the past that marijuana growers were operating in these mountains, but until now, we've never been able to find any of the patches."

Aunt Mary turned off the television set.

"There," she said matter-of-factly. "What's done is done. I don't want anyone in this house to speak of it ever again."

The firebomb came through Katie's bedroom window the next week. It was two in the morning on a Thursday. Katie had watched an Atlanta Braves baseball game with Luke before straggling off to bed around eleven. She was dreaming of swimming at the base of a massive waterfall in the bright sunshine, surrounded by brightly colored fish, when the sound of breaking glass and igniting fuel jolted her awake.

It took several seconds for her to realize the bedroom was on fire. The Molotov cocktail had landed against the wall near the door and exploded. The flames were already raging by the time Katie ripped the covers back and jumped to her feet. She heard men shouting outside her window, then heard more windows crash downstairs. She screamed. The flames were racing up from the foot of the bed, gobbling the purple quilt Aunt Mary had made and given to her for Christmas three years earlier. Smoke was already causing her to choke, the heat searing her skin and throat.

Luke. I have to get to Luke.

She couldn't go toward the door that led to the steps. It was too hot. The flames would consume her, but she had to get out. She unlatched the lock on the broken window and pushed it up. The roof above the front porch was less than ten feet below her. She crawled up into the window frame, cutting her left foot on a piece of broken glass in the process, and jumped. The steep pitch of the roof below sent her skidding toward the edge. Her elbows and knees hit the rough shingles, and she rolled onto her side, once, twice, three times . . . and then she was falling. She landed on her right side in the grass of the front yard. Her elbow jammed into her rib cage, and she heard the sickening sound of bones breaking. She tried to stand, but found she couldn't even breathe.

Katie looked up toward the front of the house. Dark smoke was billowing from beneath the soffit, and she could see flames climbing the curtains and reaching out like the devil's fingers through the windows. Katie willed herself to her knees. The heat was so intense she felt her eyebrows beginning to singe. She lay down on her back and used her feet to push herself away from the inferno.

29

A tongue lapping across her face awakened Katie, and she opened her eyes. It was night, but the sky was full of light.

"Maggie," she whispered. "Good girl."

The sound that filled Katie's ears was that of a locomotive, or maybe a tornado, close by. She tried to sit up, but the pain in her side was so excruciating, it took her breath again. She suddenly realized where she was. She turned her head and looked toward the house. Orange flames were shooting through the roof, reaching at least fifty feet into the air and throwing sparkling embers another thirty feet higher. Katie had managed to push herself a good hundred feet from the house before she passed out, but the heat was so intense, she felt as though she were slowly roasting.

Maggie bolted toward the side of the house and disappeared.

She must be going to check on the others. They must have gotten out.

Katie planted the soles of her feet firmly against the ground and began to push again, dragging herself farther away from the heat. She took shallow breaths in an effort to alleviate some of the pain. She wondered how many of her ribs had been broken in the fall, because every time she took a breath, no matter how shallow, and every time she moved her upper body in the least, it felt as if a butcher knife were being plunged into her side.

She thought briefly of the cowards who did this. It had to be the druggers. Someone had told someone about her visit to the DEA office. She thought of the eyes that watched her as she was leaving, and she wondered whether one of those pairs of eyes was responsible for what was happening now.

Aunt Mary. Lottie. Did they get out? Did they get Luke out? Are they hurt? Dead? No, please God, not dead. Not again.

She shouldn't have gone off the trail in the park. She shouldn't have let the druggers see her. She shouldn't have told Aunt Mary. At the very least, their house was burning because of her.

Katie became aware of headlights coming down the driveway. They drew nearer. She heard a door slam, then heavy footsteps approaching. Someone was kneeling beside her. She looked at the face. It was Mr. Torbett, the nearest neighbor, a friendly, white-haired farmer with the longest fingers Katie had ever seen. Kneeling on the other side of Katie was Mr. Torbett's wife, Rose.

"Katie!" Mr. Torbett cried. "Dear God, Katie. Are you all right? What happened?"

He reached behind her neck and lifted her head.

No! No! Don't move me!

Razor-sharp pain shot through Katie's body.

"The others," she whispered, and the blackness enveloped her again.

The next time Katie opened her eyes, the woman standing above her was a stranger. She was pretty, middle-aged, with sharp features and hazel eyes. Her black hair was pulled tightly into a bun, and she was wearing white. Katie thought she might be an angel. She was fiddling with a bag of liquid that hung from a stand next to the bed.

"Where am I?" Katie said. Her mouth was dry, her tongue like sandpaper, but she felt as relaxed as she'd ever felt in her life. "Am I in heaven?"

"You're in the hospital, sweetie," the nurse said. She moved next to the bed and took Katie's hand. "But you're going to be fine."

Katie smiled at the nurse and looked at her name tag. It said her name was June.

"Am I sick?" Katie said. "How did I get here?"

"You don't remember?"

Katie thought for a moment, but she couldn't remember. Truth be known, she didn't care. She felt as if she were floating. She shook her head slowly.

"You had a little accident," Nurse June said. "Just go on back to sleep now. We're going to take good care of you."

"Do you know Aunt Mary?" Katie said. "She works at the hospital."

The angel turned away for several seconds. When she turned back, Katie thought she saw a tear slip from her right eye and run down her cheek. She wondered why the woman was crying.

"Yes, honey, I know her."

"Is she here?"

"You just rest now," the nurse said. "Your aunt Mary will always be there for you."

30

It's after midnight. I've already told Caroline that Hannah is missing. She was so upset that I decided not to tell her about the information I've learned from Bates, and I didn't say anything about Ramirez. She's gone to bed, but I doubt she's sleeping. Both of us are in a state of semishock, punch-drunk from the emotional and psychological battering we've taken over the past week. Ray's suicide, the news about Judge Green and the possibility that Tommy may have been involved, Hannah's disappearance, and Caroline's continuing battle with cancer have left us wondering whether we've been infected with some sort of contagious, cosmic disease that we've unwittingly passed on to our closest friends.

I'm sitting in my study, flipping through the *Tennessee Criminal Justice Handbook*. I find the section of the Tennessee Code Annotated I'm looking for:

Section 39-16-503. Tampering with or fabricating evidence.

It is unlawful for any person, knowing that

an official investigation or official proceeding is pending or in progress, to:

(1) Alter, destroy, or conceal any record, document, or thing with intent to impair its verity, legibility, or availability as evidence in the investigation or official proceeding.

A violation of this section is a class C felony.

The statute is clear. By burning Tommy Miller's clothing and shoes after knowing that he was a suspect in a murder investigation, Caroline has committed a crime. She doesn't realize how serious it is. The penalty for a class C felony in Tennessee for a first-time offender is a minimum of three and a maximum of six years in prison. If Caroline is caught, there's no doubt in my mind she'll wind up in jail. She'll receive the minimum sentence because she's never been in any kind of trouble, but there isn't a judge in the state who will grant her probation for destroying evidence in the investigation of a murdered colleague. Even if she gets the minimum sentence and makes parole as soon as she's eligible, she'll serve nearly a year in the Tennessee State Prison for Women.

I think about the sentence Caroline is still serving, the one imposed upon her by breast cancer. She's survived, but she's been through six months of chemotherapy, nearly two months of radiation therapy, and half a dozen surgeries stretched out over twenty-two months. I'm confident she'll beat the cancer, but now she's up against the laws of man and the people who enforce them. If she's found out, she won't get any sympathy.

I know she didn't intend to do anything illegal when she collected Tommy's clothes and loaned him some of Jack's, and I'm sure she rationalizes burning the clothing later by telling herself she was merely eliminating the possibility that the clothing could somehow be used to frame Tommy. She believes he didn't kill the judge. In fact, she's so firm in her conviction that I wonder whether something else is at play here, perhaps intuition. Caroline has always been intuitive, and her judgments about people have always been spot-on. But even if she's right about Tommy, it doesn't change her having made herself vulnerable to the system. If the wrong person finds out what she's done and can prove it, they'll steamroll her.

The other problem I have, of course, is my own criminal liability. Now that Caroline's told me about burning the clothes, because of my position as an assistant district attorney, I could be charged with official misconduct if I don't report it. Official misconduct is also a felony, although not as serious as tampering with evidence. Then again, perhaps I enjoy the protection of spousal privilege. She's my wife. They can't force me to tell them anything she's said to me, and I didn't actually see the clothing.

As I sit in the lamplight, I commit to a decision. Right or wrong, legal or illegal, I'll do whatever I have to do.

There's no way in hell my wife is going to prison, and neither am I.

I walk up the stairs and lie down on the couch in the den. I keep an old blanket folded over the back of the couch because I sleep there—or just lie there—quite often. On nights when I know I won't be able to sleep or if something has happened that I think might trigger a nightmare, I head for the couch. There's no point in keeping Caroline awake while I toss and turn, and there's no point in scaring her with my dream-induced cries and ramblings in the middle of the night.

Rio crawls onto the other end of the couch and curls up. I turn the television on to Sports Center and listen as the talking heads drone on mindlessly, for the millionth time, about the long-term effects that the use of steroids by cheaters like Barry Bonds and Roger Clemens will have on the game of baseball. I think of Jack and how hard he's worked over the years, drug free, and hope that the pressure of competition at the highest level never leads him down that path.

Thoughts of Jack cause me to consider the predicament he's in. My conversations with Caroline have led me to believe that Jack had no idea what was going on with Tommy this morning. Tommy woke up before Jack did. By the time Jack saw Tommy, Caroline had already collected Tommy's clothes and shoes and provided him with replacements that belonged to Jack.

Still, I'm sure Anita White will want to talk to Jack. She'll want to know if he saw Tommy or talked to him after the funeral, and if he did, she'll want to know exactly what Tommy said and did. She'll want to know whether Jack noticed anything unusual about him. She'll ask Jack the same questions I asked him, and if he lies, he'll be in the same boat as Caroline.

Making a false statement to a police officer about a material fact in an investigation is a class C felony in Tennessee.

The key to all this, of course, is Tommy Miller. Will he go against everything he's learned from his father and what I'm sure his mother has told him and talk to the police? Will the TBI agents—who are experts at getting people to talk to them—be able to coerce him or pressure him or simply outsmart him? Will they be able to bring enough pressure or guilt to bear to loosen his tongue? If they do, what will he say? Will he tell them he was at our house during the time of the murder, hoping to use us as an alibi? Will he confess and tell them he gave his clothes to Caroline? Is there evidence the police can use against him in his car? If there is, will he be shrewd enough to get rid of the car in a way the police can't trace? What would I do in his position? Would I burn the car and report it stolen? Disable the engine, tow it to a junkyard, and have it crushed for scrap metal?

My God, what a mess.

The last time I'm conscious of the clock, it's three in the morning. I slip into sleep, and find myself running through a maze of mirrored walls, floors, and ceilings. Someone is chasing me. I come to a dead end and look at myself. I'm emaciated, nearly unrecognizable. Something has drained my body, perhaps even my soul. My skin is cracked, pale, and drawn so tightly against my bones that I resemble a skeleton. I shrink away from the image in horror and turn to run back in the direction from which I've come.

I take one step and see them. Anita White and Mike Norcross, guns up, come around the corner. I turn back and look into the mirror. I smash it with my fist.

On the other side of the mirror is a dark tunnel. I can see a dim light in the distance. I run toward it, but after only a few strides I feel myself falling, falling, falling through the darkness and down what I believe is a bottomless pit. Suddenly a parachute pops open above me. I land awkwardly and tumble, rolling onto my side as the parachute falls softly around me. I extricate myself from the chute and stand. I'm in complete darkness now, but I feel a weight on my shoulders. I run my hands up my abdomen, across my chest, and realize I'm wearing web gear now. I'm wearing boots and a Kevlar helmet. I have an M16 assault rifle strapped across my shoulders. A flashlight is attached to the strap on my web gear, and I flip it on. I'm in a cave. I hear a faint voice and cast the beam of the flashlight toward the sound.

"Fahhhhhh-eeee."

I see an elongated mound. I bring the weapon around, pull the charging handle, and aim it toward the mound. I creep forward slowly. The floor of the cave begins to tremble beneath my feet. I shoulder the weapon. The sound grows louder.

"Faaaahhhh—eeeeee."

It's the voice of a female. I suddenly realize I recognize it.

The mound begins to erode as the tremors intensify. Suddenly, the clay that covers it splits, and I can make out what I believe is a face. It's a body, slimy, in the early stages of decomposition. The lips are moving.

"Faaaahhhiiiinnnddd—mmmeeeee."

The tremors stop; the body bends at the waist and sits up. The head turns toward me, and I find myself looking directly at what's left of Hannah Mills's sweet face.

"Find me," she whispers. "Find me."

31

Anita White's plan was to execute the search warrants simultaneously, early in the morning, in Tennessee and North Carolina. Detective Rama from Durham had taken the documents Anita faxed him and drafted his own application. The primary difference in the two applications was that Rama had received information (from Anita, a fellow law enforcement officer) that Tommy Miller had returned to Durham because he was a student at Duke University, and that the vehicle was now in North Carolina. He'd called Anita late the previous afternoon and told her that the judge had issued the warrants for both Tommy's car and his apartment, that he'd obtained an address for Tommy, and that he was personally staking out Tommy's place at the Belmont complex near the Duke campus. Rama had called again around eleven at night to tell Anita that Tommy was in the apartment, but the car wasn't in the lot. Anita told him that even if he couldn't find the car in the morning, she wanted Tommy held for questioning.

Anita hung up her phone at seven a.m.

"Rama's in place," she said to Norcross. "He's going in now."

Anita pulled into Toni Miller's driveway. Norcross was in the passenger seat, and two more agents were in a separate car right behind them. She threw the car into park, killed the engine, and got out. The other two agents went around to the back as Toni and Norcross strode to the front porch. Anita rapped sharply on the front door.

"Police! Search warrant!" she yelled. She banged on the door again.

A couple of minutes later, Anita heard a voice from the other side of the door. It was Toni Miller.

"What do you want?"

"Police, Mrs. Miller! We have a search warrant. Open the door."

"Get the hell out of here!" The voice sounded tortured, as though Toni Miller had been horrifically wounded.

"Open the door, Mrs. Miller, or we'll break it down!"

"There's nothing you want here! Go away! Please! Go away!"

"Last chance, Mrs. Miller! Open the door!"

There was a long silence before Anita heard a loud click as Toni Miller slid the dead bolt. Anita pushed the door open and walked into the foyer. The ceiling in the foyer was nearly twenty feet high; the floor was marble. A large chandelier hung above Anita's head.

Toni had backed up near a decorative rail that spiraled upward along a staircase. Anita gasped when she saw her. She was naked—her robe lay in a pile at her feet—and she was crying hysterically. She spread her arms wide and screamed, "Go ahead! Search me! I have nothing to hide!"

"Walk through and let the others in," Anita said to Norcross, who had turned his back to Toni. Anita stepped toward Toni, reached down, and picked up the robe and nightgown off the floor. She wrapped the robe around Toni's shoulders and led her silently into a den off the foyer. Toni was now sobbing quietly. Anita felt deep sympathy for this tortured woman, a woman who had probably done nothing wrong, a woman whose husband—and now her son—had put her through far more than Anita suspected she deserved.

Anita helped Toni sit on a couch and knelt in front of her.

"I'm sorry to have to put you through this, Mrs. Miller, but I have a job to do. We have a warrant that allows us to search the property, inside and out. We'll do it as quickly and quietly as we can. And when we're finished, I'd still like to ask you a few questions."

Anita looked into Toni's eyes. They'd taken on a faraway look, as though she'd transported herself mentally to some other place, some other time.

"Just do what you have to do and get out," Toni whispered.

The search lasted four hours and encompassed three bedrooms, two bathrooms, a kitchen, den, dining area, laundry room, game room, basement, and garage. The agents found nothing whatsoever that could be called evidence. When Anita examined Toni's cell phone, she found that Toni hadn't made a single call to Tommy in the past twenty-four hours. There were several calls to and from someone named Caroline, however. Wasn't that Dillard's wife?

Anita had called Rama every half hour during the search to see how things were going with Tommy Miller, but Rama wasn't answering his cell. Anita figured he was either searching the car or sweating Tommy.

She told the other agents to wait outside and walked back into the den where Toni Miller had been sitting during the entire search. She hadn't said a word.

"We're finished, Mrs. Miller," Anita said. Toni didn't respond.

"I'd like to talk to you for a minute, if you feel up to it," Anita said.

"Get out of my house," came the reply. The voice was cold, full of contempt.

Anita turned and walked out the front door. As she walked toward the car, her cell phone buzzed. It was Rama.

"Talk to me," Anita said.

"Bad news," Rama said. "He spotted us first thing when we pulled into the complex this morning. I don't know what the hell he was doing out that early, but he ran like a rabbit. We've spent the whole morning looking for him. No luck so far."

"The car?" Anita said.

"No sign of it yet. We'll stay on it."

Anita closed the phone. Her only viable suspect, a kid, was staying a step ahead of her. Now both he and his vehicle had disappeared. Anita had nothing solid to tie Tommy Miller to the judge's murder. But if he had nothing to hide, why would he run?

As Anita got into the car, her cell phone rang. She looked at the number and turned to Norcross.

"It's the boss."

"Like I told you before," Norcross said, "I'm glad he didn't dump this case on me."

32

Judge Green's murder dominates the radio broadcasts as I drive through Boones Creek toward Jonesborough the next morning. Hannah's disappearance merits a brief mention. I've left home later than usual because I'm too tired to work out. I decide to take a detour and stop by my sister's house. It's several miles out of the way, but I haven't seen or heard from her since Christmas, when she suddenly announced to everyone that she was four months' pregnant. Since she's forty-four years old, unmarried, and hasn't been exactly a model citizen, the news came as quite a surprise. We had a short discussion that resulted in her storming out of the house, and I haven't spoken to her since.

Sarah lives in the house that belonged to my mother before she died of Alzheimer's a few years back. She's a year older than I, a beautiful, green-eyed, dark-haired woman who has never been able to get past my uncle raping her when she was a child. She's spent most of her adult life addicted to booze, drugs, and rotten men. She's been in jail a half dozen times.

After our mother died, Sarah pulled herself together for about a year, although she replaced her addiction to substances with a religious zeal worthy of the pope himself. During that time, she met a man named Robert Godsey and moved away with him to Crossville, Tennessee, which is about a hundred and fifty miles west of Johnson City. Godsey turned out to be a jerk and beat her terribly—twice. During the second beating, Sarah defended herself by hitting Godsey with a fireplace shovel and wound up being charged with attempted murder. The charge was eventually dropped and Sarah moved back, but I've seen very little of her since. She's working at a deli in Johnson City, slinging sandwiches for the college lunch crowd.

As I pull into the driveway off Barton Street, I see a large chopper parked outside the garage door in the shade of an old sugar maple. The first thing that pops into my mind is that Sarah's taken up a new hobby. The Harley is painted a glossy black, with shiny chrome wheels and leather saddlebags. It can't be Sarah's. She's strong, but she's eight months' pregnant now, and the bike has to weigh more than half a ton. There's no way she could handle it.

I walk to the front porch and ring the doorbell. It's a little after eight. I know she has to be at work by nine, so I figure she should be up. She comes to the door wearing an oversized black T-shirt that says "Biker Bitch" in white letters across the front. Her face is full and pink, and her pregnant belly is pushing against the inside of the shirt.

"What are you doing here?" Sarah says matter-of-factly.

"Just thought I'd stop by and say hello. Haven't seen much of you lately. Damn, you're as big as a house."

"Thanks. Thanks a lot."

"No, I didn't mean it that way. It just surprised me. You look good. You really do. You look healthy. A little tired maybe, but healthy."

"Your powers of observation never cease to amaze." Her tone is unfriendly and sarcastic.

"Caroline misses you. So do I."

"I see Caroline once in a while."

"Really? She hasn't mentioned it."

"I guess she doesn't tell you everything, does she?"

"Have I done something to piss you off?"

"Not lately."

"Well, are you going to invite me in for a cup of coffee or leave me standing out here on the porch?"

"I have company."

"So introduce me."

She shrugs her shoulders and opens the door. I follow her through the living room and into the kitchen. Standing next to the sink is one of the biggest men I've ever seen. He's a good five inches taller than I and looks to weigh in the neighborhood of three hundred pounds. He has a huge belly, but other than that, he looks like a weight lifter. He's wearing a white T-shirt under a black leather vest, blue jeans, and boots. He has a brown beard that reaches to his collarbone, and both of his thickly muscled arms are covered in tattoos. His brown hair is pulled into a ponytail that falls to the middle of his back.

"This is my friend Roy," Sarah says.

He peers at me through expressionless blue eyes. Though I'm intimidated by his size, I step toward him and put out my hand.

"Joe Dillard. Sarah's brother."

His hand is rough, calloused, and as big as a ham. He squeezes tightly, as if to let me know he could crush me if he wanted to.

"They call me Mountain," he says in a raspy bass.

"I can see why. That must be your bike out front. Nice."

He nods and drains the last of his coffee as I back away from him slowly. He looks at Sarah and says, "Gotta hit the road, babe."

Sarah walks over to him, and he bends down to kiss her. While he's at it, he grabs two huge handfuls of her butt.

"I'll stop by sometime tonight," he says, and then he lumbers past me and out the front door. As he's walking away, I see a patch on the back of his leather vest. It's a red skeleton with a wicked smile on its face and a long, pointed red tail. It's wearing a beret and carrying a rifle. Beneath the skeleton are the words "Satan's Soldiers."

Satan's Soldiers is a notorious motorcycle gang. I know they're heavy into the crystal methamphetamine business. They also deal in guns and explosives. I have to hand it to Sarah. She sure knows how to pick 'em.

I walk over to the coffeemaker, pour myself a cup, and sit down at the table. Sarah walks down the hall toward the bedroom. I sip the coffee and hear the chopper roar to life in the driveway. A few minutes later, Sarah, wearing a yellow blouse and a pair of black jeans, walks back into the kitchen.

"How long have you been dating Roy?"

"About a year, I guess."

"Classy guy. I especially enjoyed the ass grab. Where'd you meet him?"

"Tonto's."

Tonto's is a biker bar on the outskirts of Johnson City. I've never been in the place, but I've driven by it plenty of times at night on the weekends. Dozens of motorcycles—maybe up to a hundred—are always in the parking lot.

"Didn't know you ever hung out at Tonto's," I say.

"Lots of things you don't know. Did you stop by to pass judgment?"

"Nah, I just stopped by to say hello. Didn't exactly expect to find a gangbanger in Ma's house, though."

"It's my house now. And I'll invite anyone I please."

"Does he know I'm an assistant district attorney?"

"Yeah. I told him."

"Do you know what they do, Sarah? That gang? They manufacture and sell crystal—"

"I don't want to hear it," she barks. "Mind your own business. And you'd better get used to the idea of having him around. He's the father of the baby I'm about to have."

I stare at her in silence. She stands abruptly.

"I have to go to work now."

She hovers over me until I reluctantly get up. I

want to try to talk some sense into her, but I know from years of experience that I might as well beat my head against the refrigerator. I put my cup in the sink and turn around to face her, but she's already walking away down the hallway again.

"You know the way out," she calls over her shoulder, and I head out to my truck.

33

I have an appointment with the assistant United States attorney in Greeneville at ten a.m. I'm taking him my case file on Buddy Carver, the child porn aficionado. He's agreed to present the case to a federal grand jury. I'm sure they'll indict Carver, and I'm sure Carver's lawyer won't have the same success with the federal district judge that he had with Judge Green. Carver will soon be spending his days and nights in a minimum security federal prison, probably in Kentucky or West Virginia.

I stop in at the office for a few minutes to pick up Carver's file and check for phone messages, but first I dial Anita White's cell phone number, hoping she'll give me an update on the investigation into Judge Green's murder. I need to try to stay a step ahead of her if I can. Anita doesn't answer the call. I leave her a message and dial Sheriff Bates's cell number to get the latest on Hannah Mills, but he doesn't answer, either.

I check my voice mail. There's a message from Tom Pickering, the AUSA I'm supposed to meet in less than an hour. He wants me to call him before I come down. I dial the number.

"I got a call from a DEA agent in Knoxville this morning," Pickering says after he comes on the line. "He wants to drive up and meet with you while you're here."

"DEA agent?" I say. "Any idea what he wants?"

"It has something to do with the girl who worked in your office who's gone missing."

"What's his name?"

"Rider. Maurice Rider. Everybody calls him Mo. Good guy. He's been around for a long time."

"Do you know what he wants?"

"Not really. He called early. Mentioned that he'd read about the girl in the newspaper this morning. He said he had some information for whoever was looking into it, but he wanted to talk to someone he could trust. He asked if I knew anyone. I told him the sheriff seems to be a pretty solid guy, but he said he doesn't trust sheriffs. So I mentioned you. When I told him you were coming down this morning, he asked if I thought it'd be okay if he drove up from Knoxville to meet you."

"Sure," I say. "If he knows something that might help, I'd be more than willing to talk to him. Right now we're lost in the dark."

I manage to avoid Lee Mooney and leave the office around nine fifteen. So many thoughts are floating through my mind that before I realize it, I've made the thirty-minute drive to Greeneville. I park my truck in front of the federal courthouse on Depot

Street and walk past the concrete pillars designed to keep anyone from parking a vehicle within a hundred feet of the building. The pillars always remind me of that sick bastard Timothy McVeigh and the Oklahoma City bombing that killed dozens of innocent people.

Tom Pickering's office is on the third floor, and I climb the wide marble steps in the courthouse foyer after making small talk with the U.S. Marshals at the security station just inside the front door. I lay out the Carver case for Pickering, a soft-spoken, studious man in his mid-thirties. Just as we're finishing up, his secretary buzzes him over the intercom.

"Tell him to come on in," Pickering says.

Mo Rider walks through the door, and Pickering introduces us. The first thing I notice is the prominent cleft in his chin. He's fifty or so, wearing khaki pants and a brown button-down shirt. His hair, which he wears closely clipped, has already gone gray. His eyes are green, and he has the rugged look of a man who spends a lot of time outdoors. He takes a seat at the small conference table where Pickering and I have been working.

"I have a little story to tell you," Rider says after we get past the preliminaries and he's satisfied I'm not a shill for a drug cartel. "It starts about fourteen, fifteen years ago, when this young girl and her aunt came to my office. The girl's a hiker. Name's Katie, Katie Dean. She lives outside of Gatlinburg and spends a lot of time in the national forest. Sweet little gal, scared shitless the day she comes in.

"So she goes out on this overnight hike, gets way

back off the beaten path, and runs across a huge patch of marijuana. Biggest we'd ever seen in that area at the time. Her aunt brings her into the office, she shows me exactly where the patch is, and a few days later we go in and burn it."

"Sounds like a happy ending for you guys," I say, "but what does this have to do with Hannah?"

"It was anything but a happy ending," Rider says. "This kid, Katie, was only eighteen years old then. Like I said, she and her aunt were both scared about talking to us, but I assured them nobody would ever know outside of our office. Somebody leaked it, though. We had one guy from the county sheriff's department on the task force, and he must have found out who she was and leaked the information. We never could prove it, but I know he had to leak it. Corrupt bastard. The whole damned sheriff's department was in the grower's pocket. He was making millions, and he spread enough of it around to buy some loyalty.

"So anyway, a couple of days after we burned the field, the girl's house was firebombed. Katie and another woman—a black woman who lived there with them—got out, but the fire killed her aunt and a young invalid boy, the aunt's son, even the family dog."

Rider stops for a minute and shakes his head. The incident he's describing may have happened more than a decade ago, but I can see that the guilt he feels still weighs heavily on his soul.

"The group that did the firebombing was Mexican, run by a guy named Rudy Mejia," Rider says. He looks me directly in the eye. "Mejia was murdered about a month later by another grower who was trying to lock up the marijuana business for himself. The other grower's name was Rafael Ramirez. I think you have him in your jail up there, don't you?"

"Yeah. I've got him on a not-so-strong murder charge. As a matter of fact, he reached out to me yesterday. Said he knows what happened to Hannah, the girl who's gone missing from our office, but he wants a free pass in exchange for the information."

"Doesn't surprise me," Rider says. "He's branched out over the years into contract killing and kidnapping. He's a real peach."

"So what does all of this have to do with Hannah?"

"After the bombing, I felt like I had to do whatever I could to protect Katie, so I arranged for her to go into witness protection. She didn't fit the program, but I talked the suits into letting her in anyway. Gave her a new name, new social, the whole bit. The aunt had stashed a bunch of money, and the girl wound up inheriting half of it, plus the farm where they lived. Katie hated witness protection, though. She spent a couple of months in Utah and then split, but at least she kept the alias. She moved back down here, sold the farm, and got a college degree from UT. She wound up working in the DA's office in Knoxville until a few months ago. Do you see what I'm saying?"

"I think so. I think you're telling me I don't know Hannah Mills as well as I think."

"That's just the tip of the iceberg," Rider says. "Did she ever tell you that her father murdered her mother and her brothers and sister? Happened up in Michigan, when she was twelve, thirteen, something like that. That's why she moved down here in the first place."

"She never mentioned it. So what you're telling me is that the girl I know as Hannah Mills is really this Katie?"

"That's right," Rider says. "Katie Dean's her name. One of the sweetest girls I ever met."

34

Anita White was growing angrier by the minute. She felt like a schoolgirl who'd been called into the office by the principal, who was allowing her to stew before he came in to berate her. Ralph Harmon was the special agent in charge of the TBI office in Johnson City, a title Anita always found amusingly quaint. He wasn't the captain or the lieutenant or the commander. He was *in charge*. She allowed herself a brief moment to wonder what bureaucratic sycophant had come up with such a lame title.

She'd been sitting in Harmon's office for twenty minutes. He'd called her on the phone as she left Toni Miller's, asked for an update on the case, and then requested a meeting as soon as she arrived. The minute Anita walked in, Harmon walked out, saying he'd be right back. She could hear him through the open door, laughing and talking with one of the secretaries. He wasn't attending to any important business; he was insulting her in his uniquely inimical way.

Harmon had been In Charge for less than two years before Anita arrived. During her initial meeting with Harmon, she found him to be a transparent man who couldn't hide the bigotry that lurked beneath his phony smile. He'd made reference to the lack of "people of color" who were field agents in the TBI and had compounded the insult by expressing the opinion that the job was much more suited to men. He'd virtually ignored her since that first day, with the exception of assigning her cases that none of the other agents wanted.

Anita glanced around the room. The wall was plastered with certificates and photographs. She'd never looked at them closely before, but one section of the display caught her eye. There were several photographs of Harmon in military garb: a dress uniform, camouflage, a flight suit. He was smiling broadly in all of them, posing with other soldiers. In one photo, he was wearing a helmet and sitting in the cockpit of a helicopter. The photos surrounded a small, framed display of three medals backed by navy blue velvet. It was obvious that Harmon wanted everyone to know that he was in the military. Anita remembered what her daddy had said about men who displayed the memories of their military careers for all to see.

"Men like that are pretenders, Neets," her daddy had said. "Soldiers who've been in combat, those who have seen the true face of war, aren't going to put up a bunch of pictures on the wall. They don't even like to think about it, let alone be reminded of it all the time."

She smiled to herself. Thinking of her father always made her smile, and thinking of Harmon as a pretender would make easier what was undoubtedly going to be a difficult conversation.

Harmon came in a few minutes later and closed the door behind him. Anita had always thought he carried himself like one of the wise guys she'd seen in the movies. A few years older than she, he was medium height with a potbelly. His suits were always a bit too tight, and he wore his dark hair combed straight back from his forehead and held in place with hair spray or mousse.

"Do you know how many phone calls I've received about this investigation in the past twenty-four hours?" Harmon began.

"Several, I'd imagine."

"Dozens. The brass in Nashville are so far up my ass, I can feel them tickling my tonsils. They want to know what we're doing about this."

"We're doing all we can."

"But we're not getting any *results*. People want results when a judge is murdered, Agent White. They want somebody arrested. They want somebody punished. They figure, hell, if somebody can kill a judge and get away with it, none of us are safe. People call their congressmen and ask them why nobody's been arrested yet. They ask them what kind of outfit we're running up here."

"But it's only been a day and a half," Anita said.

"Doesn't matter. When people around here call the politicians, the politicians call the brass in Nashville and ask them why nobody's been arrested yet. And then guess who the brass call? Me. They ask me what we're doing. They ask me who I put in charge of the investigation. They ask me whether we have a suspect in custody, and if not, why not? And you know what I have to tell them? Lies, that's what. I tell them I've got my best agent in charge of the investigation. I tell them she's an up-and-comer, a real go-getter. I tell them she already has a suspect and she's already gotten a search warrant. I tell them she'll have someone locked up by the end of the day. And then I call her, and she tells me she doesn't have a damned thing. Not only that; she tells me her only suspect has disappeared like a goddamned fart in a hurricane. I called you in here now because I want you to explain yourself to me so I can explain myself to them. And it had better be good."

Anita thought back on what Norcross had said to her in the car yesterday. How the boss had been the first agent at the crime scene; how he must have known how tough it was going to be.

"Why did you assign this case to me?" Anita asked.

Harmon looked surprised. He laced his fingers together and rested his elbows on the desk.

"I just told you. You're my up-and-comer. My go-getter. I thought you were the right person for the job."

"Do you know what I think? I think instead of assigning this case to me, you draped it around my neck like a yoke. You were at the crime scene. You knew it was outdoors. You knew the weather was about to turn. Fire and water are two of the worst things that can happen to a crime scene, and this one had both. What evidence the fire didn't consume, the water washed away. So you dumped it on me. When the brass call, why don't you just tell them the truth? Tell them you knew it was going to be an impossible case, so you dumped it on the agent whose very existence offends you. Why don't you tell them you knew you might need a sacrificial lamb, so you dumped it on the agent you'd most like to blame if everything goes to hell in a handbasket?"

Anita took a breath. She'd stopped short of saying what was really on her mind. *Why don't you tell them you can all blame it on the woman? The black woman!* She refused to toss that card on the table. It was a card her daddy had warned her never to play. "You make your way on hard work and dedication," he'd said. "You outwork and outthink the bigots, even though you know they hate you and would do anything to destroy you. You stay true to yourself and your principles. You adapt and you overcome. *That's* how you do it."

Harmon's face flushed. His laced fingers became pink as he squeezed them tightly together.

"Are you accusing me of sexual discrimination and racism, Agent White? Are you suggesting that my decision to assign this case to you was motivated by your gender or the color of your skin?"

Anita knew she was on thin ice. She didn't want to back down, but she loved the job and wanted to keep it. She chose her words carefully.

"What I'm saying is that you've treated me like an outcast since the first day I walked through this door. I find it hard to believe that you've suddenly decided I'm some kind of wonder woman."

Harmon leaned back in his chair and began rocking back and forth. He closed his eyes and massaged his temples for a full thirty seconds before he spoke.

"I hope you understand that we're both in a world of shit here," he said. "I thought that since this judge had the reputation of being a first-class son of a bitch, nobody would pay much attention. I underestimated the political fallout. And you're right. I assigned this murder investigation to you because I knew it was a shit case and I don't like you. You're cold, Agent White, and you think your shit doesn't stink. But we're stuck with each other. We're grown-ups. We can agree to disagree."

"Is that all? Can I go now?"

"You can go as soon as you tell me how you plan to nail the bastard who did this."

"Honestly? Right now I have no idea. Perhaps you have some suggestions."

"As a matter of fact, I do have a suggestion—one that might allow both of us to keep our jobs."

35

I spend another half hour talking to Rider about Hannah Mills/Katie Dean, her background, and her tenuous connection to Ramirez. After an extra ten minutes of arguing, I finally talk him into sharing what he knows with Sheriff Bates. As I drive back to Jonesborough, I try several times to get ahold of Bates to let him know what I've found out and that he needs to talk to Rider, but he's still not answering his cell. I stop and eat a quick lunch at a little diner called the Mountain View and get back to the office around twelve thirty. Rita's out to lunch, along with everyone else, it seems, but as I walk past her desk and down the hall, I hear voices coming from Mooney's office. One of them sounds like Anita White, so I decide to walk back and see what's going on.

"Joe, come in, come in," Mooney says when I appear in the doorway. He's smiling broadly, which immediately makes me think he's going to ask me for a favor. Anita is sitting across the desk from Mooney to his right, and Mike Norcross is across the desk and to his left. "We're just having a little strategy session."

"Making any progress on the judge?" I say to Anita.

"Doing what we can."

"Any solid leads?"

"That's what we were talking about," Mooney interrupts. "We'd like to present some evidence to the grand jury, and you're just the man to do it."

"Really?" I'm immediately skeptical. He's talking in his politician voice, a sure sign that reason is being thrown out the window. "What kind of evidence?"

"Evidence of interstate flight to avoid prosecution, evidence of obstruction of justice, evidence of murder."

"I take it you have a suspect." I wonder what Anita's found out since yesterday, and I silently curse myself for not being more diligent about getting in touch with her.

Mooney motions to a chair in the corner. "Pull that chair around here. Let me bring you up to speed."

I grab the chair, turn it around, and lean on the backrest. Mooney talks for ten or fifteen minutes, occasionally assisted by Anita. He gives me a detailed description of everything that's been done in the investigation and the conclusions he's drawn. By the time he's finished, I'm quite certain he's either making a sick joke or he's gone completely insane.

"I want you to present all this to the grand jury and then persuade them to issue an indictment for first-degree murder," Mooney says.

"You can't be serious."

Mooney seems stunned, as though he would never imagine I might question him.

"I'm completely serious," he says, "and I don't think I appreciate your tone."

I look at Anita, then at Norcross.

"You guys are supportive of this?"

"We are," Anita says.

"Let me tell you a little story," I say to Anita. "There was a guy in this office a few years back, before you moved up here. His name was Deacon Baker, and he used to do things similar to this. He'd indict people for murder without sufficient evidence, overcharge people, and he filed a death penalty notice on nearly every murder case, intending to use it as leverage. And do you know what I used to do? I used to practice criminal defense, and I made a pretty handsome living taking the tactics he used and shoving them up his stupid, fat ass."

Mooney clears his throat.

"I hope you're not insinuating that I'm stupid," he says.

"What you're proposing is completely irrational. If I understand your summary of the evidence, you have exactly nothing. Zero. You have a young man who you suspect *may* be the killer. Your theory of motive is that he killed Judge Green to avenge his father's suicide. One witness saw a white car in the neighborhood; another saw a white car a mile or two from the neighborhood, but we don't even know whether it's the same car. Your suspect owns a white car. So what? Can either of your witnesses identify the car? Did they get a look at the driver? You have no weapon, no blood, no prints, no hair, no fiber, no witness to the crime, and no incriminating statements from anyone. Like I said, you have nothing."

"His mother was totally uncooperative," Mooney

says. "He's left the state, and he ran from the police in Durham this morning. This is all circumstantial evidence of guilt."

"No, it isn't," I say curtly. I'm frustrated and beginning to grow angry. I look at Anita and Norcross, both of whom have suddenly taken an intense interest in the floor. "It's diddly-squat. First of all, he had every right to leave the state. From what you've told me, no one has even talked to him. How's he even supposed to know he's a suspect?"

"His mother must have warned him," Mooney says. "The neighbor saw him come and go in a hurry."

"And you think that's evidence of guilt in a murder? Come on, Lee. You're not that obtuse. And didn't you just tell me the police executed a search warrant on the mother's home this morning and the kid's apartment in Durham and didn't find a damned thing? You'll be lucky if they don't sue you."

"This is what we do," Mooney says. "You convene the grand jury. You bring Agent White in, and you have her lay everything out: the feud between Judge Green and Ray Miller, the suicide, finding the judge's body the morning after the funeral, the fact that Tommy Miller didn't come home that night. She tells them about the mother's slamming the door in her face, how she won't give them any information at all. She tells them about the neighbor who saw Tommy come home early that morning and then leave quickly. She tells them about Tommy running from the police in Durham, how his car seems to have disappeared into thin air, and how he's now a fugitive."

He obviously hasn't listened to a word I've said.

"A fugitive? How can he be a fugitive if you don't have an arrest warrant?"

"He's wanted for questioning."

"You've just said he's a suspect in a murder. He doesn't have to answer any questions, remember?"

"Stop fencing with me," Mooney says. "Do what I say and the grand jury will indict him. We'll put out a nationwide alert. We'll have him in custody in a couple of days, tops."

"And then what? You know as well as I do that you won't be able to present any of this garbage to a trial jury. None of it's admissible. If he keeps his mouth shut, you'll all end up looking like fools."

"He's a kid, for God's sake," Mooney says. "These agents are pros. He'll cave during interrogation."

"No way. I don't want any part of this."

I stand up and start to walk toward the door, muttering under my breath. I've seen Mooney do some idiotic things over the past few years, but this tops them all.

"Now you wait just one damned minute," I hear Mooney say behind me. The tone of his voice is threatening, and I stop and turn to face him full on. I can sense where this is going, but I don't care.

"It isn't a request," he says. "You're going to take this case to the grand jury. You're going to present the evidence through Agent White, and you're going to come back with an indictment."

"No, I'm not. If you're absolutely bent on doing this, do it yourself." I stare him directly in the eye, knowing what has to come next.

"I'm your superior," Mooney says. "You work for

me. You're refusing a direct order in front of two witnesses. This is gross insubordination."

"I don't care who you are. I don't care what your title is. This isn't what I signed up for. I'm not going to be a part of a railroad job."

"Then you leave me no choice. Pack up your things. You're fired."

I turn toward the door to leave, but I can't resist saying one last thing to him. I haven't been able to shake the feeling I had yesterday when he mentioned Hannah in the past tense. I turn back around.

"By the way," I say, "Rafael Ramirez says somebody wanted Hannah Mills dead, and he says he knows who." It's a small lie. My mother would have called it a little white lie.

"He'll tell you who it is if you let him out of jail."

PART 3

36

Hannah Mills, the former Katie Dean, looked up at the waterfall and wondered what she was doing. It was the first time in years she'd been hiking, and sitting at the base of Red Fork Falls in Unicoi County, she remembered why. The memories were inevitable: the long days in the Great Smoky Mountains National Park, the beauty of the dozens of cascades and falls she'd visited, the stands of old-growth timber. But those memories triggered others, others she'd tried to keep at bay.

Pretending Aunt Mary and Luke never existed was the easiest way to get by. She'd learned to put them, along with Lottie, the farm, the animals, all of it, out of her mind. It was as though everything had turned into clouds and drifted slowly away on the breeze.

After the fire—which Hannah couldn't remember at all—her life had spun out of control for a while. She found herself with a new name, living in Salt Lake City in a downtown apartment, a few blocks from the giant Mormon Tabernacle. The agents in Knoxville had told her it was the only way they could ensure her safety, and at the time, she hadn't the will to resist. An

FBI agent named Fritz became her new best friend in Utah, but Hannah quickly grew homesick for the purple-shrouded mountains she loved so much. She packed what few things she had one day, got on a bus, and never looked back.

She wound up in Knoxville, alone and confused. The only person she had any regular contact with was Agent Rider, who, upon her return to Knoxville, had given her enough money to get a small apartment and survive until she could get on her feet. Then, a couple of weeks after she returned, Agent Rider was contacted by a lawyer from Gatlinburg who wanted to meet with Hannah. Agent Rider arranged the meeting, and it was there that Hannah learned that Aunt Mary had made her not only the executor of her estate, but a beneficiary of her will. Hannah and Lottie were each to receive one half of Aunt Mary's money—just over three hundred thousand dollars each that had been invested in U.S. Treasury bills. Hannah also inherited the farm, but the lawyer told her that Mr. Torbett, the neighbor, had made an offer to buy it. The lawyer suggested Hannah accept the offer, and she did. She had no desire to return.

Hannah spent months in a fog, staring at the walls of her small apartment, lying in bed for days at a time, unwilling and unable to start over. She cursed God, or fate, or destiny, or whatever force it was that had selected her to bear the burden of so much pain and so much shame. She didn't care about the money. It had no real value or meaning to her, especially considering how she'd come to acquire it.

It was Agent Rider who'd finally helped Hannah

crawl out of the depths of her despair. He came by her apartment regularly and finally talked her into seeing a psychiatrist, a woman named Mattie Rhea. Dr. Rhea had prescribed medication—something called a serotonin reuptake inhibitor—and gradually, the fog began to lift. Hannah enrolled at the University of Tennessee in January of that year. She made few friends because she kept largely to herself, but the routine of campus life, along with the medication, helped her to gradually put the tragedies of the past behind her. Six years after she enrolled, she earned a master's degree in sociology and got a job as the victim/witness coordinator at the Knoxville district attorney general's office. Then, after spending another six years in quiet anonymity, helping people like her, people who had been the victims of crimes, she'd met Lee Mooney at a conference in Nashville and been persuaded to make a change.

Now, as she stood gazing up at the narrow, hundred-foot falls, a hand touched Hannah on the shoulder from behind.

"Maybe we should head back," Tanner Jarrett said.

"You're right," Hannah said. "I smell a storm coming."

Later that evening, several people from the office gathered at Rowdy's, a sports bar in Johnson City, to celebrate Tanner's twenty-seventh birthday. Hannah and Tanner had become friends, but Hannah was always careful not to give Tanner the idea that she might be looking for anything more. The hike earlier in the day was the first time the two of them had been without company. They went to lunch together sometimes, but always with someone else from the office along.

Today was Tanner's birthday, and when he'd asked Hannah to hike to the falls with him and then accompany him to Rowdy's later, she couldn't say no. It would have been much easier to keep her distance if Tanner wasn't so likable. He was handsome and funny and charming, and he had a way of making Hannah feel wonderful whenever she was around him. But she couldn't get too close. She just couldn't. Not yet.

The gathering consisted of Hannah and Tanner, Joe and Caroline Dillard, Lee Mooney, Rita Jones and her boyfriend—a lawyer Hannah didn't know—and two other young prosecutors from the office and their dates. Hannah was enjoying herself. Joe and Caroline Dillard had become close friends of Hannah's. More than once, she'd found herself wondering whether she might ever be as close to a man as Caroline seemed to be to Joe. They were virtually inseparable outside the office, and they treated each other with a gentle kindness and respect that Hannah imagined could only come from a bond that had been carefully nurtured for many years.

Hannah ate lightly while Tanner laughed and joked with Joe about a DUI case Tanner was prosecuting.

"You should have seen it," Tanner said through a mouthful of chicken. "I put the police officer's videotape in the machine, and it shows this woman getting out of her car. It takes a second to see that she's stark naked from the waist down. She starts grinding on this officer and singing, 'Hey, big spender.' I thought her lawyer was going to lose his lunch right there in front of the judge."

The laughter was contagious, the conversation light and easy, and Katie decided to do something she'd never done. She decided to have a drink. Tanner was driving. Why not? She turned to Lee Mooney, who was sitting on her right, and whispered, "Please don't tell anyone, but I've never had a drink before. What should I order?"

Mooney smiled at her and bent close to her ear.

"Try a Vodka Collins," he said.

The drink arrived a few minutes later, and Hannah took a sip. Slightly bitter, a little lemony. Cold going in and warm going down.

"How is it?" Mooney said.

"Good."

As the drink disappeared, Hannah found herself becoming more and more animated. She'd never realized how funny and entertaining she could be. By the time the first drink was gone, Mooney had ordered her a replacement. After Hannah downed the second drink and just as the waitress set down a third, Mooney announced to the crowd that she was taking her maiden voyage into drunkenness.

"No kidding?" Tanner said to her. "You've never had a drink in your life?"

"Never," Hannah slurred. She was light-headed and giddy, already drunk. "Not a single one single time."

Mooney raised his glass.

"To virgins," he said. "God bless them every one."

The entire group laughed, but instead of joining them, Hannah began to sulk. As the alcohol clouded her judgment and dislodged her self-control, she began to grow angry. She wasn't a prude, after all. She just couldn't face the thought of a man discovering her reconstructed breast. He would ask questions and jostle rusty memories of death and sorrow. How dare Mr. Mooney make fun of her.

Hannah drained the third glass of vodka and slammed her glass down on the table.

"I *am* a virgin, you know!" she yelled drunkenly into Mooney's ear. The rest of the group immediately went silent. "A *real* virgin! And I don't appreciate you laughing at me!"

37

Jack Dillard hustled along West End Avenue toward his dorm room in the semidarkness. It was nearly eight p.m. in Nashville, and he felt a constant rush of wind as the traffic roared past. His backpack was weighted down with textbooks and a twenty-pound plate he'd stuck inside. The extra weight pushed him, made him leaner and stronger.

Jack had been at Vanderbilt for three years now. When he arrived, he weighed two hundred thirty pounds and thought he was strong. Now, at two hundred fifteen pounds, he was stronger than ever, a walking piece of granite. Arkansas was coming in for a three-game series this weekend, and Jack briefly visualized smashing an inside fastball over the green monster in left field. He smiled to himself. He'd done it before. There wasn't a doubt in his mind that he'd do it again.

Jack's mind drifted to the paper he had to write later that night—five pages on biological anthropology. He intended to write about the difference between the evolution of man and the evolution of apes. Many people thought men evolved from apes.

They were wrong. As he pondered his thesis sentence, Jack wondered how many papers he'd written at Vanderbilt. At least a hundred, he decided. The professors were all about being able to express yourself in writing.

Jack was sore and tired, but he was used to it. Vandy was a demanding place, and his baseball coach was a drill sergeant. His days were often twelve, fourteen hours. He was up early and off to class until noon. On game days, he'd be at the field right after lunch, hitting in the cages, throwing, shagging fly balls, lifting weights. After a two-hour warm-up, he'd play a three- or four-hour game, then do maintenance work on the field, take a shower, grab something to eat, and then study, study, study. Off days were just as strenuous, probably more so, because that's when the team conditioned, and the sessions were brutal: weight lifting, plyometrics, sprint work, endurance work. It was a never-ending assault on the mind and body. Free time was for nonathletes. Free time was for pussies.

Something ahead caught Jack's eye. A man was leaning against a tree just inside the wrought-iron fence that separated the campus from the street. Jack wasn't close enough to recognize him, but the man appeared to be watching him. As Jack approached, the figure slipped behind the tree and disappeared.

Jack walked past the spot and looked closely at where the man had been standing. There was a hemlock hedge to the right of the tree, and it appeared he had walked behind it. Maybe the guy was a student and had just walked outside the dorm for a smoke.

Jack kept walking. Because of his size and strength, mugging had never been a concern, at Vandy or anywhere else, but as he pushed on down the street, he couldn't shake the feeling that he was being watched, maybe even followed.

Jack turned right onto the circle that surrounded the statue of Cornelius Vanderbilt. He looked over his shoulder. The lighting here was poor; if someone was going to attack him, this would be the best place. He lengthened his stride and veered off the circle onto the sidewalk that led toward the Hemingway Quad. As he passed a low wall of shrubbery, he caught a quick glimpse of someone moving quickly. He was suddenly knocked off balance as the figure jumped on his back and tried to get him in a choke hold.

Jack quickly gathered himself and dropped to his left knee. He instinctively tugged the attacker's right shoulder forward with his left hand and jerked his upper body hard, downward and to his left. It was a judo throw his father had shown him years ago. Every time he'd used it when wrestling with teammates or challengers from the dorm, it had worked, and this was no different. His attacker flew over his shoulder and landed with a thud on his back. Jack quickly straddled him and was just about to unload on him with his fist, when he heard a familiar laugh. He stopped and looked closely at the face.

"Damn you, T-bone!" Jack yelled as he rose to his feet. "You scared the crap out of me!"

"What's up, Hammer?" The person on the ground slowly climbed to his feet, and Jack found himself staring into the tired-looking, smiling face of Tommy

Miller. "I should have known you'd use that judo crap on me."

Jack hugged Tommy, and they shook hands. He loved Tommy like a brother. He was fun and easygoing, constantly joking. Jack had always found Tommy to be an honest and loyal friend. And he was a fierce competitor on the baseball field. Jack had faced him dozens of times in practice over the years. Tommy had a fastball in the low nineties, a wicked slider, and a changeup that had buckled Jack's knees more than he cared to remember.

"What the hell are you doing here?" Jack said.

"I'm in the wind, man. Let's go get some coffee or something, and I'll tell you about it."

Jack knew Tommy was "in the wind." His dad had called the night before and told him he'd been fired because he refused to try to persuade the grand jury to indict Tommy for murder. He said Tommy had run from the police in Durham and that his car had disappeared. He said Tommy would probably be indicted soon.

"The police are looking for you, T-bone."

"Yeah, now I know how the runaway slaves felt."

"Follow me."

Jack led Tommy to a group of four picnic tables beneath an elm tree near the library. The tables were all vacant. Jack tossed his backpack beside him and sat down at the one nearest the tree. Tommy sat across from him.

"How'd you get here?"

Tommy's Red Sox baseball cap was pulled low on his forehead. Jack noticed that his eyes kept darting around, watching everything. "I hitched a ride."

"Why'd you run?"

"I was scared out of my mind. Mom told me they think I killed that judge."

Jack tensed slightly. He didn't want to ask the question, but he needed to.

"Did you?"

Tommy shook his head and let out a deep breath.

"I don't even know where the guy lived," Tommy said. "I went to Dad's grave that night with a gallon of bourbon. I don't drink very often, but I think I must have drunk the whole damned gallon, because the last thing I remember is sitting on the ground, leaning on the headstone, crying. I woke up in the backseat of my car around five the next morning. It was parked next to this little convenience store on Oakland, and I had no idea how I got there. I was so hungover, man. My head was splitting, and I felt like I was going to barf all over the place. Your house was a lot closer than mine, so I drove over there."

"So you don't remember anything you did?" Jack said. "You don't remember driving to the convenience store?"

"No, and that's the problem. That's why I'm so scared of the cops. If they ask me what I was doing at such and such a time, I can't tell them. Another thing that scares me is that Mom said whoever killed the judge burned him. I had freaking gasoline all over me when I woke up at the convenience store, and I don't remember how it happened. I must have gotten gas somewhere, because my car was almost empty when I drove to the cemetery, and the next morning it was full."

"So maybe you filled up with gas at the convenience store and spilled gas all over you, and then you decided to get in the backseat and go to sleep."

"Maybe."

"You should go back there and see if somebody remembers you. You had to pay for the gas, and if you were that drunk, you were sure to make an impression."

"I'm afraid to go back there. I'm afraid to go anywhere near Johnson City."

"Where's your car?" Jack said. "Dad said the police can't find it."

"You'll love this. I gave it to this black guy about fifty miles outside of Durham. He was working on this old piece of junk in his driveway when I drove by. He lived in this little shack. So I turned around and pulled into his place, got my suitcase and my backpack out of the car, took the tag off, and handed him the keys. You should have seen the look on his face. Then I hitched a ride the rest of the way to Durham."

"Why'd you do that?"

"Because I knew the cops would be looking for the car. I didn't want to drive it into a lake or something like that, so I just figured I'd give it to somebody who needed it more than I did."

"Listen, T-bone, you need to go back and face this. Running makes you look guilty."

Tommy's head dropped. He stared at the table for a long minute. "Maybe I am, Hammer. God knows I thought about beating that son of a bitch to death with my bare hands at least a hundred times since Dad killed himself. Maybe I got plastered and went nuts, found out where he lived somehow, and drove over there and killed him."

"Don't say that, even if you're just joking. Don't even think it."

"I can't go back there, man. Not yet, anyway. If I go back and tell the police I don't remember what I did that night, they'll arrest me for sure. I think I'll just stay on the road for a while, then go back after things have settled down a little. Maybe in the meantime they'll find out who really did it."

"Do you have enough money? Do you need anything?"

"I'm okay. Mom gave me fifteen hundred dollars before I left. That should last me a little while."

Jack reached over and touched his friend lightly on the hand. "I haven't really had a chance to tell you this, but I'm sorry about your dad," he said. "I'm sorry about everything."

Tommy's eyes began to glisten, and Jack saw tears begin to roll down his cheeks.

"Can you believe he killed himself because he thought we'd be better off with money than with him?" Tommy said. "He must have been in so much pain. I just wish I could hug him again and tell him everything will be all right."

Tommy laid his head on his forearms and began to sob quietly. Jack wanted to offer him comfort but didn't know how. He was accustomed to the banter that goes on in a locker room, jousting verbally with his friends and teammates. Trying to comfort a friend after such a terrible loss was foreign territory. He reached over and squeezed Tommy's shoulder tightly.

"How about that coffee?" he said. "I'll just run across the street to the cafeteria and get us some."

Tommy raised his head slowly and wiped his eyes with the backs of his hands.

"Sure, Hammer, coffee sounds good."

Jack was gone for less than ten minutes. As he was hurrying back up the sidewalk carrying the coffee, he saw a campus policeman emerge from the shadows near the spot where the picnic tables were located. Jack smiled and nodded as he passed the officer, but he knew what he'd probably find when he got back to the tables.

He was right. His backpack was still lying on the table where he'd left it, but Tommy was gone.

38

Hannah Mills laid the slim, elongated tube on a paper towel on the back of the toilet and began to pace around the house. She picked up Patches, the cocker spaniel–mix puppy she'd adopted from the animal shelter a couple of weeks earlier, and carried him along with her.

"It can't be," she kept saying to the pup. "It just can't be."

With all that had happened to her, Hannah had become an expert at putting things out of her mind, and that's exactly what she'd done with the memory of her drunken night at the restaurant. What else could she do? Accuse Tanner of raping her? Perhaps, in her drunken state, she'd consented and simply didn't remember.

Tanner had called the next afternoon to check on her and ask how she was feeling. She'd casually asked him how she got into bed, and he said he'd carried her into the house, laid her on the bed, removed her shoes, and tucked her in. Hannah couldn't bring herself to believe otherwise.

The fatigue had started less than a week later.

There were times when her legs felt as though they were made of concrete. She would suddenly find herself barely able to move, barely able to stay awake. There'd been several times when, out of nowhere, she'd felt like crying and would have to run off into the bathroom to sob. Last week, the waves of nausea had begun to wash over her in the mornings, even when her stomach was empty. Her breasts were tender. She urinated far more often than she ever had in the past. She'd missed her period.

Hannah walked back into the bathroom. The pregnancy test was sitting there, waiting. She knew what the result was going to be, but she had no idea what she was going to do. She held the puppy close to her chest with her left hand and reached down with her right. . . .

Hannah decided to call Lee Mooney. Mr. Mooney had hired her, after all, and had treated her extremely well since she'd made the move from Knoxville. He also knew Tanner well and might be able to give her some advice in that regard. She'd thought about calling Joe and Caroline Dillard and asking their advice, but she found she was too embarrassed. She hadn't told Mr. Mooney the problem over the phone, just that she needed to speak with him as soon as possible. He'd arrived at her house in less than half an hour and was sitting in a chair in her den.

"I hope you're not going to tell me you've decided to leave," Mooney said as Hannah handed him a glass of sweet iced tea.

"No, no, I'm not leaving," Hannah said nervously. Actually, the thought of leaving suddenly appealed to her. "At least I'm not planning on leaving. Not any time soon, anyway."

"That doesn't sound too promising," Mooney said.

"I'm sorry. It's just that . . . It's just that what I'm about to tell you is terribly difficult, not to mention embarrassing. You can't tell a soul."

Mooney twisted the end of his handlebar mustache with the fingers on his right hand.

"I've never really asked you about your family, Hannah," he said. "If I remember correctly, I asked you a couple of things when I first met you at the conference, and it seemed to make you uncomfortable. Isn't there anyone in your family you can talk to?"

"I don't have any family. My parents and brothers and sister were killed. I'm all that's left."

"Do you want to tell me about what happened to them?"

"Thank you, but no."

"All right. Well, I hope you know you can trust me," he said.

"You've been good to me."

"And it's been my pleasure."

Hannah took a sip of her tea. Her hand was shaking, so she set the tea on a coaster on the coffee table in front of her. She folded her hands and began to rock back and forth.

"I'm pregnant," she said.

Hannah fought to maintain her composure, but the shock of actually saying the words caused her to break down. She covered her face with her hands and began to sob quietly. A few seconds later, she felt Mr.

Mooney's presence beside her. He sat down on the couch and gently took her hands.

"It's all right," he said. "Everything's going to be fine."

Hannah looked at him through watery eyes. He was smiling warmly. Both his touch and his voice were reassuring.

"Do you feel up to talking?"

Hannah calmed herself as best she could. Mr. Mooney handed her a handkerchief, and she tearfully recounted her symptoms of the past few weeks and the results of the pregnancy test.

"It had to happen the night I got so drunk," she said tearfully. "It had to be Tanner."

"You have no recollection of what happened after you got home that night?" he said.

"None. None whatsoever."

"There are certainly ways to find out if Tanner's the father," Mr. Mooney said. "Paternity tests. You could ask him to take a paternity test."

"I know. I've thought of that."

"If he refuses, you could force him."

"Yes, I know. But what then? What if he takes a test and I find out it's his?"

"Then I suppose you have him arrested for rape."

"I can't be certain he raped me. Maybe I let him. Maybe I wanted him to."

"Hannah," Mr. Mooney said, "I was there that night. I saw how intoxicated you were. As a matter of fact, I felt guilty about my role in contributing to your condition. But sex is something that's supposed to occur between two consenting adults, and there's no way in the world you were capable of consenting. If Tanner had sex with you that night, it was a rape under the law. And if he raped you, he needs to face the consequences."

"No," Hannah said. "I can't. I won't. I've worked with dozens of rape victims in the past six or seven years, Mr. Mooney. I've seen what they go through. I can't put myself through that."

"I understand, Hannah. I truly do. The system can be harder on victims than criminals."

Mr. Mooney rubbed Hannah's hands gently. She found herself glad that she'd made the decision to call him. It was good to have someone to talk to, especially someone as experienced, not to mention as compassionate, as Mr. Mooney.

"Have you considered the alternative?" Mr. Mooney said.

Hannah looked at him and blinked, not quite sure what he meant.

"You could terminate the pregnancy. It happens more than you might think, especially in cases of rape."

The thought of abortion hadn't entered Hannah's mind. It was out of the question. She wouldn't—she couldn't—even begin to entertain the notion of destroying the life she knew was growing inside her. Rape or no rape, abortion was not an option.

"No," Hannah said quietly. "I could never do that."

"Are you sure? It's no sin, Hannah, especially considering what seems to have happened to you."

"No," she whispered. "No, Mr. Mooney. I won't destroy my own child."

"Of course you won't. I hope you'll forgive me for even bringing it up."

Hannah was silent after that, lost in the maze of thought that surrounded her latest predicament. Mr. Mooney continued to rub her hands and softly reassure her, and she was content to let him do so. A half hour passed, maybe more. Mr. Mooney knelt in front of her and pushed back from her face the hair that had matted in the tears on her cheeks.

"It's getting late, Hannah," he said. "I have to go now. Why don't we sleep on it for a day or two and then decide the best course of action? There's no sense rushing into anything."

Hannah nodded, and shortly thereafter, Mr. Mooney left.

When Hannah had decided to switch jobs, she'd sensed she was doing the right thing. She wasn't so certain about the decision now, but at least she'd been right about one thing.

Mr. Mooney was a kind and decent man. If anyone could help her, it would be him.

She picked up Patches, who was whining at her feet, and began to rub his belly.

"I wonder if it'll be a girl," she said. "No, I *hope* it'll be a girl."

39

Hannah opened the refrigerator and pulled out a cold bottle of water. She noticed the package of chicken she'd purchased at the store on Tuesday. She'd better do something with it tonight or it might spoil. She decided she'd make herself some stir-fry later and closed the door. Patches was barking excitedly in the bedroom, and Hannah called him. She poured some of her water into Patches's bowl and bent down and petted his head as he lapped it up. She'd come to love him dearly in the short time she'd had him. He was so sweet and docile. He'd make a wonderful playmate for the baby.

It had been a difficult week. After her conversation with Mr. Mooney last Saturday, he'd called her on Sunday and said he'd completely forgotten he was leaving for vacation. He asked her to keep their conversation private. They would call Tanner into Mr. Mooney's office when he returned to work on Monday, have a conversation, gauge Tanner's reaction, and go from there.

Hannah had avoided Tanner the entire week. He'd called and left messages on her answering machine—

the last one asked whether he'd done something to offend her—but she'd ignored him. She was looking forward to Monday and the opportunity to confront Tanner. She might not like what he had to say, but at least she'd have some answers.

She stood and walked into the bedroom, removing her red Windbreaker along the way. She dropped it, along with her purse, onto the bed.

The strap went around her neck before she could step away from the bed. Hannah felt herself being pulled back and upward. Her feet left the floor. Her hands went immediately to her throat. Something was choking her. She couldn't breathe. What was it? Who was it?

Whoever it was, he was powerful, far more powerful than she. Hannah could feel the hair of his beard against her face as he pulled her tightly against him. She could smell the musty odor of his breath, feel the air rushing from his nostrils into her right ear. But she couldn't get free. She kicked and wriggled and squirmed, trying her best to break his hold, but he slammed her face-first into the floor and pinned her there. She felt something warm trickle from her mouth. *Blood, I must be bleeding.*

When Hannah accepted the inevitability of her own death, she relaxed. She saw her mother's smiling face, the expanse of Lake Michigan from a sandy bluff, the majesty of the purple Smoky Mountains. Lottie called to her from the kitchen. Supper was ready. Luke jerked in his bed, his eyes alight, a sure sign that he understood the joke she'd made. Aunt

Mary patted her hand on the front porch swing on a moonlit summer night.

As the darkness overtook her and the white light appeared, Hannah found herself a bit surprised, even puzzled, by her lack of fear. The thought passed through her mind that perhaps she should thank this man who was taking her life. True, he was taking her unborn child along with her, but since she'd learned of the pregnancy, Hannah had caught herself—more than once—regarding the thought of a child as another tragedy in the making.

Hannah's heart stopped beating, and the light grew brighter.

The last emotion she felt was relief.

40

The biker who killed Hannah Mills raised a beer can toward the sky.

"To gettin' 'er done," he yelled. Cyrus "Red" McKinney was in a celebratory mood. "The job" had gone off without a hitch. The girl had been missing for two weeks, and the cops didn't have a clue. He was certain they would never find her.

Sitting across the table from Red was his cousin, Ricky "Barrel" Reed. Barrel had been the only person Red trusted enough to help him with the job. Red knew what they were doing was strictly forbidden by the gang's code, but he also knew Barrel would keep quiet about it. He'd cut him in for five thousand of the twenty thousand he'd collected from the Mexican. Barrel had wanted an equal share, but because Red had done the actual wet work, he figured he earned the extra money.

It was Saturday, the last night of Bike Week in Myrtle Beach, South Carolina. The news had quickly spread through the ranks of Satan's Soldiers that the officers had negotiated a fat deal with a gang in Charlotte, and the booze and drugs were flowing. They were hanging out at a bar called Dante's, a run-down hellhole in Garden City that they took over for a week in the spring each year. Rock music was blaring, bitches were dancing topless on the tables, and two dudes had already ridden their choppers through the place. Red had downed nearly a case of beer during the day and had made two trips to the bathroom in the past hour to snort crystal meth. He was feeling like a conqueror.

"Me and you are two badass motherfuckers," Red hollered.

"Fuckin-A!" Barrel replied.

"That bitch was just the beginning! We're gonna be the next Murder Incorporated. Hit men, by God! I always wanted to be a hit man. Fuck this Mickey Mouse shit we been doing! We're going big-time, baby!"

"Keep your voice down, Red! People can hear you."

"I don't give a shit!"

Red rose from his chair and raised both fists into the air.

"Yea though I walk through the valley of the shadow of death, I shall fear no evil," he yelled, "for I'm the baddest motherfucker in the valley!"

It took less than a week for word to reach the officers. Inquiries had been made, meetings held. And now Red found himself in a barn in Unicoi County, tied securely to a metal chair, surrounded by men he thought were his friends. Barrel was next to him, whimpering like a child.

Red watched the man circling him. He was known

as Bear, the president of Satan's Soldiers. He was six feet tall and thick as an Angus bull. Muscles rippled beneath the tight black tank top he was wearing. Everything on him was covered with thick black hair—his head, face, shoulders, back, and chest—and he was wearing the gang's signature black bandanna. The rest of the officers were leaning against a stall about ten feet away, watching as he toyed with a length of braided rawhide and the knot at its end. They were known as Turtle, Rain Man, and Mountain.

"Know why you're here?" Bear asked.

"We ain't done nothing," Red said.

The knotted piece of rawhide smashed into his temple. Red saw a bright flash as pain shot through his head and down his spine.

"Don't lie to me, Red. It'll go a lot easier on you. That girl you killed worked for the DA. You think they're gonna stop looking for her, you damned fool? Now *we* gotta clean up the mess you made."

"Ain't no mess," Red said. "Ain't nobody gonna find nothing."

"We got rules. You break the rules, it affects us all. What the hell were you thinking? Going on your own. And a girl! She hadn't done a damned thing to us. And now, all this heat."

"There won't be no heat. *They ain't gonna find nothing.*"

"Won't be no heat? How do you think we found out about it? Because you're too goddamned dumb to keep your mouth shut. You and this fat lump of shit next to you."

"We won't say nothing, Bear," Barrel cried. "I swear to God we won't say a word."

Red heard the whiz of the rawhide and the dull thump as it struck his cousin. Barrel screamed.

"Shut your mouth, lard ass!" Bear yelled. "Now, I've known the two of you long enough to know that ol' Barrel here doesn't have brains enough to get in out of the rain. So you must have been the one who set it up. Right, Red?"

Red nodded his head and closed his eyes. He listened as Bear's boots crunched the dirt floor as he continued to circle.

"Who paid you?"

"Some Mexican down in Morristown."

"What Mexican? How'd he get in touch with you?"

"Don't know his name. I found out about the contract from another Mexican dude I party with. I told him I might be interested, so he gave me a number to call. I set up a meet and went to Morristown."

"How much? How much did it take to get you to betray us?"

"I didn't betray y'all, man. All I did was a job. It put fifteen grand in my pocket and didn't cause nobody no harm. Like I said, they ain't gonna find her."

"What'd you do with her?"

The interrogation lasted another fifteen minutes. The more Red talked, the less hostile Bear's voice became. Red told him everything: how they'd cased her place, how they'd killed her, where they'd put the body, what they'd done after the murder.

Bear squatted down in front of Red and put his hands on Red's knees.

"Anything else you can think of?"

"No, man. I told you everything."

"Good."

Bear stood up and turned around.

"Rain Man, you and Psycho hook the chipper up to the pickup and haul it down to the pigpen. I want you to shoot these two pieces of shit, then shred 'em. The pigs will take care of what's left."

41

Thirty-six hours after a judge is found dead and twenty-four hours after Hannah Mills is discovered missing—two of the biggest mysteries I can remember in the district—I find myself on the outside.

Fired. Sacked. Terminated.

Caroline says she isn't surprised. She's tells me she's never much cared for Mooney, something she's kept to herself since I made the decision to go to work for him. He leers at her, she says, and even made a drunken pass at her at last year's office holiday party. She didn't mention it to me for the simple reason that she believed I might do something rash, like kick his sorry ass. She was right about that.

Mooney's public relations campaign against me was anything but subtle. The afternoon he fired me, all of the local television channels featured me front and center on the evening news. Mooney refused interviews, but Rita Jones called me a couple of hours after I left the office and told me Mooney had faxed to the media a press release he'd drafted himself.

The TV news reporters showed up at my house immediately. They parked in the driveway and tried to get me to come out and talk to them, but I just opened the back door and turned Rio loose. They scattered like so many frightened geese. That evening, they did a mini-history of my career as a defense attorney and then as a prosecutor. Aside from the phone's ringing off the hook, it really wasn't that bad. The next morning's newspaper carried a front-page story with the headline "Prosecutor Dismissed for Insubordination," but outside of the fact that I'd been fired, they didn't have anything negative to say.

A week later, there was another round of press when Tanner Jarrett went into court and announced that the district attorney's office was dismissing all charges against Rafael Ramirez. Mooney told the media that my prosecution of Ramirez was "overzealous." He actually apologized to Ramirez on the evening news. It made me so angry, I threw a shoe at the television and cracked the screen.

Another week quickly passes. I fall back into the same routines I had before I went to work for the district attorney's office. Caroline and I drive to Nashville to watch Jack play baseball. I piddle around the house. I run, work out, and play with Rio.

I talk with Bates daily, but nothing has developed with Hannah Mills/Katie Dean. It's the same with Judge Green's murder. Silence. I've tried several times to call Anita White to ask whether they indicted Tommy Miller, but she refuses to speak with me. There hasn't been a word about it in the news, though, which makes me think Mooney didn't go through with it. Someone would have leaked the information to the press. A cop, a prosecutor, a grand juror—a piece of news that juicy would have hit the streets in banner headlines.

Then, on Thursday evening, I'm walking back up to the house from a run along the trail by the lake with Rio when I see a car in the driveway. It's dusk, and I can see an outline of a figure leaning against the car. It looks just like one of those cowboy cutouts people put on their lawns. Rio begins to bark and strains against the leash, but as I get closer, I recognize who it is. It's Bates, wearing his cowboy hat and his boots and leaning against his confiscated BMW.

"Didn't think you'd want to be seen with me." Rio takes a quick sniff of Bates, calms down, and I let him off the leash.

"I don't, at least not in public. That's why I came all the way out here."

"Want to come inside? We've got beer and tea, water, soft drinks, whatever you want."

"You know what? A beer sounds good right about now."

Bates follows me in. I grab a couple of beers from the refrigerator and lead him out to the deck.

"Where's the missus?"

"Teaching a dance class."

"She doing all right these days?"

"Yeah, she's good. Thanks for asking. So what brings you out here?"

Bates sits at a table and takes a sip from the beer. The weather is warm, in the low seventies, and the light from the rising moon is reflecting soft yellow light off the channel below. The low roar of a bass boat can be heard in the distance. It would be a perfect evening to get half crocked with Bates and listen to his stories, but he seems to be in a somber mood.

"I've got some news, Brother Dillard. We found Hannah."

"Is she—"

"Gone. I'm sorry."

I drop my head in silence. I've thought about her every day since she disappeared, and since I learned about her past from Agent Rider, I've thought about her even more. Poor kid. Family killed by a crazy father. Aunt and cousin killed by a drug dealer. I knew I saw pain in her eyes, but I had no idea how deeply it ran.

"Where'd you find her?"

"In an abandoned mine shaft up on Buffalo Mountain."

"How did she die?"

"Strangled. I've got an old buddy of mine, a forensic pathologist, doing an autopsy as we speak."

"An old buddy? What's wrong with the medical examiner?"

"Nobody knows we found her yet besides me, an undercover deputy, and my buddy the pathologist. And now you. I intend to keep it that way for a while. My buddy's gonna store her for me until we get this sorted out."

"Where?"

"In a big cooler in his garage. He tells me he's got a bunch of other body parts in there."

"Is he some kind of wacko?"

"Aren't most pathologists? He's a little on the strange side, but sharp as they come. Don't worry about it. It's a heckuva lot better than the place we found her."

It takes me a minute to digest this piece of information. Nobody knows they've found her? How could that be possible? When a body is discovered, everybody and his brother shows up at the scene—police, EMTs, coroner, gawkers. I've never heard of anyone in law enforcement concealing the discovery of a body.

"What's going on, Leon?"

"Let's just say there are certain people who don't need to know about this."

"Talk to me."

Bates takes a long pull off his beer, removes his hat, and sets it on the table in front of him. He runs his long fingers through his hair and breathes deeply.

"I've had a guy undercover for a couple of years," he begins. "We're trying to take down a motorcycle gang, Satan's Soldiers. My guess is you've heard of them."

Not only have I heard of them; my sister is pregnant by one, a tidbit I decide to keep to myself. I nod at Bates.

"Pretty rough bunch," Bates continues. "So last night, my undercover comes to me and tells me a little story. Seems that one of the gang members heard about a contract being put out on a girl. He decided to do a little freelance work, you know, outside of his regular drug dealing and gun running with the gang. Pick up a little extra cash. So he meets with this Mexican who's offering the contract, takes ten grand down, gathers up his cousin, and goes and does the deed. The girl turns out to be Hannah. They strangle her in her bedroom, carry her out, and put her in the trunk. Then they take her up to Buffalo Mountain, dump her in this old mine shaft, and pour a couple of sacks of lime down the hole on top of her. Me and the undercover had a helluva time getting her out of there. It was a mess. So when they're done, these two geniuses go buy a bottle of liquor and drive around in her car for a few hours before they take it back.

"They collect another ten grand a couple of days later and manage to keep quiet about it for about a week, but then one of them gets drunk and runs his mouth. You have to understand, now, this is a breach of code. You don't go around killing folks without the approval of the officers, and you damned sure don't go around killing folks who haven't done anything to disrespect the gang. Bad for business. So word spreads among the gang, the officers hold a meeting, and they decide these two have to be punished for what they've done. Not for killing Hannah, mind you, but for taking this contract without the knowledge or consent of the hierarchy."

"So what's the punishment?"

"Death. They're both dead. Shot in the head, dismembered, and run through a wood chipper into a pigpen on a farm in Unicoi County."

"You know who they are?"

"I know who they *were*. Not that it does me any damned good."

"So why the secrecy with Hannah's body?"

"The contract came from a Mexican who is a known associate of your ol' buddy Rafael Ramirez.

The undercover says the contract didn't come *from* Ramirez's guy; it came *through* him. The undercover has worked his way up to treasurer of the gang. They trust him. He was there when these two guys were interrogated. The president of the club wanted to know what else they'd been doing on the side before he killed them, so he tortured them awhile. Turns out they weren't really doing anything else on the side, but the guy who actually met with the Mexican and took the contract said whoever was putting up the money was someone important."

"Someone important? He didn't say who?"

"The Mexican didn't tell him."

"Any ideas?"

"A couple, but first I need to ask you a question. You remember when I asked you whether Hannah had said anything about being pregnant? You told me she was a virgin. How would you know a thing like that?"

I immediately think again about the night at the bar.

"I probably should have told you this before, but maybe four or five weeks before she disappeared, I went to a little birthday party for Tanner Jarrett up at Rowdy's. Mooney kept buying drinks for Hannah, and before we knew it, she was plastered. Then out of nowhere she blurted out that she was a virgin."

"Who was there?" Bates says.

"Caroline and I, Tanner, Mooney, Rita and the guy she's dating, a few others."

"Who took her home?"

"Tanner."

"Well, she wasn't no virgin. My forensics boys dug up one of those early-pregnancy tests in a trash barrel outside her house. The lab guys were able to get prints, skin cells, and some urine off the tube. The DNA matched Hannah, and the test was positive. She was pregnant."

"Okay," I say. "So she was pregnant. What does that have to do with a contract killing?"

"The Mexican who paid this gangbanger said Hannah was pregnant and was blackmailing someone important. So before I release any news about finding her, there are a couple of things I want to do. My pathologist buddy says he thinks he can extract DNA from the embryo. We need to do whatever we can to find out who the daddy is. That should go a long ways toward telling who the killer might be. The other thing we need to do is go find Mr. Ramirez and try to get some answers out of him."

"Ramirez is gone, Leon. You're not going to find him. And even if you do, you're not going to get anything out of him. You don't have any leverage."

"I said *we. We're* going to find him. I've been talking to Rider some. He'll help me. He hates Ramirez with a passion."

"Anything I can do?"

"As a matter of fact there is, but I want you to take your time and do it right. No screwups. If this turns out the way I think it's going to, there are going to be some big changes around here. Big changes, and I want you right in the middle of it."

"I assume you have a suspect."

"Two of 'em, brother. Two of 'em."

42

A little while later, after Bates has gone, I look through my cell phone for Mike Norcross's number. He answers after the second ring.

"My ID tells me a former prosecutor is calling," Norcross says.

"How are you?"

"Fighting for truth, justice, and the American way. You?"

"Can't complain. Listen, first off, I want to tell you I'm sorry you had to witness the little meltdown in Mooney's office."

"Sorry? Are you kidding? That was one of the best shows I've ever seen in my life. You've got some set of balls on you, Counselor."

"I've heard that before, and every time I hear it, it's because I've done something stupid."

"Well, between you, me, and the fly on the wall, I thought what you did was right. No way we could have made a case on what we had. Harmon was just trying to shake things up."

"Harmon? You mean it wasn't Mooney's idea?"

"It was Harmon's. He strong-armed Anita and me

into doing it. He's getting a lot of pressure from Nashville on this case."

"Yeah, I can imagine. Listen, I need to talk to Anita. She won't pick up when I call. I've left her a few messages, but she hasn't returned the calls."

"I know," Norcross says. "She's a little freaked out by what happened with you. I think she wishes she'd told Harmon the same thing you told Mooney."

"Are you with her? You guys working tonight?"

"Nah, we knocked off about an hour ago. Not much going on, to tell you the truth."

"Do you know where she is?"

"She isn't exactly a party girl. My guess is she's at her place."

"Mind telling me where that might be?"

"You're going to show up unannounced?"

"Maybe. I have something on my mind that's been bothering me. I want to talk to her."

Norcross is silent for a few seconds.

"Sure, why not? Just don't tell her where you got the address, okay?"

"I won't, as long as you don't call her and tell her I'm coming."

"Deal," Norcross says, and he gives me Anita's address.

I leave Caroline a note and get in my truck. The address Norcross has given me is a new condominium complex called Pointe 24, across the Bristol Highway from Winged Deer Park. The buildings sit high on a ridge above Boone Lake, just a few miles from my place. I pull in and find her condo without any problem. She answers the door a few seconds after I ring the bell.

"Sorry to show up out of the blue like this, but I'd like to talk to you," I say.

She's wearing a pair of jeans and a frayed blue hoodie with "Memphis State" written across the front. The light from the lamppost outside her door catches her green eyes, and they sparkle. I'm worried she'll shut the door in my face, but she smiles.

"Come in."

I follow her through a foyer highlighted by a chandelier and immediately notice the smell of incense—jasmine, maybe. There's a stairwell on the left and a kitchen with an island and stainless-steel appliances to the right. She leads me into a den dominated by a bookshelf that covers half the wall to my right. It goes from floor to ceiling and is full. The other half of the wall is covered by an upright piano. The tastefully decorated room is warmly lit by a lamp in the corner. Classical music is playing softly. There are framed photographs on a couple of small tables and more on the walls. I notice there is no television.

"Sit, please," Anita says, motioning to a couch.

"Have you read all of these books?"

"I have. I've read most of them twice."

"What do you like best?"

"I lean toward the classics, but I get a kick out of some of the genre fiction. Especially cop stuff."

"Do you have a favorite writer?"

"Dozens of them. Did you come over here to ask me about my tastes in literature?"

"I came to tell you something, but to be honest, I'm feeling a little awkward."

"Would you like a glass of wine? Maybe that would help. I've already had one myself, but after the past couple of weeks, I wouldn't mind another."

I drank two beers with Bates, but it's been more than an hour. I don't think a glass of wine will put my blood-alcohol level over the legal limit, but the last thing I want to do is catch a buzz and start blathering. The room is so cozy, though. So warm. And she's so damned easy to look at.

"Sure, a glass of wine would be nice."

"I'm drinking Chablis. Do you like Chablis?"

"I have no idea. Not much of a connoisseur, I'm afraid."

"I'll be right back."

She goes to the kitchen, and I wander around the room and look at some of the photos. Most of them are of a handsome black man. In a couple of the photos, the man is young, wearing the uniform of the United States Air Force. I notice silver bars on his collar. He's a captain. In another photo, he's older, wearing a police officer's uniform.

"Is this your father?" I ask when Anita comes back into the room.

"Yes. He just retired from the Memphis Police Department. He worked there for more than thirty years."

"And your mother? Is this her?" I point to a photo of a middle-aged woman sitting on a porch swing.

"That's my grandmother. My mother left us when I was very young."

"I'm sorry. I didn't mean to pry."

"It's all right. It was difficult at the time, but I learned to deal with it. I didn't hear from her until I graduated from law school. Turned out she didn't go any farther than Collierville. She was living with a man there. My father never divorced her, though. I think he still loves her."

"Why did she leave?"

"She was lonely, I suppose. My father worked all the time. He thought he was doing what he was supposed to do. It's all he's ever known."

Anita walks back over to her chair and sits down. I take a sip of wine. It's warm going down my throat.

"How do you like it?" Anita says.

"Excellent."

"Do you like Chopin?" She waves her hand slightly. "I think it's beautiful."

"I like classical music in small doses. I'm more of a rhythm and blues guy."

"So what did you come to tell me?"

I take another sip of the wine and look at her. I've been struggling with this for weeks now. Before I start to talk, I raise the glass to my lips and take a long swallow. I set the glass on the table, rest my elbows on my knees, and fold my hands.

"I saw Tommy Miller the morning Judge Green was killed. I found him sleeping downstairs on a couch at my house before I left for work. I didn't really think anything about it at the time. I thought he probably just didn't want to go home the night they buried his dad. But later, after I found out what had happened to the judge and after I talked to you at the crime scene, I guess I should have told you."

She's holding the wineglass under her nose with both hands, gently swirling the liquid and breathing in deeply.

"Now you've told me," she says quietly. "It doesn't really change anything, does it?"

"There's more. I found out later that the clothes he was wearing when he woke up smelled like gasoline. He had what seemed to be a reasonable explanation at the time, so I didn't say anything to anyone."

"What was his explanation?"

"He was drunk, and he spilled gas on himself when he stopped at a station."

"That should be easy enough to verify, provided we can ask him which station he went to."

"You'll have to find him first."

"Did he tell you all of this?"

"No. I haven't talked to him. It's all secondhand."

"And what became of this clothing?" Anita says.

"I'm not sure. I think it might have been destroyed."

"Intentionally destroyed?"

"I'm not sure."

"By whom?"

"I can't tell you that."

"Why not?"

"Because it could potentially harm someone I love very much."

"Your son?"

"Someone I love very much. That's all I'll say."

Anita leans forward, the wineglass still dangling from her slender fingers.

"You realize you're telling me you may very well be

guilty of a crime, Counselor. And this person you love so much, he or she could be guilty of a crime as well."

"I know."

"What do you want me to do?"

"I don't know." I hesitate for several seconds. "I still don't think Tommy killed the judge, but I guess I just wanted to apologize for not being honest with you from the beginning."

She's silent for a minute, and then she does something that takes me completely by surprise. She gets up from the chair, walks over, and sits next to me on the couch. I feel a tightness in my stomach, a rush of excitement. My face flushes, and I immediately feel guilty.

"I owe you an apology, too," she says. She smells like lilac.

"Really? For what?"

"For getting you fired. Indicting Tommy Miller was my boss's idea. But sitting there listening to you rip the case apart and thunder away at Mooney made me realize I should have stood up to him. I guess I was feeling a little desperate with all the pressure to make an arrest. Judges and politicians from all over the state were calling my boss, and he was starting to lean on me. You know how cops are. The last thing you want to admit is that you have nothing, that you can't prove a single thing. So when Harmon came up with this bright idea to go to Mooney, I went along with it. I shouldn't have done it. I'm sorry."

"You're not the first cop who's given in to the temptation to use the power of the grand jury prematurely," I say, "and I'm sure you won't be the last."

"I never dreamed it would cost you your job," she says.

She places her hand on my thigh, and my skin tingles. I take another drink of the wine.

"I'm fine," I say. "We're fine. Don't worry about it. Listen, I need to get going. Caroline should be home by now. Thanks for talking to me."

I set the empty wineglass on the table and stand. Anita leads me back through the condo to the door. She opens it and I step out into the night air. Relief washes over me. I've escaped. But I turn back.

"May I ask you a personal question?"

"Sure."

"Why aren't you married? I mean, you're bright, you're beautiful, you're talented. I can't believe they're not standing in line to snatch you up."

"I'm waiting for a man like my father," she says. "I've only met one who could even come close, and he's taken."

She smiles at me and winks, and gently closes the door.

43

The next morning I'm at the grocery store, leaning over the fresh chicken comparing prices, when I suddenly feel uncomfortable. I can see someone in my peripheral vision standing about ten feet to my right. I glance over and see a blond, overweight, middle-aged woman I vaguely recognize. She's staring at me. I try to place her but can't. The look on her face is one of contempt, and I turn back to the chicken, hoping she'll go away.

I pick out a small packet of breasts, place it in the basket I'm carrying, and glance back toward her. She's still there, and she's still staring. I turn and start walking in the opposite direction. I've taken about five steps when I hear a voice behind me.

"We missed you at the execution."

I keep walking.

"Hey, superstar lawyer! I said we missed you at the execution!"

I suddenly realize who she is, and my throat tightens. It's Brian Gant's wife, Donna. I'd read the cursory account of Brian's execution in the newspaper a few days earlier with a deep sense of regret. With everything that had been going on, I'd forgotten about it completely. I remember mentioning it to Mooney the morning Judge Green was killed, but after that, Brian had faded from my consciousness like fog being warmed by the sun. I stop and turn to face her.

"I'm sorry, Donna. I'm truly sorry."

She steps up close to me, her eyes filled with fury.

"You're right about that," she says. "You're the sorriest damned excuse for a lawyer I've ever seen. How does it feel to be responsible for the death of an innocent man?"

"I can't explain how it feels," I say honestly. "I wish I could have done more."

"Brian told me you came down to the prison a few weeks ago and tried to unload your guilt on him. He said you told him you were sorry. You're just sorry all over the place, aren't you?"

"What do you want from me, Donna? I did all I could."

"You know what the worst part of this is? The only reason Brian ended up with you as his lawyer was because we were poor. Tell me something. When the judge appointed you to represent him, why didn't you tell the judge you didn't have enough experience to handle a death penalty case?"

"I thought I was ready."

"You *thought* you were ready? You thought wrong, didn't you? You got your ass kicked by a confused five-year-old girl. And now my husband is dead."

I look at the floor in shame. The same thing has passed through my mind a million times. I was young,

I was eager, and I wanted to make my mark. But she's right. I wasn't ready.

"Look at me, you son of a bitch," she says.

I raise my head slowly and look into her eyes. There are no tears, only the stark face of hatred.

"My husband was innocent," she says. "Say it!"

"Your husband was innocent." The words come out weakly. I feel so ashamed, I'm barely able to speak.

"And you killed him. Say it!"

"And I killed him."

She moves even closer to me, so close I can feel her breath on my cheek. Then she spits in my face.

"I hope you rot in hell."

She abruptly turns and walks away.

44

At some level, I'm conscious that I'm dreaming, but my mind won't allow me to wake up.

I jump from the door of the C-130 Hercules and tuck. The static line snaps me backward as it rips the cover off my pack and deploys the parachute. I take a quick look up at the green canopy and then look down. I'm dropping toward a narrow peninsula on an island, thousands of miles from home. An airstrip extends far out beneath me. The green ocean is beating against jagged rocks no more than thirty feet on either side of the strip.

Two hours earlier, I'd never heard of Grenada. All they told us when we left Georgia was that we were going to war.

During the long flight, they've given us a quick briefing. The Grenadian government has been overthrown by left-wing radicals. Russian, Cuban, and North Korean advisers have been spotted on the island. They're completing a ten-thousand-feet-long airstrip. A military buildup is suspected. There are hundreds of Americans on Grenada, most of them students at the Grand Anse area's True Blue campus of St. George's University School of Medicine. President Ronald Reagan has issued an executive order. We're going in.

Our mission is to jump from only five hundred feet above the airstrip at a place called Point Salines. We're to neutralize any resistance and secure the airstrip so our planes can land. Once we've done that, we're to evacuate the students from the medical school. They've told us that a small number of Delta Force operators are already on the island, along with a few Navy SEALs. A U.S. Marine amphibious force has been diverted from a mission in Lebanon and will be mounting an assault. The Air Force is sending AC-130 Spectre gunships and combat controllers. Two battalions of Rangers are going in, and fighters from the Eighty-second Airborne Division will land as soon as we clear the runway. They've told us that Grenada is roughly one hundred twenty square miles, but that the fighting will concentrate around a city called St. George's. The entire country has a population of one hundred thousand. I remember shaking my head when the lieutenant said that. *All this for a country with a population roughly the size of Knoxville?*

I'm only twenty-one, and despite having been through Ranger school and feeling bulletproof, as soon as the sound of machine gun fire below reaches my ears, I feel fear welling in my stomach. Ten seconds later I hit the tarmac, roll, shed my chute, unstrap my weapon from my ruck, and make for a rally point just east of the airstrip.

I dive behind a berm as small arms and machine gun fire whizzes by overhead and kicks up sand near my feet. The steady thump of antiaircraft fire echoes off the hills beyond the airstrip. I belly crawl to the edge of the berm and shoulder my weapon. Other Rangers are running and yelling around me. I look for a target and am just about to fire when something falls on my back, nearly knocking the wind out of me. It's a fellow Ranger. I push him off me, and when he rolls, I see that his face has been blown off. I scream, stand up, start firing, and run straight toward the enemy.

"Joe! Joe! Wake up! Joe!"

I open my eyes. Caroline is sitting up, shaking my shoulder.

"You're screaming. Are you all right?"

I shake my head in disbelief. It seemed so real. "Yeah, baby, I'm fine. I guess it was just a nightmare."

"*Just* a nightmare? You're soaking wet."

I sit up on the edge of the bed as Caroline rubs my back.

"Why don't you go dry off and come back to bed?" she says.

I look at the clock. Almost four in the morning. I stand up and walk around the bed to Caroline's side. I tuck the comforter in around her and kiss her on the forehead.

"Go on back to sleep," I say. "I think I'll just stay awake."

I walk out to the couch, turn on the television, and try not to think about the dream. But it won't go away. A year after I jumped into Grenada, I learned that the U.S. State Department had issued a warning to the Grenadian government that we were coming.

They, in turn, told the Russians and the North Koreans, who immediately left the island. All that was left were a few Cuban engineers and the People's Defense Force, but they were armed to the teeth, and they were waiting for us.

That was the day I knew I would leave the army, and that was the day I knew I'd never trust my own government again.

45

Anita White believed Tommy Miller would show up at his mother's house before long. He was a kid, after all. His father had just been buried. He'd want to be near his mother, and he'd need money. Anita formulated a simple but effective plan for finding out if Tommy came around. She gave her cell number to the nosy neighbor, Trudy Goodin, and told her to keep a close eye out.

Mrs. Goodin called late on a Tuesday night.

"I saw him through the window," she said. "I'm sure it's him."

Anita and three other agents took Tommy down at six the next morning when he and his mother backed out of their garage. Toni Miller was driving, with Tommy in the passenger seat. The agents made the usual show of force on a felony arrest—the guns drawn, the yelling, the threats. When Special Agent in Charge Ralph Harmon discovered that Tommy had an airline ticket to San Francisco and five thousand dollars in cash in his backpack, he became infuriated and arrested Toni for obstructing justice. Both Tommy and his mother were handcuffed, taken to the TBI office, and placed in separate interrogation rooms. Agent Harmon tried to interview Toni Miller first, but she immediately demanded to speak to an attorney.

"What are we going to do with her?" Anita asked as Harmon walked out of the room.

"Let her sit. We can hold her for up to seventy-two hours before we have to get her in front of a magistrate. There's no way I'm letting her anywhere near a phone. The first thing she'll do is start calling lawyers."

Anita watched on the monitor as Harmon walked in and read Tommy his Miranda rights. To her surprise, Tommy didn't mention anything about an attorney. Harmon then left Tommy alone for three hours. Toni Miller was still in the other interrogation room down the hall. During the entire three hours, the only peep the agents heard from Tommy was when he asked to go to the bathroom. Other than that, he simply sat with his head down on the table.

Just before Anita, Norcross, and Harmon entered the interrogation room to interview Tommy, Harmon called them into his office.

"I'll handle the questioning," Harmon said. "The two of you just watch and learn. The only satisfactory conclusion to this interview will be a signed confession and an arrest for first-degree murder, and I intend to make sure it happens."

When they walked into the room, Harmon took a seat directly across the table from Tommy. Anita sat down to Tommy's right, Norcross to his left. Anita looked at Tommy closely. What she saw was a frightened boy who looked very much like his father. Anita had seen pictures of Ray Miller in the newspaper, and she immediately noticed the similarities. He had a young handsomeness about him, with dark hair and eyes, a slight lump in the bridge of his nose, high cheekbones, and well-defined facial lines.

"Where have you been, son?" Harmon said in a friendly tone. "We've been looking all over for you."

"I was on the road for a little while," Tommy replied.

"I want you to understand something from the beginning, Tommy," Harmon said. "It's okay if I call you Tommy, right? I want you to know that we're here to help you. We're willing to do anything we can to help you help yourself. You believe that, don't you, Tommy? You believe we're here to help? We're your friends, son. We don't want to see anything bad happen to you."

Tommy nodded his head silently. Anita thought she saw a look of relief cross his face. She wanted to tell him that Harmon wasn't his friend. She wanted to tell him he should ask for a lawyer, but she sat there silently, just as Harmon had ordered.

"I read your Miranda rights to you earlier, correct?" Harmon continued. "I know your dad was a lawyer, so you should be familiar with your rights, but there's been a change in the law recently. The United States Supreme Court says you no longer have a constitutional right to have an attorney present during questioning. You still have a right to an attorney, and you don't have to talk to me if you don't want to. Do you understand that?"

"I understand," Tommy said.

"Are you sure you don't want a lawyer present during this interview?"

"I've been thinking about that ever since you picked me up," Tommy said. "I don't have anything to hide. I just want to get this behind me."

"Of course you do. Besides, only a person who's done something wrong needs a lawyer, am I right? Only guilty people need lawyers."

"Where is my mother?"

"She's just down the hall. She's fine."

"Is she going to go to jail?"

"A lot will depend on how our conversation goes," Harmon said. "Can we get you anything? Something to drink? Eat? A cigarette?"

"Some water would be good," Tommy said.

Harmon nodded at Anita. "Get the boy some water."

Anita returned quickly with a bottle of water, stung by the cavalier manner in which Harmon had ordered her out of the room. She watched as Tommy lifted the bottle to his lips. His hands were trembling slightly, which was understandable, given the circumstances.

"I guess you know why you're here," Harmon said to Tommy.

"Yes, sir, I think so. I think you want to talk to me about Judge Green's murder."

For the next twenty minutes, Tommy gave Harmon the same answers he'd given Jack Dillard a couple of weeks earlier. He recounted the evening as best he could but was unable to answer any specific questions about his actions after he left the cemetery that night.

He told Harmon about waking up outside the convenience store and driving to the Dillards'. He told him about how his clothing smelled like gasoline and that Mrs. Dillard had offered to wash the clothes for him. He said he ran from his home because his mother told him the police suspected him of being involved in the judge's murder. No, he didn't know how she found out about it. As soon as he returned home that morning, his mother told him he should leave. He ran from the police in Durham for the same reason he left Johnson City—fear. He didn't think the police would believe his story about not being able to remember. He explained how he gave his car to a stranger in North Carolina, knowing the police would be looking for the car, and how he hitchhiked and rode buses around the Southeast for two weeks, staying in cheap hotels and flophouses along the way. When he was finished, Harmon sat back and folded his arms.

"Say your clothing smelled like gasoline?" he said.

"I must have spilled some on me when I was pumping gas. I don't remember it, though."

"Where is this convenience store where you say you woke up?"

Tommy gave him the location, and Harmon and Norcross went into the hall for a few minutes.

"Agent Norcross is going over to the convenience store right now to see whether anyone remembers you," Harmon said when he returned. "In the meantime, tell me how you felt when you heard about what Judge Green had done to your father."

"I don't know," Tommy said. "Confused, surprised."

"Were you angry?"

"Not really. When Dad first told me about it, he said he'd fix it. He said everything would be fine and for me just to go about my business at school and not worry about it. So that's what I did."

"But then things got worse, didn't they? How did you feel then?"

"My dad didn't tell me much about it. I didn't know how bad things really were until my mom called me and told me my car was going to be repossessed. That's when they bought me the Honda."

"What were you driving before?"

"A Jeep."

"A new one?"

"It was a couple of years old. My dad got it for me when I graduated from high school."

"So you go from driving a new Jeep to an old Honda," Harmon said. "That must have bothered you, at least a little."

"I got used to it."

"Tommy," Harmon said, "if I'm going to help you, you have to be honest with me. Please don't try to tell me you felt absolutely no anger toward Judge Green."

"I can't honestly tell you I felt no anger toward him, especially after Dad killed himself," Tommy said.

"And that's only natural," Harmon said. "Anyone in your situation would feel the same way. On a scale of one to ten, how angry would you say you were?"

"On a scale of one to ten? Twelve."

Anita cringed. Tommy obviously didn't know it, but by being honest, he was hanging himself.

"So you were angry enough to kill him."

"I didn't say that. I didn't kill him."

"Really? How do you know? You say you don't remember what happened. You say you were angry. I know if some jerk had caused my father to kill himself, I'd want him dead. Maybe you drank yourself a bunch of liquid courage and went over and got a little revenge."

"I didn't. I couldn't. I could never do something like that."

"We have two witnesses who saw your car in the judge's neighborhood right after the murder. One of the witnesses got a good look at the driver, and the description the witness gave matches you."

Anita shifted uneasily in her chair. Harmon was lying. It was perfectly legal for a police officer to lie to a suspect, but the tactic sometimes backfired.

"Really?" Tommy said. "You have people who say they saw me?"

"Tell you what I'm going to do, Tommy," Harmon said. "Agent White and I are going to take a little break so we can check on Agent Norcross. You take the time to think about things. Think hard, Tommy. You seem like a good kid to me, and I don't want to see you go down the wrong path. If you tell us what happened that night, we'll talk to the district attorney for you. We'll tell him you were cooperative and remorseful. It could be the difference between a long sentence and the death penalty. And who knows? After everything you've been through, you probably have some kind of mental defense. Diminished capacity, that kind of thing. So you just think things through carefully, and we'll be back in a bit."

It went on like that all night. Anita knew what Harmon was doing. He was wearing the boy down, trying to get him to agree that he must have been the killer. Norcross's trip to the convenience store revealed that no one who worked at the store remembered seeing Tommy. Norcross had even made a side trip to visit the employee who had worked the graveyard shift. He showed the employee Tommy's photo and described his car, but the employee said he didn't recall anyone who looked like Tommy in or around the store that night. There was no record of any credit card transaction with Tommy's name on it.

Harmon would leave Tommy sitting for hours at a time, then go back into the room and question him again. With each visit, he'd reveal another detail about exactly how the judge had been killed, how someone had lain in wait, cut down a tree across the driveway, ambushed the judge with a blunt instrument, dragged him across the yard, doused him with kerosene, and hanged him from a maple tree. The intensity of the conversation increased with each visit. Anita noticed the physical and mental changes in Tommy as the grueling hours passed and the questioning became more confrontational, more accusatory. The boy was exhausted. Dark circles had formed under his eyes, which had taken on a forlorn, empty look. His speech had grown slow and deliberate, as though he had to search for every word. He was easier to confuse.

Finally, at ten minutes past three in the morning,

after nearly twenty hours of questioning, Harmon leaned across the table to within a foot of Tommy's nose.

"I just talked to your mother," Harmon said. "She says she thinks you did it."

Tommy burst into tears, and Anita knew that Harmon had broken him.

"My mother thinks I did it?" Tommy said slowly.

"Your own mother," Harmon said, shaking his head.

Tommy's head dropped to the table. His shoulders shuddered as he sobbed loudly, uncontrollably.

"Oh my God!" Tommy cried. "Oh my God! I'm a murderer!"

46

Roscoe Stinnett pulled into the gravel driveway of a small bar outside Morristown. He'd been here before, but that didn't mean he was comfortable. The place was a dump. It was in the middle of nowhere. But Rafael Ramirez owned it and refused to meet anyplace else. Since Stinnett's relationship with Ramirez had been so profitable, he ignored his misgivings, got out of his Jaguar, and walked through the gravel. He'd brought his briefcase along, just in case. He didn't know what Ramirez wanted, but he hoped it was something that would involve another fat fee. Perhaps he needed help moving his cash around. Stinnett had some experience in that regard, but he'd never dealt with a drug dealer as wealthy as Ramirez.

Stinnett pushed through the heavy front door and stepped into the bar. Ramirez was waiting in the corner booth, the same seat where Stinnett had met with the person he knew only as the Mexican. It was there, in that very same booth, where Stinnett had set in motion the murder of Hannah Mills. He immediately put his hands on the table of the first booth inside the door and waited for the two men to frisk him and check him for recording devices. When they were finished, he walked back to Ramirez's booth.

"How about a scotch on the rocks?" Stinnett said as he sat down.

"No scotch here," Ramirez said.

"Beer then. Whatever's on tap."

Ramirez motioned to a white man behind the bar and told him to bring Stinnett a draft beer. The man brought the beer around the bar and put it down in front of Stinnett.

"So how's life on the outside?" Stinnett said.

"I want my money back," Ramirez growled.

Stinnett nearly choked on the beer. He put the glass back down on the table.

"I don't understand," he said.

"The money I paid you for the murder case. A hundred and fifty thousand dollars. You didn't earn it. I want it back."

"But I fulfilled my obligation under the contract," Stinnett said. "The case against you was dismissed. I earned the fee."

"I'm willing to let you keep twenty thousand," Ramirez said. "But I want the rest of it."

"That's ridiculous," Stinnett said. "It's unheard of. You signed a contract. The fee is nonrefundable. Nearly all fees in criminal cases are nonrefundable. I couldn't run my business otherwise. I have to pay my bills, plan my budget—"

"Live like royalty?" Ramirez interrupted. "I saw the Jaguar when you pulled up."

"I don't see what that has to do with anything."

"I think I'm being generous," Ramirez said. "More than fair."

"I don't see how you can call giving you a hundred and thirty thousand dollars of my money—money to which I have a contractual, legal right—*fair*," Stinnett said. "The contract called for me to represent you to the disposition of the case, whether it be trial, plea bargain, dismissal, whatever. I got the case dismissed."

"I was responsible for the case being dismissed," Ramirez said. "Not you."

Stinnett heard the door open and looked around. Another Mexican had walked into the bar. He looked at Ramirez and shook his head.

"But I was the one who brought you the proposal in the first place!" Stinnett said.

"And for that, you're being paid twenty thousand dollars."

"But when I first mentioned the deal, you didn't say anything about refunding the fee for the murder case. I was under the impression it wouldn't be an issue."

"You were wrong."

Stinnett sat back in the booth and ran his hands through his curly hair. The truth was that he no longer had the money. He'd used it for a down payment on a used Cessna Skyhawk. He'd been flying for most of his adult life and had had his eye on the plane for a long time. Ramirez had given him the means to go ahead with the purchase.

"This isn't right," Stinnett said. "What if I refuse?"

"It wouldn't be a good idea."

"What if I told you I don't have it? That I've already spent it?"

"I'd think you're either a liar or very stupid. I want my money, and I want it in the next twenty-four hours."

"But that's impossible! I'm telling you I don't have it."

"What if your life depended on it?"

"So now you're threatening me? I don't think you know who you're dealing with. I'm not some criminal you can kill and nobody will care. If you do anything to me, there'll be hell to pay."

Ramirez began to laugh.

"Did you hear that, *muchachos*? There'll be hell to pay!"

Stinnett squirmed in the booth as the laughter continued. He started to get up, but Ramirez's hand caught his forearm.

"Relax, my friend. Relax. I should have known better than to try to get money back from a lawyer."

"You don't understand," Stinnett said nervously. His leg was beginning to shake uncontrollably. He suddenly felt nauseated. "It's just that we had a contract. A *contract*, you see?"

"Yes, yes, a contract," Ramirez said.

Ramirez reached beneath the table, and Stinnett suddenly found himself staring down the barrel of a pistol equipped with a silencer.

"Speaking of contracts," Ramirez said, "I'm afraid you're the only person who might be able to tie me to the contract on the girl. The only person I don't trust, anyway."

"What are you talking about?" Stinnett said. He felt his bladder give. Warm urine was running down the inside of his thigh. "I'd never do that. Think about it. If I ever said anything about you, I'd be right in the middle of it, too. It would be professional suicide. I'd wind up in jail."

"This friend of yours, this friend from the district attorney's office who gave you the money for the contract," Ramirez said. "He knows who I am, that I arranged the murder."

"So what? You didn't touch the money. You didn't talk to the people who actually killed the girl. You're clean on this, Rafael."

"I don't like loose ends."

"Will you please get that gun out of my face?" Stinnett was trying to remain calm, but he felt himself on the verge of tears.

"I'll give you the money back," Stinnett blurted.

"No, you won't. You're lying." Ramirez pulled the hammer back on the pistol.

The last words Roscoe Stinnett heard were, "You're all the same. Fucking lawyers."

47

Special Agent Mo Rider felt his adrenaline surge as the UH-60 Black Hawk banked and began its descent into the valley below. It was just before dawn. There was enough light to see, but the sun hadn't yet climbed over the mountain peaks to the east. As the wind whistled and the blades beat like war drums, Rider was thankful that someone up the chain at the Department of Justice had finally listened.

Through the network of informants he'd developed in more than twenty years with the DEA, Rider had been able to gather enough information to convince his superiors that if they committed the assets, they'd get their man. Satellite time had been approved, which was a rarity in the mountains of East Tennessee, and the images they relayed had confirmed the informants' information. The patch was there. Their man was there.

Two helicopters had been assigned and had arrived from Fort Campbell, Kentucky, at five that morning. They were equipped with state-of-the-art thermal-imaging capabilities. And now nineteen men—seven FBI agents, eleven DEA agents, and Sheriff Bates from Washington County—were about to rock Rafael Ramirez's world. Each of them wore a black Kevlar helmet and vest, black utilities, and black boots. Each carried the weapon of his choice.

Rider had both planned the mission and conducted the preraid briefing. He was confident every man knew his job. They knew exactly where the Mexicans were sleeping. Rider even knew which space on the tent floor was occupied by Ramirez.

The choppers came in low and fast, one on each side of the small campsite. The Mexicans were just beginning to scramble from the tents when the pilot pulled the nose into the air and dropped the skids onto the deck. Rider launched himself from the door and ran straight toward Ramirez's tent. He was carrying a sawed-off Beretta semiautomatic twelve-gauge shotgun. There was no time for taking careful aim on this mission. If he had to use the weapon, it'd be point and shoot.

Rider could hear the agents behind him shouting, ordering the Mexicans to get on the ground. A man ran from Ramirez's tent, tripped, and fell to the ground. Two agents were on him before he could get back to his feet. Another man suddenly appeared in the opening of Ramirez's tent. He was carrying a pistol in his right hand.

Rider stopped in his tracks. It was Ramirez. The scar was unmistakable.

"Drop it!" Rider screamed. The Mexican hesitated.

"Drop the weapon!"

Ramirez's eyes tightened. The pistol started to

come up, and Rider pulled the trigger. The shotgun roared, Ramirez's right leg jerked backward, and he fell to the ground on his face. Rider stepped quickly to Ramirez and tossed the pistol away while two more agents entered the tent. Rider pulled Ramirez's hands behind his back, pulled a pair of handcuffs from a pouch on his web belt, and tightened them securely on the Mexican's wrists.

"I should have blown your fucking head off," Rider said, and he meant it. Rider knew Ramirez was a violent sociopath, and he believed him to be directly or indirectly responsible for at least a dozen murders, but the two that stuck in Rider's craw were the murders of Katie Dean's aunt and her son. And now, according to Sheriff Bates, Ramirez had been involved in Katie's murder. Bates had only circumstantial proof and had told Rider he didn't think Ramirez would ever be convicted of the murder, but Ramirez didn't know that. Ramirez also didn't know how far Rider was willing to go to get him to talk. He was about to find out.

Rider moved to Ramirez's side and knelt. He placed his boot on the bloody crater in Ramirez's thigh. The Mexican moaned.

"It looks like you'll live," Rider said. "That is unless you don't talk to me." He leaned close to Ramirez's ear. "Now I swear to God, asshole, if you don't tell me exactly what I want to know, I'll stake you out over there and leave you for the animals."

48

I'm dreaming of sitting in an electric chair with a hood over my head and Brian Gant standing with his hand on the switch, laughing maniacally, when my cell phone awakens me. I pick it up and see that it's 4:12 a.m. The caller ID tells me Anita White is on the other end of the line.

"I need to talk to you," she says when I answer.

"Now?"

"Yes. Can you meet me?"

I crawl out of bed, throw on some clothes, and drive to Perkins restaurant in Johnson City. Anita is sitting at a booth in the corner, alone. She's drinking coffee, looking haggard and exhausted.

"I didn't want you to hear this on the news," she says after I've sat down and ordered coffee and ice water. "Tommy Miller confessed a little while ago to killing Judge Green."

The words stun me, as though I've just been hit in the face with a shovel. I stare at Anita, unable to speak. When my senses begin to return, I'm left with feelings of betrayal and confusion. How could I have misjudged him so fundamentally? Why did he have to drag my family into this mess? I think of Toni Miller, and wonder just how much more emotional devastation she can take.

"Tell me about it," I say, barely able to speak. "Tell me everything."

Anita spends nearly an hour telling me about Tommy's interrogation. She goes into great detail about Harmon taking over and the tactics he used, which included planting the details of the crime scene in Tommy's mind. She tells me that Harmon wrote out the confession himself, and that Tommy initialed each page and signed it. By the time she's finished, I've become angry.

"It sounds to me like this confession was coerced," I snap.

The tone of my voice surprises her, and she folds her arms defensively.

"Maybe," she says.

"So what are you going to *do* about it?"

"What do you mean? What *can* I do about it? I'm sure Harmon has contacted every media outlet within a hundred miles by now to let them know we've made an arrest and have obtained a signed confession. The bosses in Nashville will know as soon as they show up for work. What's done is done."

"What's done is done? That's all you can say? You should have done something to stop it."

"Like what? Harmon didn't beat him. He didn't threaten him. He didn't deprive him of food or water."

"What about sleep? You said you guys picked him up at six in the morning and were still interrogating him at three the next morning. That's twenty-one hours straight. It's over the line."

"Harmon took breaks. He could have slept during the breaks."

"You said Harmon lied to Tommy. That's coercion."

"No, it isn't, and you know it. Courts have held time and again that the police can lie to a suspect during interrogation."

"And I suppose none of this is on videotape." The TBI doesn't use video or audio tape during interrogations. Neither does the FBI. It gives the agents more leeway during questioning. It also allows them to deny that they've stepped across lines. If a suspect claims coercion, it's his word against the police.

"Harmon is a pro," Anita says. "He did what he's trained to do."

"Really? When did the TBI start training agents to sweat confessions out of innocent boys?"

"Maybe he did it and really doesn't remember. His alibi didn't check out. Norcross went to the convenience store on Oakland where he said he woke up that morning. Nobody there remembers him."

"You're sure about that?"

"Norcross wouldn't lie."

"What did Tommy say about his clothing?"

"He said he must have spilled gasoline on himself when he was pumping gas. He said he gave the clothes to your wife so she could wash them."

"Which means Caroline will wind up getting a subpoena if Tommy goes to trial. She'll be a witness against him."

Anita nods her head slowly. I suddenly find her

unattractive, almost nauseating. She's given me the distinct impression that she doesn't believe sincerely that Tommy is guilty; yet she stood by and did nothing while her boss browbeat him into a confession. Tommy is in a nearly impossible position now. Nothing is harder to defend than a false confession, because jurors have a hard time believing that anyone would confess to a crime they didn't commit, especially a murder. But jurors don't understand the extreme psychological pressure the police can bring to bear during an interrogation. They don't understand that a person's psyche can be systematically broken down to the point where the accused begins to believe he must have committed the crime, even though he's completely innocent.

"Where's Tommy now?" I ask.

"Probably being booked into the jail."

I lean forward and look into Anita's eyes.

"Why did you call me and ask me to come down here, Anita? And don't say you wanted me to hear the bad news from you instead of reading it in the paper or hearing it on the radio. Why did you really call me?"

She looks down at the table and starts running her finger around the top of the coffee cup. She doesn't seem to have an answer.

"You don't think Tommy did it, do you? You wanted to tell me because you want *me* to do something. You want me to help him."

Her eyes remain on the table, and I stand.

"You should have spoken up," I say. "He needed you in that interrogation room, and you should have helped him. But keeping your precious job means more to you than doing the right thing. I misjudged you, Anita. I thought you were one of the good guys."

I turn and walk out of the restaurant. As I'm walking by the front of the building toward my truck, I look through the window. She's still sitting at the table, her head in her hands. She appears to be crying.

Several hours later, I'm knocking on the cheap aluminum front door of a small trailer in Cash Hollow. I've already broken the bad news to Caroline and been to the jail to see Tommy. Caroline is with Toni Miller now. The TBI held Toni for more than twenty hours on a bogus obstruction of justice charge. As soon as Tommy confessed, they released her.

My conversation with Tommy at the jail confirmed my belief that he'd been coerced. At first I couldn't believe he'd talked to Harmon, but I soon became convinced his decision was a mixture of fatigue and confusion caused by being on the run, coupled with a young man's naïve belief that if he told the officers the truth, everything would turn out okay.

Anita had told me that Harmon lied to Tommy about witnesses seeing him near the crime scene, but she failed to mention that Harmon broke Tommy when he told him that Toni said she believed Tommy committed the crime. After visiting with Tommy and offering whatever comfort I could, I drove straight to the convenience store on Oakland and was directed to this trailer. I feel certain that Norcross has been here earlier, but Tommy was so adamant about waking up in his car at the convenience store, I feel obligated to be here.

An overweight young woman holding a baby answers the door. She wears the hopeless, defeated look of the impoverished. I introduce myself and ask to speak to Ellis Holmes.

"The police have already been here," she says hatefully.

"I'm not the police, ma'am, and I'm sorry to bother you, but it's extremely important."

She turns away from the door. "Ellis! Get your ass out here!"

A young man, mid-twenties, appears in the doorway a few seconds later. He's short, less than five and a half feet, and extremely thin. He's wearing orange shorts, a white tank top, and flip-flops. His hair is thinning, stringy, and dirty blond. He looks like an orphan, an emaciated, unkempt child of the streets.

"Mr. Holmes?" I say.

"Yeah. What do you want?" His voice is nasal and unpleasant, and I find myself feeling sympathy for him. Life can be cruel in so many ways, and in the few seconds that I've known Ellis Holmes, it appears that there isn't a single attractive thing about him.

I'm holding a photograph of Tommy Miller in my hand, and I show it to him.

"Have you ever seen this young man?" I say.

"Another cop already asked me that."

"I'm not a cop. I know they've already been by here. But I want you to take a closer look and think.

Did the officer who came by yesterday tell you why he was asking about this?"

"Nah. He just wanted to know if I'd ever seen him before. Said something about him maybe being outside the store where I work a few weeks ago."

"Do you keep up with the news, Mr. Holmes?"

"Not really. Don't care for it much."

"Did you hear anything about a judge being murdered a little while back? He was hanged and burned in his front yard."

"Oh yeah, yeah, I heard about that."

"This young man right here—his name is Tommy Miller—has been arrested and charged with murdering the judge. I've know Tommy for most of his life, and I don't think he could kill anybody. Tommy's father committed suicide about a week before this happened. He buried his father the day before it happened. He says he got drunk that night and wound up parked outside the store where you were working. He doesn't remember driving there. He says he spilled gasoline all over himself, but he doesn't remember that, either. If he was there, it means he's telling the truth and could go a long way toward proving that he's innocent. So take a close look at this photo, and I'll ask you one more time. Did you see Tommy Miller that night?"

Holmes looks nervously over his shoulder into the trailer.

"Let's talk out in the yard," he says, and he closes the door and starts down the steps. We walk over to my truck, about thirty feet away.

"I might have seen him," Holmes says, "but I can't be getting involved in no murder."

"Please. His life could depend on it."

"I could lose my job."

"Why would you lose your job for telling the truth?"

"I need my job, man. It don't pay shit, but it's all I got, and I have to take care of that baby in there."

"I'm a lawyer, Mr. Holmes, and I promise I'll do whatever I can to help you keep your job. If you get fired because of this, I'll give you a job. You can work out at my place. I have ten acres, and there's always something that needs to be done. And I'll pay you more than you're making at the convenience store."

He looks at me suspiciously. "No joke? You swear on your life?"

"I give you my word."

"Okay," he says. "I don't want to see nobody get hung for a murder if he didn't do it. Your boy showed up at the store about eleven o'clock that night. Business was slow as hell, so I was taking a bag of trash out to the Dumpster. I'm walking back around the building, and I see this little white Civic pull in, but it stops about three, four feet from the pump. I'm wondering whether the hose will even reach that far. Then your boy gets out, and he's wobbling all over the damned place. I see plenty of drunks during my shift, but this dude was really shit-faced. I walk on back into the store and turn the pump on, and I'm telling myself that he ain't gonna be able to pump no gas. So I'm standing there watching him, laughing, you know? He gets the nozzle off the pump, but it takes him a while to figure out which grade he wants. He finally pushes the button and staggers over to the car. He opens the lid where the gas cap is, but then he loses his balance and starts backing up like a crab. He runs into the pump and gets his balance back. About this time, I decide I'd better go on out there and help him. So I'm coming out the door, when I see him start pumping gas. But he forgot to take the damned gas cap off, so gas goes flying all over the place. By the time I get to him, he's freaking soaked. I'm afraid he's gonna blow the whole damned place up. I get the nozzle away from him and lean him up against the side of the car. He's so drunk he can barely talk. I ask him if he has any money, and he can't even answer me. So I pull his wallet out of his back pocket. He's got about fifty dollars, so I fill his car up. Twenty-five dollars' worth. I take the money out of his wallet and stick it back in his pocket. By this time, he's leaned over the hood and passed out. So I open the back door and wrestle him into the backseat, and I'll tell you something—it wasn't no easy task. He's a pretty big dude. Then I park his car next to the building, take his keys, and leave him out there to sleep it off. I check on him every hour or so to make sure he ain't choking in his own puke or something. Along about four in the morning, I see him stirring in the backseat. I figure he's sober enough to drive by that time, so I take the keys out and put them in the ignition."

"So he left around four?"

"Nah, he didn't leave until after five. My relief, this dude named Oscar, came in at five. I shot the shit with Oscar for ten, fifteen minutes before I left. I saw your

49

The next night, I walk into the Chop House in Kingsport and look around. Her car is in the parking lot, but I don't see her. I walk through the tables quickly. She isn't there. When I get back to the lobby, I look into the bar. She's sitting at a small table in a darkened area of the room. I walk in and sit down across from her. She smiles seductively.

"Damn, you look good in those jeans," she says.

"Thanks. You look pretty hot yourself."

She's wearing a bloodred dress that matches her hair. The neckline dives so deeply that it reveals all but the bottom portion of her large breasts. She's leaning forward on the table, which makes matters even worse. Or better, depending upon one's point of view. She's rubbed cream on her skin, and it shimmers in the candlelight. Her face looks as though it's been made up by a professional. Her lips are full, her cheeks high, her jaw strong and angular.

Rita Jones, the receptionist at the DA's office, is one of the sexiest women I've ever known. I've asked her to do me a favor—a huge favor—and she's agreed, but with Rita, there's always a price. Tonight, the price is dinner. She'll do her best to seduce me, but both of us know it isn't going to happen. She's been trying to seduce me for fifteen years, since the very first time I met her. It's become more of a joke these days than anything, but I've been around her long enough to know that if I drop my guard for a second, she'll have me out of my clothes and into her bed before I've realized what's happened.

"Did you tell your wife where you were going?" she says coyly.

"No. I value my marriage."

"But isn't that deceptive?"

"I'd rather think of it as prudent."

"Are you going to get drunk with me?"

"Not likely."

"Aren't you at least going to have a drink?"

A waiter stops by the table and drops off two menus. I order a vodka martini, as much to quiet my nerves as anything else. I'm worried that someone will see me here with Rita and tell Caroline. I'm worried that someone from the office might walk in. I would have never picked this spot to meet, but she insisted.

"This is wonderful," Rita says. "My favorite restaurant and my favorite man."

"I'm glad you're having a good time. Were you able to do what I asked?"

"Of course."

"Where is it?"

"Not until we're finished."

I spend an hour eating and talking with Rita. She regales me with stories of her many conquests and bemoans the fact that she can't stand the man she's dating now, a personal injury lawyer named Steve Willis. When I ask her why she's with him, she gives me an answer that's pure Rita: "He's loaded, and he's hung like a horse."

She's funny, down-to-earth, and beautiful, but as she starts on her fourth glass of wine, her eyes begin to glaze over and her speech becomes slurred. The change is sudden, and it isn't attractive.

"So whaddaya gonna do with this stuff?" she asks.

"What stuff do you mean?" I'm wondering whether there's a sexual connotation to what she's saying. There usually is.

"This stuff I brought you."

"I'm sorry, Rita. I can't tell you."

"Well, I hope you nail his hide to the side of the barn with it. He's a fucking pervert, you know."

"No. I don't know. And would you please keep your voice down?"

"Ooooohhh." She giggles. "Ssshhhhhh!"

"Come on, Rita. Let's get out of here."

I pay the tab and manage to walk her out before anything too embarrassing happens. She begins to hiccup.

"You can't drive," I say.

"Sure I can."

"No, you can't. I'll take you home. Can Steve bring you up here to pick up your car tomorrow?"

"The lazy bastard will probably pay somebody to pick it up," she says. "He's got more money than sense, you know."

"Yeah, you told me."

"But he's got a fantastic schlong. Oops, wait just a second, sweetie. I almost forgot."

She stumbles across the parking lot toward her car, a sharp little Chrysler Crossfire convertible that I'm sure she's earned. I hear a beep, and the trunk pops open. She reaches in and pulls out a brown paper bag, then makes her way back toward me. I help her into my truck and pull out of the parking lot.

"I sealed every—" A hiccup catches Rita's breath. "I sealed everything in plastic Baggies and labeled it, just like you asked me to."

"Thanks."

I take the bag from her hand and put it in the glove compartment. She slides across the seat, cuddles up next to me, and puts her head on my shoulder.

"You don't mind, do you?" she says. She hiccups again, and within thirty seconds, she's fast asleep.

50

Bates is waiting for me at six the next morning at the Waffle House near Boones Creek. It's still dark outside as I carry the paper bag into the restaurant and set it down on the table in front of him.

"How'd you do it?" Bates says as he opens the bag and peers inside.

"I took advantage of an old friend."

"Everything's labeled?"

"Just like the doctor ordered. How'd it go with Ramirez?"

"It was an excellent adventure, Brother Dillard, a truly excellent adventure. I got to ride in a helicopter and carry an assault rifle. Reminded me of the old days. And I gotta tell you, I have a whole new respect for them federal boys. They know what they're doing."

"So Ramirez was there?"

"He was there, all right. Got himself shot right off the bat."

"Shot? Is he dead?"

"Nah, he ain't dead, but I guaran-damn-tee you he wishes he was. I've never seen an interrogation quite like the one ol' Rider did yesterday. I don't think you would have approved."

"What makes you say that?"

"Let's just say Ramirez's constitutional rights weren't given a whole lot of consideration. We hit 'em right at dawn. Come screaming in there like something out of *Apocalypse Now*. Rider heads straight for Ramirez, but Ramirez is stupid enough to point a gun at him, so Rider blows a chunk out of his leg with this sawed-off scattergun he's carrying. We get things settled down, and one of the guys patches up Ramirez's leg, but he doesn't give him anything for pain. They load six Mexicans and a bunch of agents up in a Huey, and then everybody climbs into one of the Black Hawks and takes off. The only ones left on the ground are the pilot who's flying our chopper, me, Rider, another agent, named Lucas, and Ramirez. They've already got Ramirez cuffed, but they drag him over to this little tree, sit him up against it, and recuff his hands around the tree trunk. Then they put another set of cuffs around his ankles and go to work on him. Rider starts asking him questions, and if he didn't like the answer, Lucas would stomp on Ramirez's wound. I swear, Dillard, they had me believing they were gonna kill that ol' boy right then and there. Ramirez must have believed it, too, because he sure did start talking."

"What did he say about Hannah?"

"Stinnett comes to him at the jail about a week before she was killed and tells him he needs a job done. Stinnett says someone in the DA's office, a very wealthy man with some serious political connections, has gotten this girl pregnant, and now she's blackmailing him. He tells Ramirez that if he'll see to it that this girl is taken care of, the murder charge against him will be dismissed. So Ramirez puts Stinnett in touch with this other Mexican who works for Ramirez, a man named Arturo Gutierrez. Gutierrez gets the word out and hooks up with the biker, and Hannah winds up dead."

"Who was it? Who paid the money?"

"He said Stinnett didn't tell him—just that it was somebody from the DA's office. And, believe me, if he'd known, he'd have told."

"So you can ask Stinnett."

"That's a bit of a problem."

"Why?"

"Stinnett's dead. Ramirez shot him in the face."

"He admitted that?"

"Damn straight. Rider and Lucas had his mind right."

I think about the day Ramirez tried to get me to dismiss the murder charge against him. If he already had some kind of deal in place with Stinnett's connection at the office, why would he try to strong-arm me? Then I remember the way Stinnett looked after we went outside. Ramirez had surprised him, maybe tried to double-cross him. I ask Bates about it.

"My guess is he didn't trust Stinnett," Bates says, "so he tried to get you to let him out by telling you he knew where she was and who wanted her killed. He was lying."

"And then Mooney lets him out a week after he fires me."

"Exactly. But we don't know whether Mooney paid for the contract, whether he did somebody a favor or maybe got paid for letting Ramirez out, or whether he really thought the case wasn't strong enough."

"The case was strong enough, Leon."

"What we've got in this bag here will go a long way toward giving us some answers. The pathologist was able to get a DNA sample from the embryo. I was worried that Hannah might have been too far along in the decomposition. . . ."

He chokes up briefly, which surprises me. But then I realize Bates actually witnessed the inhuman way Hannah was discarded. He's poured his soul into this case, and he and his informant climbed down into the abandoned mine shaft and carried her battered and rotting body back up to the light. It's become personal.

He coughs a couple of times, then continues. "If one of the samples in this bag matches the baby, somebody's going to have a lot of explaining to do. So what do you have for me?"

"A couple of coffee cups from the trash can in Mooney's office, and a soft drink can from Tanner's desk. I hope Tanner didn't have anything to do with this."

"He may not have. Even if it turns out he's the father, Hannah could have been trying to blackmail his daddy."

"Hannah wouldn't have blackmailed anybody. There's no way."

"You're sure about that. You knew her so well that you can say that without any doubt."

"I'm sure."

Bates drains his coffee, stands, and picks up the bag off the table.

"We'll see, Brother Dillard. I'll let you know what the lab boys say as soon as I can."

51

An hour later I'm back at home, sitting on the edge of the bed, cleaning Caroline's wound. She'd barely spoken to me after my clandestine dinner with Rita, and she hasn't said a word to me this morning.

"Something wrong?" I ask as I begin to swab. "You've been awfully quiet."

"No, Joe. Everything's just peachy. I love lying here while you dig around inside this horrific piece of trash that used to be my breast. I love the smell, especially. Don't you? It's so sexy."

"It isn't bad, baby. I don't mind it."

"You don't mind it? That's nice, Joe. I'm so glad *you* don't mind it."

Her tone is heavy with sarcasm, which is definitely a bad sign, because Caroline rarely resorts to sarcasm. I continue to work on the wound quietly, wondering whether she's going to tell me what's on her mind or whether she'll need prodding. I don't have to wait long.

"Where were you last night?" she asks.

There are things I don't tell her occasionally, but

I've never been able to lie to her. I opt for a compromise.

"I had dinner with a friend."

"Which friend?"

"An old friend. What difference does it make?"

"And what about the other night? Just like last night. I came home and you were gone. All the note said was, 'Back in a while.' "

"I went to see somebody. What's wrong with you?"

"And this morning? You left early, but you didn't go to the gym."

"I had a cup of coffee with Bates."

"Why?"

"Why not?"

"Because you don't work for the district attorney anymore, so why would you have coffee with the sheriff?"

"I don't know. I didn't have anything else to do."

"Stop it!"

She's upset now. She turns on her side to face me and pushes my hand away from her breast. She grabs me by the wrist and squeezes.

"Why can't you give me a straight answer? What are you hiding?"

"I'm not hiding anything, Caroline."

"Stop lying to me!"

"I'm not lying."

"Are you having an affair?"

I nearly fall off the edge of the bed. I can't believe I'm hearing this. Caroline and I have been married for more than twenty years, and being unfaithful to her has never entered my mind.

"Have you gone crazy? Of course I'm not having an affair."

"Then where were you last night?"

"I told you. I had dinner with a friend."

"Which friend, damn it. Which friend?"

I lower my eyes. I have to tell her.

"Rita Jones."

She throws her legs over the side of the bed and stomps off toward the bathroom. "I knew it! I knew it!"

I get up slowly and follow her. Explaining dinner with Rita to her means I'm going to have to explain a lot more. I don't really know why I haven't told her about Hannah. I suppose it's because I just didn't want to upset her. She's been dealing with cancer for such a long time now that I've probably become overly protective of her. But I should know better. She knows me so well.

The bathroom door is locked. I can hear her sobbing inside.

"Caroline, it isn't what you think."

"Stay away from me! I hate you!"

"Open the door and let me explain."

"Explain what? How you're fucking another woman?"

"Hannah's dead, Caroline. I've been trying to help Bates find out who killed her. Rita helped us out, that's all. We needed DNA samples from a couple of people in the office, and I called her and asked her if she'd collect some things for me. I met her last night and picked them up. That's all it was. I'm sorry I didn't tell you before now. Please open the door."

The crying stops, and a few seconds later I hear her feet shuffling across the tile on the other side of the door.

"Hannah's dead?" she says weakly.

"Bates found her the other day. He's not going to tell anyone until we figure out what happened."

"I knew she was dead. I knew it the night you told me she was gone."

"Open the door, Caroline. Please?"

"Why did you have dinner with Rita? Why couldn't you just pick up whatever it was she had?"

"You know how she is. I bought her dinner and took her home, that's all. I swear it."

"You took her home?"

"She was too drunk to drive."

"Did she make a pass at you?"

"Several."

"You promised me you wouldn't keep things from me anymore, Joe. You promised."

"I know. I'm sorry."

"I wouldn't blame you, you know," she says through the door. "I mean, I'd kill you, but I wouldn't blame you. I'm a freak."

"I love you, Caroline. Nothing will ever change that."

I hear the lock click, and the door opens slowly. She's standing there with her robe hanging open and tearstains on her cheeks. She's so beautiful, so vulnerable, that it nearly moves me to tears.

"You promise you love me the way I am?" she says. "Mutilated ..."

I step toward her and take her in my arms.

"I love you just like you are, baby. I wouldn't change a thing."

52

Anita White walked quickly through the front door of the Tennessee Bureau of Investigation's forensic laboratory in Knoxville. The same day Tommy Miller was arrested, Dillard had left her a message on her cell phone saying he'd talked to the night clerk at the convenience store. The clerk had identified Tommy. He also said Tommy slept off a drunk in the parking lot that night and didn't leave until after five in the morning. The next day, Anita learned that the DNA sample they obtained from Tommy Miller didn't match the DNA the lab technicians had taken from the cigarette butts found near Judge Green's body. With each passing hour, Anita's belief that they'd arrested the wrong person intensified.

She'd been hurt and angry following her conversation with Dillard at the restaurant, but after hearing his message, reading the DNA report, and spending a sleepless night deep in thought, she realized Dillard was right. She should have voiced her concerns over Harmon's tactics during the interrogation. She should have helped the boy. But as she told Dillard, what was done was done. She couldn't undo the confession, but she could keep on working, keep on digging. If someone else killed the judge, Anita intended to find him.

She walked into a small office on the third floor. The office was occupied by Harold Teller, a forensic computer analyst. Teller had called Anita early that morning to say he was finished with his analysis of Judge Green's computer and would be mailing a hard copy of his report. When Anita asked him whether there was anything interesting in the report, his reply was, "Several things," so Anita asked Teller if she could meet with him later in the day. She'd driven the ninety miles to Knoxville in just over an hour.

"Agent White, I presume," Teller said from behind a stack of reports on his desk.

Teller was in his late twenties, much younger than he sounded over the phone. His light brown hair was cut neatly and parted on the side, his eyes were the clearest blue Anita had ever seen, and he wore a pleasant smile on his anguiar face.

"Have a seat," Teller said as he rolled in his chair to the corner, picked up a bound stack of papers, and rolled back to his desk. "Why are you so interested in the report? Don't you already have a confession in this case?"

"Let's just say I'm not totally convinced by the confession and leave it at that," Anita said.

"Ah, you suspect a false confession. How intriguing."

Teller's eyes were gleaming mischievously, and Anita smiled. She'd been expecting a geek, a nerd with acne and thick glasses, someone so smart he would have difficulty talking to a mere mortal. But this was a good-looking young man who apparently had a sense of humor—a nice surprise.

Teller slid the report across the table, and Anita picked it up.

"There are some pretty disturbing images in there," Teller said. "The judge had eclectic tastes in pornography. He favored prepubescent boys and adult gay sadomasochism."

Anita set the report back on the desk. She had no desire to view lurid images of pornography.

"You said you found several interesting things on the computer," Anita said. "What kind of things?"

"He visited a lot of pornographic Web sites, and there were some bizarre e-mails," Teller said. "But the thing you're probably most interested in, especially since you're still on the hunt, is that someone hacked into his computer five days before he was killed. Someone who knew what he was doing. He used four different proxies."

"What are proxies?" Anita said.

"It's complicated," Teller said, "but basically, a proxy is what hackers use to hide their identities. Every PC on the Internet has an identification number, called an IP, which stands for Internet Protocol number. Each one is unique, like a fingerprint. Typically, a hacker sends a virus or tries to find an IP address. Then he finds a way to exploit the computer's security program. Once he does that, he's got full control. Now he'll use that computer to hack into another by doing the same thing. They call them proxies."

"So what you're telling me is that this person

hacked into four different computers before he got to the judge?"

"Right. He was pretty good."

"So it had to be somebody who knew the judge, or at least someone he corresponded with by e-mail?"

"Normally, yes. But the county maintains a Web site that has e-mail addresses for all of the judges. The judge checked that e-mail address regularly from his home computer. That's how the hacker got in."

"And once he got in, what did he do?"

"Nothing, which is strange. He didn't download any viruses. He didn't copy or destroy any files. He didn't use the computer as a proxy. It appears that he just looked around and left."

"I still want to talk to him," Anita said. "Do you know who he is?"

"Assuming it's a he, I know where his computer is," Teller said. "I didn't bother to track down the owner of the address since I knew you'd already made an arrest."

Teller opened the report, found the page he was looking for, and set it down in front of Anita. "Here it is," he said, pointing.

Anita felt the familiar surge of adrenaline that occurred whenever she got a break in a case.

"Thank you," Anita said as she stood and picked up the report.

"What? You're leaving?" Teller said. "Just like that? We were getting along so well."

"Gotta go. I have work to do."

PART 4

53

"Stay, boy. Stay."

It's nearly nine o'clock and darkness has fallen. I step onto the deck and close the door behind me. Rio is standing on the other side, eyes bright, tail wagging. He loves this nightly ritual of ours. I'm holding a ragged tennis ball, and I throw it as far as I can into the backyard. I open the door, and he leaps out.

"Go get it, Rio."

He races down the steps, and I lean on the rail and watch. I can barely see him as he begins his search for the ball. He trots back and forth across the yard, nose to the ground, instinctively creating a grid. He's invariably successful, and in just a few minutes, he's back on the deck with the ball in his mouth.

"Good boy, Rio. Good boy."

He drops the ball at my feet, and I pick it up. I throw it into the darkness again. He'd run and search all night if I'd stay out here with him. As I'm watching, Caroline walks out the door and hands me the phone. It's Bates.

"Put on a suit," he says. "I'll pick you up in twenty minutes."

"A suit? Where are we going?"

"To meet somebody important."

"Who?"

"Just put on the suit, all right? I'm on my way."

I reluctantly follow his order. He pulls into the driveway a little while later, and I climb into the BMW. He backs out without saying a word, and a in few minutes we're heading west toward Jonesborough.

"So when do you tell me where we're going?" I ask.

"We're in for a busy night. Just sit back and enjoy the ride."

A few minutes later he pulls the BMW into a high-dollar residential area called the Ridges. It's the latest example of one-upmanship among the rich in the community, full of elegant homes surrounded by a championship golf course. I've never been inside any of the homes at the Ridges, but I know several people who live here. One of them is Lee Mooney.

Bates pulls into the driveway of a sprawling white mansion. He turns off the ignition and opens the door.

"You coming or is your ass glued to that seat?" Bates says.

"Is this Mooney's house?"

"Sure is."

"I don't think I'd be welcome here."

"Neither one of us will be welcome in a few minutes. Now get your butt out of the car and come on. You don't want to miss this."

We walk onto the front porch and Bates rings the doorbell. Lee Mooney opens the door a minute later, wearing a navy blue robe that appears to be made of silk and a pair of house shoes. He reeks of booze. The look on his face when he sees Bates is a mixture of consternation and confusion.

"What do you want, Sheriff?"

When he sees me, the look turns to anger.

"And what's *he* doing here?"

"We need to speak to you in private," Bates says.

"About what?"

"It's important. I wouldn't be standing here if it wasn't."

"This is private enough. Tell me what you want."

"If you make me stand out here on the porch, I'm going to say what I have to say loud enough so your neighbors and your wife can hear me," Bates says loudly. "And believe me, it won't go good for you."

Mooney looks around nervously and opens the door. As he steps back so we can walk through, he stumbles slightly and catches himself on the door.

"You remember where the study is, I assume," Mooney says.

"I do," Bates replies with mock civility.

"Go ahead. I'll be right up."

Mooney disappears down a hallway and Bates leads me up a wide staircase. I look around in awe: marble tile, cherry molding, cathedral ceilings, expensive art, a huge chandelier in the foyer. I've always heard that Mooney's wife was extremely wealthy, and from the looks of the house, she must be. We walk into a study filled with plush leather and expensive wood. There's a large cherry desk to my right and a leather couch to my left. Bates and I sit down on the couch.

"He's deep in the bottle," I say.

"No kidding. I thought he was gonna fall on his backside when we came in."

"You've been here before?"

"Once. It's been a while, though."

"What's going on, Leon?"

"You'll see. Just let me do all the talking."

Mooney walks in a couple of minutes later and closes the door behind him. He's carrying a martini. He sits down behind his desk, sets the drink down, laces his fingers around the back of his neck, and leans back.

"What's so damned important that it can't wait until morning?" he says in a drunken, belligerent slur.

Bates leans forward and rests his forearms on his thighs. He stares at Mooney for a long minute—so long that even I begin to become uncomfortable.

"We finally got a break in the Hannah Mills case," Bates says.

"We?" Mooney says. "What do you mean, 'we'?"

"Me and Mr. Dillard, here. We've been working together. Well, that ain't exactly right. I've been doing most of the work, but Mr. Dillard did help me out with one little detail. It was important, though. It surely was."

Mooney unlaces his fingers, takes a drink from the martini, and crosses his arms.

"Why is he wearing a suit?" Mooney says.

"I'll get to that in a minute. Don't you want to know about Hannah? I thought you'd be tickled to hear that we found her."

"You found her? Where? Is she alive?"

"She was in a mine shaft up on Buffalo Mountain.

Somebody killed her and dumped her down that hole like a bag of trash."

Mooney shakes his head and lowers his chin. He reaches for the martini glass again and misses, then finds it. I don't know exactly where Bates is going with this, but I can feel a slow burn beginning in my stomach.

"Do you have any suspects?" Mooney asks.

"Oh yeah, I've got a suspect, all right. As a matter of fact, I know exactly who's responsible for her death."

"Then I assume you've made an arrest."

"Well, I've got a little problem with that. I was hoping maybe you might help me out, but I kinda doubt it, to tell you the truth."

"What do you mean?"

"I don't reckon you're gonna confess, are you?"

Time freezes momentarily. I see Mooney draw in a long, slow breath, as if trying to gather himself. I've suspected since the beginning that Mooney was involved in Hannah's death, but I didn't want to believe it. Bates must have gotten his DNA test results back. Mooney must be the father of Hannah's baby.

"Is this some kind of joke, Sheriff?" Mooney says. "You're making jokes about Hannah's murder?"

"Oh no, it's no joke. I'll just go ahead and tell you the way I see it. After you got Hannah drunk up there at Tanner's birthday party and she made her little announcement about being a virgin, I reckon you just couldn't stand it. You had to help yourself. So the way I figure it is, you followed Tanner and Hannah home and raped her while she was passed out."

Mooney stands abruptly, his face twisted in anger. He points toward the door.

"Get out!"

Bates doesn't move. He seems perfectly calm, but I feel myself growing angrier with each passing second.

"I ain't going nowhere," Bates says. "Not until I've said my piece. Now, you can either sit your ass back down in that chair, or I can go downstairs and tell your wife what I'm about to tell you."

Mooney sits, slowly. Beads of sweat are forming on his forehead. He takes a long drink of the martini.

"You didn't think about getting her pregnant, though, did you?" Bates says. "You damned fool. You see, ol' Dillard here got me a sample of your DNA. It matches the DNA sample from the embryo the pathologist found in Hannah's body. Tough luck for you, huh? If Hannah had stayed in that hole for a couple more weeks before we found her, we wouldn't have been able to get DNA and you would've been in the clear. The only thing I don't know is how you found out about her being pregnant, but that don't really matter, does it? I'll bet you were in a panic. You had to do something, and you had to do it fast. So you went to your old buddy Stinnett and made a deal with Ramirez."

Mooney remains quiet. He's taken on the look of someone who has just been forced to eat a pile of dung.

"Ramirez is locked up again," Bates continues, "but this time ain't nobody gonna let him out. One of his cronies hired a couple of bikers to kill Hannah.

They're as dead as she is. Stinnett's dead, too. So you can relax, Brother Mooney. I can't prove any of this."

Mooney's expression changes slowly to one of smugness. He clears his throat and leans back in his chair again. I can feel my heart beating inside my chest. Pressure has been steadily building at my temples, and my field of vision has narrowed. All I can see is Mooney. I'm thinking about his sneaking into her bedroom, sweating over her while she lay helpless and unaware. I'm thinking about what a sick, perverted bastard he is. I'm thinking about how good it would feel to snap his neck like a twig.

"Get up," I say.

"Get away from me," he mutters.

"I said *get up*, you fucking coward!"

I'm conscious of movement to my left, and I realize it must be Bates. I crack Mooney across the bridge of the nose with the back of my right hand before Bates can get to me. He yelps like a puppy and tears immediately fill his eyes. Bates is pulling me backward while talking in my ear, but my eyes stay on Mooney. I feel a sense of satisfaction as blood begins to run from his nostrils onto his mouth and his chin. Bates keeps talking, but the words are like white noise. They mean nothing to me. He pushes me into the chair and kneels in front of me.

"Brother Dillard, you with me?" The voice sounds as though it's coming from far away. "Brother Dillard? You've got to come out of it, now. We've got business to take care of."

The rage begins to subside, and I slowly become conscious of where I am. I feel sick, and I suddenly want nothing more than to leave this place. Mooney's presence in the room nauseates me. I nod weakly at Bates. He stands and turns toward Mooney, who is holding his expensive robe against his bloody nose.

"This can go one of two ways," Bates says. "What I could do is run straight to the media folks around here and tell them that Hannah Mills was pregnant with your child when she was killed. I *can* prove that. Then I might start leading some of them reporters down the same road I've been traveling for the past few weeks. My guess is that they'll draw the same conclusions I've drawn. It'll be real embarrassing for you. No way you'll be able to stay in office once they get through with you.

"But what I'd rather do is keep this between you, me, and Mr. Dillard here. All you have to do is write out a letter of resignation right now and give it to me. I'll see to it that it goes straight to the governor. He's already got your replacement picked out. He's already signed the paperwork for the appointment. You're finished either way. Pick your poison."

"You're lying," Mooney says.

Bates reaches inside his jacket and pulls out a piece of paper. He tosses it onto the desk in front of Mooney.

"There's the lab report," Bates says. "Read it and weep."

He reaches back into his pocket and pulls out a pen. "That resignation needs to be effective immediately."

54

Bates and I are riding through the darkness in silence. I'm stunned by what's happened, not so much by the fact that Mooney is guilty, but by the fact that he's going to get away with it. Losing the district attorney's office will devastate him—he's become addicted to the power and prestige—but I can't stop thinking that he needs to be punished. He needs to be dragged through a public trial, convicted, and sent off to prison. There he should be gang-raped for ten years before they finally stick a needle in his arm.

I know Bates is right. The only way to prove that Mooney was involved in Katie's death would be to bring a string of witnesses into court to testify how the contract came about and how it was executed. But the only direct link to Mooney—Roscoe Stinnett—is dead. So are the two bikers who actually murdered Hannah. Ramirez is in a federal prison, but the prosecution couldn't force him to testify at a trial without leverage. Even if he did testify, Stinnett apparently never told him precisely who was putting out the contract on Hannah. There's simply no direct evidence that Mooney was involved, and the only circumstantial evidence is that he's the father of Hannah's child. It's not enough.

I think back to the day I went out to Hannah's house, discovered she was gone, and then went back to the office and talked to Mooney. He was so emotional, such a skilled actor. What was it he said? Something about being protective of her, fatherly. And then he said, "That's the way I *felt* about her." He knew she was dead. He knew it.

"I can't believe he's going to get away with it," I say to Bates.

"He ain't gonna go to prison, but he ain't gonna get away with it, either."

"What do you mean?"

"I ain't one to lie much, but I'm afraid I had to lie to him a little. I already mailed a copy of that DNA report to every newspaper and television station within fifty miles. In three days' time, they'll be on him like jackals. He'll have to find him a cave to live in."

"I wanted to kill him back there."

"Can't say as I blame you for that. At least you got a good lick on him."

I look down at the back of my hand and clench and unclench my fist. The knuckles are bruised. It feels good.

"Don't you want to know where we're going next?" Bates says.

"I can't wait."

"You're about to become the new attorney general of the First Judicial District."

I turn and look at him. He's smiling as if he just won the lottery.

"What the hell are you talking about?"

"Mooney's out, which means somebody's going to have to take his place. Now, since the attorney general is an elected state official, not a county official, his replacement is appointed by the governor. Under normal circumstances, an interim would be appointed, there'd be nominations, and the governor would choose whoever he thinks would benefit him the most come the next election. But these ain't normal circumstances. Since me and the governor are such good buddies, I've already got the fix in for you, brother. We're on our way to the airport to meet him right now. All you have to do is say yes."

"You're nuts. I'm not a politician, Leon. I don't want to be the district attorney general."

"Sure you do. It'll be grand. You don't even have to run for office. Instead of some dipstick making all the important decisions, you get to make 'em. You'll make a hundred and fifty grand a year, and you know what the best part will be? You'll have some real power. You can mess with the judges to your heart's content."

"I—I'm grateful. I appreciate the confidence. I really do. But this is too . . . It's too quick, Leon. Too much responsibility."

"What else are you gonna do, Dillard? Sit at home and twiddle your damn thumbs? You're the right man for this job, and I aim to see you take it. Me and you will make a great team. If it turns out you don't like it, don't run for election when the term is up in four years."

"You could have at least told me about this, given me a chance to talk to Caroline."

"She'll be glad to have you out of the house again. Besides, you really ain't got no choice now. The governor's already signed the appointment, and he's flying all the way up here from Nashville just to meet you. His jet should be landing right about now. That's why I asked you to wear the suit, brother. I wouldn't want you to meet the governor looking like a heathen."

"He knows about Mooney?"

"I told him everything."

I lean my head back on the headrest and close my eyes. Despite my protests, I find the idea intriguing. I've always been critical of the men who occupied the position of district attorney general, and this would give me the opportunity to run the office the way I think it should be run—the right way. Ultimately, I'd control all of the decisions about whom to indict and what crime to charge in a four-county district. But what intrigues me even more is Tommy Miller's situation. I'll be in a position to make sure the same thing doesn't happen to Tommy that happened to Brian Gant. And then there's Caroline. If the evidence she destroyed ever comes up as an issue and if Anita White or Ralph Harmon or anyone else ever attempts to bring a case against her, they'll have to get past me. I open my eyes and turn to Bates.

"Okay, Leon," I say. "You talked me into it. Let's go see the governor."

55

The private jet that has carried the governor of Tennessee to Tri-Cities Regional Airport has been pulled into a hangar about a quarter mile from the main terminal. Bates pulls inside the huge opening slowly. Three men in suits—the governor's security detail—are waiting. They talk to us briefly, wave wands over our bodies, and then lead us across the floor to a set of steps that ascends to the interior of the plane.

I'm a bit startled by the luxury, and by the space, once we get inside. An attractive young woman gives us a brief introduction to the pilot, shows us the kitchenette and the bar and the soft, reclining leather seats—three on each side of the aisle. There's a flat-screen television on the wall in front of the seats and two computer workstations behind. She leads us down a short hallway past the bathrooms to the back of the plane, opens a door, motions us inside, and closes the door behind us.

James Lincoln Donner III, the governor of Tennessee, is standing behind a sprawling oak desk. I've never met Donner, but I know he's a multimillionaire from Nashville who made his money the old-fashioned way—he inherited it. Donner is the first Democrat to hold the office in sixteen years, but he wasn't elected because of any noble ideal he represented or because of a rock-solid political platform. He was elected because the two Republican administrations that preceded him used the state treasury as their personal piggy banks. I remember reading a quote from Donner during his campaign in which he said corruption was so rampant at the state capitol in Nashville that his first order of business would be to go into the Senate and House chambers with a fire hose and clean them both out.

I'm surprised by the governor's size as he walks around his desk to embrace Bates. He looks much bigger on television. Considerably under six feet tall, he's wearing a tailored gray suit with white shirt and navy blue tie. His hair is chestnut brown and cut short. His cheeks are oddly hollow. His eyes are gray—like Lee Mooney's.

"Leon, so good to see you," he says as he pats Bates's shoulders after he releases the hug. "Is this your man?"

"Sure is," Bates says. "Joe Dillard, meet Governor Jim Donner."

"Governor," I say as he shakes my hand vigorously.

"A pleasure, Mr. Dillard," he says, "or should I say General Dillard?"

"Call me Joe, please. I never made it past sergeant, anyway."

"Yes, a veteran," he says. "We've put together a

file on you. Hope you don't mind. It says you were a Ranger, combat experience, decorated with a Silver Star in Grenada."

"That was a long time ago, sir."

"Leon here tells me you're as honest as anyone he's ever met. Says you're a helluva lawyer, too. Just the kind of man we need under these trying circumstances."

"I have my reservations, to be perfectly honest, but I'm willing to try."

The governor walks back around the desk and sits in a leather swivel chair. He motions to us to do the same, and I notice he's looking down on us. He's obviously installed a platform under his seat to make himself appear taller. I want to snicker or say something, but I know Bates will kick me in the balls if I do. The governor picks up a file in front of him.

"Let's see here. Born in Johnson City, father was killed in Vietnam, raised by your mother. One sister, Sarah, who seems to have had some problems with the law." He glances up at Bates and then back down at the file. "Graduated Science Hill High School. Then joined the army. Decorated, honorable discharge. Then graduated East Tennessee State University and the University of Tennessee College of Law. Practiced both as a defense attorney and a prosecutor. Married to the same woman for twenty-two years. Two children, both in college. With the exception of your sister, you're perfect."

"My sister won't be a problem, sir."

"Let's hope not."

He turns back to Bates.

"You've spoken to the outgoing district attorney?"

"Just came from his house, Governor," Bates says.

"Any problems?"

"He was too drunk to give us any guff. I have his resignation right here."

Bates hands the paper across the desk, and the governor reads it out loud.

" 'I hereby tender my resignation as Attorney General of the First Judicial District, effective immediately.' Short and sweet, signed and dated. I wonder what he'll tell his wife."

"That's the least of his problems," Bates says. "By the time I get through with him, he's gonna have to leave the state."

"Republicans," the governor says. "Just can't seem to keep their peckers in their pants, huh?"

I want to say something—something about Hannah and what a beautiful human being she was, something to remind him of what this is really about. It isn't about sexual misconduct. It isn't about Republicans and Democrats. It's about a public official being responsible for a murder, and I don't appreciate his cavalier attitude. But this is Bates's show. I keep my mouth shut.

"I don't think the inability to keep the pecker in the pants is an affliction that's unique to Republicans," Bates says. "Ever heard of Bill Clinton? Eliot Spitzer? Gary Hart?"

"Ah, touché, my friend, touché."

The governor turns to me.

"So, Joe, I understand you're not particularly interested in politics."

"My plate's always been full just trying to make a living and raising my family," I say. "I'm not really interested in trying to run things."

"Well, you're going to be running something now. The district attorney's office. Do you have any plans to rehabilitate the image of the office after the public learns of Mooney's demise?"

"I really haven't had a chance to think about any plans, Governor. The sheriff just dropped all of this on me about a half hour ago. But I don't think it's rocket science. People commit crimes, the police arrest them, and the district attorney prosecutes them under the law."

"So you're a black-and-white kind of guy."

"I guess I am, but the older I get, the more gray I seem to see."

Governor Donner opens a desk drawer and pulls out a legal-sized piece of paper. He holds it up in front of him and stands.

"This is a copy of the appointment that will be filed with the Supreme Court in the morning. It makes you the new district attorney general. I've already signed it. Thought you might want to frame it. Congratulations."

He extends his hand again. Bates and I stand, and I grasp it.

"Thank you, Governor. Thank you."

"Thank Leon," he says. "I have a file on you, but I really don't know you from Adam."

Bates and I turn to leave. Just as I'm about to clear the door, I hear the governor clear his throat.

"Mr. Dillard," he says."

I turn to face him. "Yes, sir?"

"Don't make me regret this."

56

A sound awakens me. I open my eyes in the darkened bedroom and look at the digital clock on the dresser. Almost three in the morning.

I hear it again, a low growl coming from the foot of the bed. It's Rio. Something has startled him.

"Shhhh, Rio. Go to sleep." I lay my head back on the pillow and close my eyes. I can hear Caroline breathing rhythmically next to me. I start to drift off, but Rio growls again, this time louder. I sit up and slide my legs over the side of the bed. I've heard him growl thousands of times. This one is different.

I flip on the lamp beside the bed and stand up. Rio has also gotten to his feet and is standing near the closed bedroom door. His ears are laid back flat against his head, and he's quivering. I walk over to him and pat him on the shoulder in an attempt to calm him, but he ignores me. Something is wrong; definitely wrong. I take hold of his harness and look over toward Caroline. She's sitting up now, rubbing her eyes. I put a finger to my mouth and open the bedroom door.

"Go get 'em!" I whisper, and I let go of the harness.

The dog launches himself into the darkness beyond the door as though he's been shot from a cannon.

I hear a deafening gunshot about three seconds later, followed by a pitiful wail. Caroline screams. The first thing that enters my mind is that someone from Brian Gant's family has come for a little revenge. I dive across the bed and turn the lamp back off. I can hear the dog whining somewhere in the house. I grab Caroline by the arm.

"Be quiet," I whisper, and I pull her toward the walk-in closet between the bedroom and bathroom. There's a semiautomatic Remington twelve gauge standing in the closet corner. I always keep it loaded. My fingers find it immediately, and I flip the safety off.

I help Caroline down beneath the clothes and boxes and so that she's facing the door. I hand her the gun.

"Stay here. It's ready to go. All you have to do is pull the trigger. When I come back, I'll say something before I get to the door. Anybody else comes through, blow them away."

"Where are you going?" The whisper is almost desperate. She doesn't want me to leave her.

"I'm going to go kill the son of a bitch who broke into my house and shot my dog."

A quiet rage is building within me. This is my home. It's the middle of the night. My wife is terrified. I'll be damned if I'm going to let whoever has invaded us walk out alive. I creep back into the bedroom for the nine-millimeter Beretta I keep in the drawer with my socks. I ease the clip out, check it, and push it back in.

The pistol is loaded and I'm ready, though my heart is thumping against my chest and my hands are trembling slightly. I take a few deep breaths and try to focus.

Let them come to you. Whoever it is has come this far; they'll come the rest of the way.

I crouch on the floor next to the dresser for a couple of the longest minutes of my life and listen. I hear a thump, then mumbling. It's coming from the kitchen. He's run into the counter or the island.

After another moment—an eternity in the dark—I hear what I think is a creak in the floor. Screw this. I can't wait any longer. I go down, flat on my belly, and slide toward the sound. Once my head is around the corner I can just barely make out a pair of legs, two dark shadows on the far side of the kitchen table, but nothing else. If I stand, I'll expose myself. I wait just a couple of seconds to make sure he's alone. I ease my elbows out onto the floor in front of me and aim through the legs of a chair. He's mumbling again. He's maybe fifteen feet away.

The muzzle flash is blinding, and the explosion rattles my eardrums. He screams and falls in a heap. I hear his gun clatter against the tile as it skids away from him. I leap to my feet and run toward the intruder. I reach out and flip on the kitchen light as I pass the switch. His gun is lying near my feet, and I kick it away. He's on the floor on his side, groaning, his face away from me. Both of his hands are wrapped around his knee, and blood is running through his fingers. A strong urge grips me, an urge that tells me to stick the barrel of my gun next to his temple and pull the trigger. I take a couple of steps toward him. I raise my foot, plant it in his shoulder, and roll him onto his back.

"You!"

I turn my head toward the bedroom and yell, "Caroline, come out here!"

She appears in a couple of seconds, carrying the shotgun, and walks tentatively toward me. She looks at the man on the floor and her mouth drops open.

"Are you capable of shooting this piece of shit if he moves?"

She nods her head. By the look in her eye, she means it.

I turn and walk into the hallway near the stairs that lead down to Jack's room. Rio is lying a couple of feet from the door. A small pool of blood has formed beneath his chest. I kneel down beside him. His breathing is slow, but his eyes are open. I stroke him between the ears, and he moans.

"It's okay, buddy. It's okay."

I examine him quickly. The bullet looks to have entered at the shoulder and broken his leg. I need to stop the bleeding. I remove my T-shirt and wrap it tightly around the wound. The bleeding slows, but I still need to get him to a vet.

I stand, and he whimpers.

"I'll be right back, big guy. You just stay with us."

I run back through the kitchen where Caroline is still holding the shotgun on the intruder. I pick up my cell phone off the bed and find Dr. James Kruk's number. He's been taking care of my animals for years, and he's accustomed to being awakened. He answers after the fifth ring, and I tell him what's happened. He says he'll be right over.

I walk quickly back to the kitchen. The man has rolled onto his side again, but now he's facing toward me. His hands are still wrapped around his left knee. Caroline is standing over him with the shotgun pointed at his head.

"I'm bleeding," Lee Mooney says quietly. I can smell the strong odor of liquor in the air. He was trashed earlier. He must have kept drinking, the effects of which eventually led to the irrational decision that I needed to die.

"I don't care if you're bleeding," I say.

"I needa ... go ... ta hospital."

"How about the morgue?"

I kneel next to him and hold the barrel hard against his forehead. His head moves with the trembling of my hand. "You couldn't just leave it alone, could you? All you had to do was crawl into a hole somewhere."

"You don't unnerstand," Mooney says in the whiny voice I've heard more times than I care to remember, now thick with drunkenness. His dilated pupils look like black holes.

"You're the one who doesn't understand," I say. I feel something I've never felt before, and I realize it's indifference. I don't care about him. I don't care that he's bleeding. "You broke into my house, you son of a bitch. You know the legal standard for defending yourself in your own home, don't you?"

I see a glint of understanding. He knows what I mean.

"That's right. Deadly force. I can use deadly force defending myself against someone who invades my home."

I stand and back up a few steps, my mind whirling. *If they look closely, they'll see the amount of blood on the floor and know he bled for a while before he was shot the second time. They'll analyze the angle of the trajectory of the bullet and know I was standing over him when I shot him. They'll accuse me of murdering him.*

He's garbage. He raped Hannah and then had her murdered, and he's going to get away with it. He shot my dog. He needs to be dead.

I pull back the hammer on the pistol and take a deep breath.

A hand wraps around the gun barrel and pushes it down gently. I come out of the trance and recognize the voice.

"Don't," Caroline says. "You're not like him."

I lower the gun to my side and nod my head. A thought pops into my mind, something Bates told me about Ramirez. I step back up next to Mooney, raise my heel off the ground, and stomp on his wounded knee with all the force I can muster. He screams in agony. I dial 911 on my cell phone and tell them there's been a shooting. The cavalry is on the way.

"Take care of Rio, will you?" I say to Caroline.

I walk to a drawer next to the sink, pull out a clean dish towel, and walk back over to Mooney.

"Here," I say as I toss it onto his forehead. "You're going to jail. Try not to bleed to death before you get there."

57

The following week is a blur. My first order of business is to reassure the employees in the office that I won't be making any dramatic changes, that everyone will keep their jobs. I tell them as much as I can about Mooney's resignation and my appointment. I don't see any point in keeping anything from them. After all, I want them to trust me. They're all shocked at the news of Hannah's violent death, especially Tanner Jarrett. When he hears that she was pregnant with Mooney's child, that Mooney paid to have her killed, and that we can't prosecute Mooney because all the witnesses are dead, he excuses himself from the room and doesn't come back.

The pressure from the media becomes so intense on the first day that I agree to a press conference in one of the courtrooms at one o'clock. News about Hannah has leaked, probably from Bates, and the conference is brutal. They ask about Hannah. How was she killed? Who killed her? When was she killed? When was she found? Is it true she was pregnant? I refer all those questions to the sheriff. They ask about Mooney, question after question after question. I refuse to tell them anything other than to confirm that he resigned last night and that the governor has appointed me to replace him until the end of the term. I refer all of the questions about the break-in at my house and the shooting to the sheriff. One of the reporters even asks whether it's true that my dog was shot. I swallow hard and tell him to talk to the sheriff.

Late that afternoon, I'm sworn into office by the judge the governor has appointed to replace Leonard Green. Sixty-year-old Terry Breck made a fortune in medical malpractice law. He's retired now, but the governor has apparently seduced him into taking the job. He has a reputation as an even-tempered, scholarly man. I hope that turns out to be true. It'll be such a pleasant change from what I'm used to dealing with.

On Wednesday, Leon Bates appears before the grand jury with Tanner Jarrett. He comes out with indictments against seventeen members of Satan's Soldiers for charges ranging from possession with intent to distribute methamphetamine, to murder. Bates and his SWAT team conduct a raid early the next morning, and thus far, six of the seventeen have been taken into custody. None of the indictments contain the name "Roy" or the alias "Mountain," and I wonder what Sarah's boyfriend's real name is and whether he's on the run.

Late Thursday afternoon, Tanner Jarrett, Caroline, and I get on a plane to Knoxville. There we meet a black woman, Lottie Antoine, who looks to be in her mid-sixties. After Hannah's death was made public, I was contacted by a lawyer from Gatlinburg and told that Hannah Mills had a will, and that Lottie was the executor of her estate.

After a short, emotional introductory meeting, the four of us board a plane to Kalamazoo, Michigan. Lottie is silent during the flight. She carries herself with a sense of quiet dignity, but I can see in her dark eyes that she, too, has endured more than her share of sorrow. We rent a van and drive to South Haven the next morning. We hold a brief service for Hannah and bury her alongside her mother and brothers and sister in McDowell Cemetery near Casco Township. Lottie speaks of Hannah's gentle nature and kindness, her love of family and the outdoors, her relationship with Luke Clinton, and her almost superhuman ability to carry on through unspeakable tragedy. Her words move all of us to tears, and I find myself thinking, once again, about how unjust life can be. We board another plane that same afternoon and fly home. On the way, Lottie tells me that Hannah's will set up a trust that would benefit her beloved Smoky Mountains National Park.

On Sunday evening, Caroline invites a group of people, around twenty or so, over to the house to celebrate my appointment as district attorney. I have mixed feelings about it. I'm looking forward to what I know will be a challenge, but at the same time, the circumstances under which I inherited the job give me no cause for celebration. Rio is limping around in a cast. The shot shattered the upper part of his right leg, but Dr. Kruk repaired the damage and says he'll be fine in a couple of months.

I'm standing on the deck around eight o'clock. The sun has just dropped behind the hills to the west, and the evening air has taken on a bit of a chill. I'm talking to Jim Beaumont, a well-respected local defense attorney and close friend, when I catch a glimpse of my sister, Sarah, through the window in the kitchen. Caroline must have invited her. She looks like a tick about to pop. Towering above her is Roy, the biker boyfriend.

"Oh shit," I say to Beaumont. "Excuse me for a minute."

I hurry through the door into the kitchen, catch Sarah by the elbow, and lead her into the same hallway where Rio was shot.

"Are you crazy?" I say. "Don't you know the sheriff is here? Your boyfriend's about to go to jail."

Sarah gives me a curious look. "Why?"

"Why? Don't you read the papers? Listen to the news? Bates indicted a whole slew of his gang this week. He's bound to be one of them."

"You think so?" she says. A hint of a smile is beginning to form on her face.

"Damned right, I think so. Now get him out of here before Bates spots him and a gun battle breaks out."

"Too late," she says, and nods back toward the kitchen. I turn to see Bates walk up to Sarah's boyfriend and give him a big slap on the back. I'm dumbfounded. I walk into the kitchen and stare. Bates notices me and grins.

"Come on over here, Brother Dillard," Bates says. "Let me introduce you to Roy Walker, the best undercover agent I've ever had the pleasure of working with."

I stand there looking at him stupidly, and Walker winks and sticks out his massive hand.

"Howdy again," he says. "They call me Mountain."

58

On Monday morning, I'm sitting at my new desk at seven o'clock sharp. I'm alone. The rest of the crew won't arrive for another hour.

I've removed everything from the office that reminds me of Lee Mooney: the desk, the furniture, the photos on the wall. I've boxed up all of his personal property and mailed it to him. The United States and Tennessee flags that framed his desk have been moved to the reception area. The large photograph of George W. Bush has been replaced by a framed copy of the preamble to the United States Constitution. I've painted the walls myself. Caroline told me that Hannah Mills's favorite color was gold and helped me pick out a shade that isn't too bright. I've brought a few small framed photos of my family into the office, but outside of that, I've chosen to keep it sparse.

There's a large sealed envelope on the desk in front of me. To my right is a thick file I've retrieved from a storage room in my house.

Last week, I made two important phone calls. One was to Brian Gant's appellate attorney, and the other was to the director of the Tennessee Department of Correction. I was amazed at how easy it was to get the director on the phone. Being a district attorney general certainly has its advantages. Brian's lawyer faxed me a copy of the DNA profile of evidence from the scene where Brian's mother-in-law was murdered and his niece was raped, and the director readily agreed to run the profile through their database. All he needed was a case number, he said, and he'd see to it that it was taken care of. In less than forty-eight hours, I received a telephone call from a Department of Correction DNA specialist. She had a match to the profile I faxed her, she said. The DNA belonged to a man named Earl Gaines. He'd been convicted twice of aggravated rape and was currently serving a thirty-year sentence. I asked her whether she could send me a copy of the DOC's records on Gaines, and she said she'd get it in the mail right away.

The package in front of me is Gaines's records. The file to my right is Brian Gant's. I open the package, remove the thick sheaf of papers, and begin to read them carefully. Gaines was born in 1966. He was first convicted of aggravated rape at the age of nineteen. He served ten years, and was paroled in February 1995, just two months before Brian Gant's mother-in-law was murdered.

I find the section that contains Gaines's parole records. They show that in February 1995, he moved in with a woman named Clara Stoots. As I look at Clara Stoots's address, an alarm bell goes off inside my head. I grab Brian Gant's file and quickly locate a copy of the original police report of the murder. I'm

59

Anita White walks unannounced into my office an
hour and a half later wearing a smart-looking navy
blue pantsuit but seeming a bit frazzled. She sits down
across the desk from me without saying a word. I've
called her a couple of times since our conversation
at Perkins the morning they arrested Tommy Miller,
but she hasn't answered and hasn't returned the calls.
I wonder whether she's looking for another apology
from me.

"I've been trying to get ahold of you," I say.

"I've been out of the country."

"Vacation?"

"I took a few personal days, but I worked the entire time I was gone."

"Really? On what?"

"It started with the forensic analysis of Judge
Green's computer. Our analyst found out that someone had hacked into the judge's computer not long
before he was killed. He investigated, like all good
TBI agents do, and found that the computer the
hacker used was located in another country."

"And what country was that?"

"Canada."

The look on her face is almost, but not quite, smug. There's a gleam in her eye that tells me she knows something that I don't. I can tell she's dying to spit it out, but first she wants to enjoy her little game.

"Canada's a big country," I say.

"Yes, and Vancouver's a big city."

The thought germinates in my mind and begins to grow quickly. Vancouver. Canada. Judge Green. Computer hacker. What do they have in common? It dawns on me suddenly, but I'm afraid to be too optimistic. What has she learned? How far has she taken it?

"Talk to me," I say.

"When I saw the Vancouver address, I remembered the case against the pedophile that Judge Green threw out on a technicality, so I got online and looked it up. David Dillinger was the witness the judge held in contempt that day, so I started doing my job. I checked with the airlines at Tri-Cities Airport and found out that David Dillinger flew back here three days before Judge Green was murdered. He took a plane home the morning the judge was discovered. I checked with the rental agency at the airport. Guess what model car David Dillinger rented? A white Subaru Legacy. I checked the hotels and found out he stayed at the Doubletree, the same hotel the state put him in when he came down to testify at the hearing. The Doubletree has security cameras at all of the entrances and in all of the hallways. When I went through the tapes, I learned that Dillinger had a tendency to sleep all day and stay out all night. On the morning of the murder, he showed up at the hotel at exactly 5:12 a.m. Shall I keep going?"

"By all means," I say. "So far I've heard a fairly good circumstantial case, but I'm not sure there's enough for a conviction."

"Did I tell you about the part where I got his credit card bill and found that he'd charged some items at Wal-Mart in Johnson City the night before the murder? Let's see, what was it? Oh yes, a bow saw, a length of rope, and a five-gallon plastic gasoline container. Wal-Mart had a tape, too. Dillinger is easily recognizable."

The excitement is building. I'm picturing the look on Tommy Miller's face when I walk into court and ask the judge to dismiss the charges against him.

"So you went to Canada to arrest him?"

"First I called the Vancouver police, and based on the information I provided, they arrested him and got a DNA sample. It matched two cigarette butts we found at the crime scene. So I flew up there and interviewed him. As soon as I showed him the DNA match, he knew he was dead in the water. He said when he got back to Vancouver, he hacked into Green's computer. It was full of child pornography, along with a lot of other obscene material. Dillinger was so enraged that he started planning the murder that very minute. He confessed to everything, and I have it on video. He's in the Washington County jail as we speak. I brought him back with me."

She's grinning broadly now. I get up from behind the desk, walk around in front of her, and reach out my arms.

"Give me a hug, Agent White."

She stands and wraps her arms around my neck.

"Thank you," I say. "Thank you from the bottom of my heart."

"Would you like to know what the best part of all this is?" she says. "Harmon doesn't know anything about it. He thinks I'm on vacation."

Also Available

from

Scott Pratt

AN INNOCENT CLIENT

A preacher is stabbed to death in a Tennessee motel and the suspect is a waitress at a strip club. Defense attorney Joe Dillard's too burnt out to defend anyone he knows in his heart is guilty. Then he meets the vulnerable Angel—the accused, incriminated by circumstantial evidence. Dillard's sure she's not capable of killing anyone. What he doesn't count on are the others drawn into the storm of the stunning crime—from the vindictive detective to the victim's avenging son to Dillard's own deeply troubled sister—all of whom will help to erase the line between guilt and innocence, and between an unthinkable lie and the unbelievable truth.

"Artfully plotted, carefully nuanced, and immensely readable."
—*New York Times* bestselling author Sheldon Siegel

Available wherever books are sold or at penguin.com

Also Available

from

Scott Pratt

In Good Faith

A family is slaughtered in rural Tennessee. Two goth teens stand accused of the murders, and now it's up to prosecutor Joe Dillard to convict them. A former defense attorney who spent way too much time defending people he knew were guilty, Joe is determined to win this case to atone for his past. But a young woman named Natasha, who apparently inspired the slayings, is walking around free because the boys are afraid to implicate her. Now, Joe must risk everything—including the safety of his family and his own good faith— to bring a guilty woman to justice.

"Pratt is a talent to watch."
—Jeff Abbott, national bestselling author of *Collision*

Available wherever books are sold or at penguin.com

The *New York Times* bestseller from

John Lescroart

BETRAYAL

Dismas Hardy agrees to take an appeal to overturn the murder conviction of National Guard reservist Evan Scholler. Scholler had plenty of reasons for revenge—but as Dismas delves into the case, he begins to uncover a terrible truth that drops him right into the complicated world of government conspiracy, assassination, and betrayal.

Also Available

Treasure Hunt
Betrayal
The Suspect
The Hunt Club
A Certain Justice
The 13th Juror
Hard Evidence
The Vig
The Motive
Dead Irish
The Second Chair
The First Law
The Oath
The Hearing
Nothing but the Truth

**Available wherever books are sold
or at penguin.com**

Penguin Group (USA) Online

What will you be reading tomorrow?

Tom Clancy, Patricia Cornwell, W.E.B. Griffin,
Nora Roberts, William Gibson, Robin Cook,
Brian Jacques, Catherine Coulter, Stephen King,
Dean Koontz, Ken Follett, Clive Cussler,
Eric Jerome Dickey, John Sandford,
Terry McMillan, Sue Monk Kidd, Amy Tan,
J. R. Ward, Laurell K. Hamilton,
Charlaine Harris, Christine Feehan...

You'll find them all at
penguin.com

*Read excerpts and newsletters,
find tour schedules and reading group guides,
and enter contests.*

Subscribe to Penguin Group (USA) newsletters
and get an exclusive inside look
at exciting new titles and the authors you love
long before everyone else does.

PENGUIN GROUP (USA)
us.penguingroup.com